DESTROYER

Chris Fox

ISBN: 1530628504
ISBN-13: 9781530628506

For Saul. If you hadn't forced me to start writing again, none of this would have been possible.

Exiled

Sign up for the mailing list

and read the the prequel for free!

Chapter 1- Debris

Commander Nolan ducked through the hatch into the combat information center of the UFC *Johnston*. It was smaller than he was used to, the consoles set closer to each other than they'd been back at the Office of Fleet Intelligence. Seven people made the room positively claustrophobic, and he imagined that this was what sailors had experienced aboard submarines just a few centuries past.

"Captain, we're clearing the sun's corona. Inductive field down to twelve percent. I'm bringing thrusters online," Emo called over his shoulder in a strange southern drawl, completely at odds with his appearance. Waif-thin and pale, he wore black lipstick and white makeup. The left side of his head had been shaved, while the shiny black hair on the right side drooped over his face. He sat near the far end of the CIC, his simple chrome chair aimed at the view screen.

That view screen showed the most breathtaking vista Nolan had ever seen. Pillars of flame hundreds of miles high shot up around them, more than one coming perilously close to their destroyer class vessel. Emo deftly maneuvered around the flares, slowly gaining distance from the star. The fact that it was even possible to escape a sun's gravitational pull was nothing short of miraculous, but the Helios drives made it commonplace. They simply harnessed the sun's own energy.

"Commander, are you going to join us?" called a gruff voice. Nolan turned toward the voice, which had come from a chair on the opposite side of the room--one that was set a little higher than the rest, a subtle reminder that the person sitting there was in charge.

In this case, that person was a short man in his early sixties, a person Nolan had revered his whole life. The legendary Captain Dryker, hero of the Tigris war. His white beard was scraggly and his hair hadn't seen a brush since Nolan had boarded three days past, but the captain's eyes were sharp and his leanly-muscled physique was still that of a much younger officer.

"Yes, sir," Nolan said, realizing he was still standing just inside the narrow hatchway. He threaded between the communication consoles, wishing he knew the names of the two techs working there. He stepped up next to the Captain's chair, folding his hands behind his back.

"You're two minutes early," the Captain said, though his eyes were fixed on the view screen.

"Yes, sir. I prefer being early," Nolan said, though he had

the impression that the captain wasn't really listening.

"Captain," Emo called, spinning his chair to face them. "You're going to want to see this. Check grid 729, sir."

"Noted," Dryker said, scanning a data pad sitting in his lap. He loosened the collar of his uniform, revealing a coffee stain on the cotton shirt underneath. Nolan waited for several moments while the captain scanned. Dryker finally looked up, meeting Nolan's gaze. "What do you make of this, Commander?"

He handed the pad to Nolan, who quickly scanned the data. "It's a debris field, sir. From the alloy, I'd suggest it's probably the remains of a Tigris vessel. It's smaller than I'd expect, though. A science vessel, maybe?"

"Very good," Dryker replied, giving a tight nod. "And what can you deduce from the situation?"

Nolan was silent as he glanced between the view screen and the data pad. There were a lot of disparate pieces, but he knew they added up to something--something the Captain was already aware of. "There was a battle, and that battle was recent. Tigris don't generally send their science vessels outside their own space, and they certainly don't send them to a human colony like Mar Kona."

"Good, but there's a more urgent fact you're missing," Dryker said, eyeing Nolan frostily.

Nolan resisted the urge to blush. He'd only been aboard the *Johnston* for a few days, and didn't mind admitting that the war hero intimidated him. "Sir?"

"The debris is close, maybe three hundred thousand clicks from the sun's corona," Dryker supplied, raising an eyebrow.

"Ahh, I should have caught that," Nolan replied, finally understanding. He tensed. "The battle was recent. *Very* recent. If this had happened even a few hours ago the debris field would have already been pulled in by the sun's gravity."

The *Johnston* had cleared the corona, and was accelerating toward the debris field. As they approached the view screen's magnification shifted to provide a close up. Large chunks of bronze-colored alloy floated in space, sinking gradually closer to the sun.

"Set condition one throughout the ship," Dryker barked.

A blonde lieutenant in her early twenties gave a quick nod and a murmured response, then the lighting changed. The bright halogens faded to soft red, and a single warning klaxon rang across the deck. Nolan had never seen a ship of the line enter combat readiness, but he'd been trained for it back at the academy. He moved a step to the left, clipping himself to a handle on the side of the bulkhead.

"Captain, do you think whoever did this is still here?

Wouldn't we be able to see them?" Nolan asked. It might be a stupid question, but he was genuinely curious.

"It's possible they could have retreated back into the sun, and they may have already used the Helios Gate," Dryker conceded, his eyes never leaving the view screen. "I don't think so, though. I'm guessing they're still in system. Emo, give me a system scan. Where could a vessel run to?"

"There are only two real choices," Emo said. "They could go for that asteroid field that used to be a moon, or they could be hiding in Mar Kona's shadow."

"They'd have to be damned quick to make it to the planet already," Dryker said, rising from his chair and crossing the deck to stand next to Emo. Nolan considered following, but chose to stay clipped to the bulkhead.

"Sir, if they *are* in the asteroid field, what are we planning to do about it?" Nolan asked.

"Captain," the blonde snapped, drawing Nolan's attention. Her blue eyes had gone wide. "Another vessel is emerging from the Helios Gate. It's clearing the sun's corona now. It's broadcasting an ident. Looks to be a Tigris Warship."

"Battle stations," Dryker barked.

Chapter 2- You're In Charge

Nolan tensed as the Klaxon blared a second time. That was the only sign that anything had changed. The techs manning the comm stations didn't so much as flinch, instead keeping their focus and continuing to monitor the individual metrics that every warship needed in combat.

"Commander Nolan," Dryker said, brushing lint from the arm of his uniform. He looked up to meet Nolan's gaze. "You have the bridge."

"Excuse me? Uh, sir," Nolan said, trying to keep the shock from his voice. The idea that a Captain would desert his bridge during a battle was unthinkable.

"Did I stutter? The shift has changed. It's 0800 and you're scheduled to take command, aren't you? I'm going to go get some chow," Dryker said. His tone was flat, completely devoid of emotion.

Nolan paused, glancing at the view screen. The Tigris warship loomed behind them, slowly clearing the sun's corona. The spike-shaped vessel dodged a solar flare, disappearing for a moment before returning to view. The thing looked like a high-caliber bullet: long, lean, and deadly. Three ports ringed the midsection, each capable of launching one of the dart fighters the Tigris so loved to employ. Above those ports were a smaller ring of turrets, designed to launch harpoons that would pin their foes long enough to grapple them.

"Sir, I'm not sure that's appropriate. I've only been aboard ship for three days, and I--" Nolan began.

"Nolan," Dryker snapped, taking a step closer. Nolan could smell coffee on the captain's breath. "You're an officer of the UFC, are you not? You're trained to command in combat--by OFI, no less. If the Office of Fleet Intelligence hasn't prepared you for battle, then why the hell are you on my ship?"

"Well, yes, I have been trained," Nolan began again. "But, sir, you've seen at least a dozen battles. Are you certain that--"

"I'm going to see about breakfast," Dryker said, ducking past Nolan and through the hatch. He paused to poke his head back inside. "Figure it out, Nolan. Or we're all dead."

Nolan took a deep breath and focused on the view screen. The warship was closing, but because it was exiting the sun's corona it hadn't had time to accelerate yet. They still had a little time to react. That time would be critical. The Tigris warship was three times their size. It was faster, better armored, and packed wall to wall with a race that lived for combat.

"Pilot," Nolan barked, trying to affect the same tone of authority Dryker had used. "Set course for the asteroid field around Mar Kona."

"Acknowledged, Commander," Emo replied in a lazy drawl. Nolan couldn't feel the ship accelerate, but the asteroids loomed larger as the *Johnston* made for them.

"You," he said, pointing at the blonde comm tech. "What's your name?"

"Lieutenant Juliard, sir," the woman said, blinking at him.

"Juliard, open a channel to the Tigris vessel and put it on screen," Nolan ordered. He moved to the Captain's chair, pausing to inspect the smooth chrome. Then he sat, resting his arms on the cold metal. The chair had been designed for function, not form. Just like everything else on this rust bucket. The *Johnston* had been old when the war with the Tigris began, and should have been retired when that war ended.

"On screen, sir," Juliard said. Nolan glanced up as the screen shimmered. The asteroid disappeared, replaced by a very feline, very angry face. This Tigris had black fur and large yellow eyes. Its shoulders, arms, and chest were corded with thick muscle, and Nolan was thankful they weren't in the same room. This thing could probably tear him apart.

"You will die for this atrocity, ape," the creature snarled. When it spoke, Nolan caught sight of wicked two-inch fangs. A thickly-furred tail flicked over its shoulder, as though it had a mind of its own. "The Leonis Pride will be alerted to your cowardly actions."

Nolan attempted to explain. "We didn't destroy your science vessel. We--"

The view screen went dark.

"They've cut connection, sir," Juliard said, quite unhelpfully.

"Lovely," Nolan snarled. He leaned forward in the chair, thinking quickly. "Emo, how close are we to the asteroid field?"

"Not close enough, sir. I've plotted the Tigris intercept course. They're going to reach us about forty seconds before we make that field," Emo said, glancing over his shoulder at Nolan. Nolan had a hard time taking Emo seriously, and hoped his style of dress didn't mean the young pilot was bad at his job. They were going to need some top-notch flying in the next few minutes.

He considered his strategy for all of three seconds. Tigris had greater acceleration, which fit their MO. Their vessels had dense tritanium along the spike at their prow, which was perfect for ramming enemy vessels. Once they'd done so, hatches opened all along the tip to allow them to disgorge boarding parties. Tigris loved hand to hand combat, and their vessels didn't have any ranged weaponry beyond their harpoons and dart fighters. That had proven to be more than enough during the eight-year war.

"Full burn for those asteroids, Emo," Nolan ordered. He turned to a dark-skinned man he'd yet to meet. The man was standing at the gunnery station. "You, Lieutenant...Ezana? Bring turrets one through eight online, and prepare for dispersal firing. See if you can make them wary, at least."

"Yes, sir." The man bent back to his console.

Nolan punched a button on the tablet the captain had left him, and the view screen shifted to show the pursuing Tigris vessel. It had already exited the corona, and was accelerating toward them.

"Commander, they're gaining rapidly," Juliard said, her voice rising half an octave.

"Damn it," Nolan cursed, knowing they were playing right into the Tigris hands. Should they stand and fight? No, that way lay death. He needed a way to even the odds.

"Commander, they've launched three darts," Ezana shouted. "I'll try to intercept."

The entire ship shook as the starboard and aft turrets

began firing. Each turret was a miniature gauss cannon, little brothers to the forward-facing main cannon underslung along the hull. Unfortunately, that cannon required them to be facing a foe, and Nolan wasn't about to risk that.

Three sleek, missile-like ships were rapidly closing the distance to the *Johnston*. Nolan held his breath as all eight turrets fired. White streaks shot into space--visible evidence of the breakup of the projectile housing, as each turret fired a depleted uranium core accelerated to lethal velocity with powerful magnets.

One of the darts exploded, but the other two took evasive maneuvers. The darts had no armaments, but their massive engines allowed them to rapidly close with their targets. Like their parent vessel, they had dense tritanium armor, which meant that only a direct hit would bring one down.

"Brace yourselves," Nolan roared, grabbing onto the side of the chair. The ship shuddered, then shuddered again, as both darts impacted.

Unlike the Primos, the Tigris didn't generally use conventional ordinance. Those missiles were troop transports.

He stabbed a button on the right arm of the Captain's chair to send his voice across the entire ship. "This is commander Nolan," he said. "All hands prepare to be boarded."

Chapter 3- Hannan

Hannan settled her combat helmet over her bare scalp, flicking the switch that illuminated the targeting HUD. Her Head-up Display could be set to show a variety of things, but for this engagement, targeting was what she needed. She tucked her sidearm into the holster strapped to the leg of her TX-11 body armor, then picked up her her assault rifle. Around her the rest of the squad was doing the same.

"Mills, you're on point," she said, tucking two more clips into the largest pouch on her belt.

"Sure," the handsome sniper said. He peered at her with those frosty blue eyes, expression as emotionless as a shark's. He didn't salute, and she didn't ask him to. He did his job, and that was enough.

"Edwards, keep your cool, all right? Wait for them to come to us." Hannan turned to face the largest member of the squad, a beefy man with a thick red beard and a shaved scalp. The private had a slightly vacant expression, which matched his demeanor. Edwards wasn't smart, but he was loyal and took orders well.

"Yes, sir," Edwards said, giving her an eager nod. He picked up his heavy assault rifle, the TM-601. It weighed nearly sixty pounds, about three times her own TM-30.

"Paterson," she said, addressing the oldest member of the squad. Paterson wore a neatly trimmed beard that was beginning to gray, and had been in the 14th even longer than Hannan. For some reason he'd never advanced beyond private, and seemed happy with that. "I want you to keep an eye on the kid." She didn't wait for a reply, exiting the armory and starting up the corridor.

"I've got your back, Duncan. Just stick close to me," Paterson said, clapping the newest member of the squad on the back.

"I don't need a babysitter," Duncan said, eyes flashing. The kid trotted up the corridor until he was even with Hannan. "Just show me where the Tigris are. I've been wanting a new lion-skin rug."

"Don't be an idiot," Hannan said, eyes narrowing. "Stay in position, and listen to Paterson. If you get out of line again, I'll toss your ass into the brig, private. Am I clear?"

"Yes, sir," Duncan said, sullenly.

"Sarge," Mills called from up the corridor. He dropped to one knee next to the hatch leading down to B deck, one fist raised to indicate they should stop.

The squad froze, each making their profile as small as

possible. Hannan glided forward, trying to be stealthy as she knelt next to Mills. "What have you got?"

"See for yourself," Mills whispered.

Hannan peered down the corridor. About forty meters away a bronze spike had shot through the hull. It filled the corridor, and the tip punched through the inner wall. The area around the breach was thick with viscous black fluid, which the Tigris used to prevent attacked vessels from depressurizing. She could see an outline along the metal spike, and knew immediately what it was.

"Boarding tube. They're going to pop out of there any second," she whispered. Hannan turned back to the quad, raising her arm and gesturing to the squad. They trotted forward, assuming defensive positions. Hannan waited until they were settled before speaking. "We'll have contact in a few seconds. As soon as that hatch opens they'll start pouring out. Let Mills pick them off. When they rush our position, cut them down. Let them come to us."

A sharp hiss sounded behind her, and Hannan whirled with a curse. The hatch along the spike slid down, and the first Tigris dropped into the hallway. It wore midnight armor that matched its fur well enough that she had a hard time knowing where the armor ended and fur began. The beast was taller than Edwards, and about twice as wide. It cradled a huge shotgun, a weapon the Tigris had adopted during the eight year war.

"End it, Mills," she whispered.

Mills brought the stock of his rifle to his shoulder, sighting down the scope. The motion was as smooth as it was fast, and less than two seconds later a sharp report echoed down the corridor. The bullet caught the Tigris above the left eye, and blood sprayed the bronze tube behind it as the beast collapsed to the deck.

Hannan ducked to the left side of the hatch as answering fire came from the Tigris. The corridor filled with the hot smell of gunpowder, and the pings of slugs biting into the other side of the hatch.

"They're going to rush us," Hannan called over the gunfire. "Get ready to push back."

She risked a glance around the hatch, and cursed when she saw the Tigris charging. Four black-furred cats bounded up the hallway, covering ten feet with every jump. She brought up the muzzle of her assault rifle and loosed a three round burst at the closest target. It caught the cat in the chest, but the heavy armor shunted the impact. The cat was knocked prone, but was otherwise unharmed.

Its companions bounded over it, and the first one leapt

through the door. Edwards was waiting, and the deep angry booms of his TM-601 were deafening. The stream of slugs caught the cat in the face, sending it into a backwards spin. It flipped back through the doorway with a pitiful mew, but the next cat was already through. It landed next to Edwards, grabbing the barrel of his assault rifle with one hand.

It yanked the weapon from Edwards's grip, tossing it to the deck. Then the beast raked his armor with its claws, sending up a shower of sparks as Edwards toppled backwards. The cat leapt, pinning the big Marine to the deck as it savaged his neck armor with those massive jaws.

Another cat came through, but Duncan and Paterson were ready. Their combined fire drove the cat back, then a lucky shot from the kid caught the cat in the face. It slumped to the deck, its body straddling the hatch.

Hannan took a split second to assess, then decided that Edwards was most in need of help. She darted forward, ripping her sidearm from its holster. She planted the weapon against the back of the Tigris's skull, and squeezed the trigger. The beast's skull was thick, but not thick enough to take three high velocity rounds at close range. It collapsed onto Edwards, who groaned as he tossed the body aside.

"Thanks, Sarge," Edwards panted, his face and neck covered

in blood. She hoped most of that was from the Tigris.

"Get some," Duncan yelled. Hannan's head snapped up, her stomach sinking when she saw what was happening.

Duncan had advanced past the hatch, into the hallway. There was no cover there, and he was completely unsupported. She was still rising to her feet when a black form flashed into view. It leveled its shotgun at Duncan's chest, and the weapon boomed. Duncan was picked up and hurled backwards, landing in a heap.

Paterson rushed into the corridor, unloading three-round bursts at the Tigris who'd shot Duncan. That Tigris went down, but answering fire from the other Tigris lit Paterson up. His body jerked as rounds punched through his armor, and he finally collapsed to the deck. Hannan knew he was dead.

"Mills," she snarled. "I'll lay down suppressive fire. I want dead cats, and I want them now."

"Dead cats I can do," he said. It was all he had to say. Hannan knew that Mills had more cause than most to hate the Tigris. His parents had been on a freighter wiped out by Tigris, during the war.

Hannan dropped to one knee, shielding her body with the hatch as much as possible. She switched her weapon to full auto, and sprayed the corridor with a quarter clip's worth of rounds. There were only three targets remaining, and all three ducked when she began firing.

Mills brought his rifle up. It coughed once. Twice. Three times. All three cats collapsed to the deck.

Hannan stopped firing, her chest heaving as she surveyed the carnage.

"We did it," Duncan said, stumbling awkwardly to his feet. His armor had been punctured over his right shoulder, which explained how he'd survived a Tigris shotgun blast. His gap-toothed grin made Hannan want to punch him. "We downed a Tigris boarding party. Hell yes."

"Shut up, kid," Mills said. "We got lucky."

"What do you mean?" Duncan said, blinking. He was unaware of the blood coming from Paterson's body, just a couple feet away.

"These weren't elites," Hannan said, wearily. She moved down to Paterson, gently closing his eyes. She gave Duncan a hard look. "These are nothing more than privateers, not true Leonis Pride. If we'd fought elites all of us would be dead, thanks to that stunt you pulled."

Chapter 4- Cat and Mouse

"Emo," Nolan called, rising from his chair and moving toward the pilot's chair. "I want you to decelerate."

"You want me to do what? Are you crazy?" Emo said, darting a look Nolan's way that left no doubt how he felt about Nolan's sanity. He looked around to the rest of the bridge crew. "Where's the captain? This guy is going to get us killed."

"Ensign Gaden, I gave you a direct order," Nolan snapped. He seized the back of Emo's chair, the adrenaline surging through him. "Do it. Slow down to seventy-five percent acceleration."

Nolan spun to face the comm officer. "Juliard, tell Engineering to shut down engine number four."

"Aye, sir," Juliard responded, her voice calm. Though her expression showed a healthy dose of fear, she bent to her terminal and began punching in commands.

Nolan released Emo's chair and moved back to his own, eyes fixed on the view screen as he waited to see if his tactic would work.

"Sir, the Tigris are closing the gap between us. They'll be in range to grapple in nine seconds," Emo said, spinning his chair to face Nolan.

"I'm aware of that. When they're three seconds out, I want you to do a full burn in the three active engines. That should get us into that asteroid field," Nolan ordered, forcing himself to lean back in the chair.

"Ahh, I see what you're up to," Captain Dryker said, ducking through the hatch. He carried a plate of the yellow protein that passed for eggs, but tasted a lot more like styrofoam. "You want them to think we're more wounded than we are, that their boarding teams disabled an engine. Don't let me interrupt."

Nolan clenched a fist, then took a deep breath. Putting him in charge had been the worst kind of recklessness, but he'd only have a chance to be angry about it if they survived the next three minutes.

"The Tigris warship is following us into the asteroid field," Emo warned. He tilted the stick, and the *Johnston* bucked wildly as it swerved around an asteroid that dwarfed both itself and the pursuing warship.

Nolan was silent as Emo expertly threaded their way through the asteroid field. They passed within a dozen feet of chunks of rock large enough to crush their vessel. The Tigris warship showed up as a red blip on the mini-map in the corner of the display. It was close, but no longer gaining.

"Juliard, connect me to Engineering," he ordered, again forcing himself to relax in the chair. His next move was a gamble. If it paid off, they had a chance. If not--well, at least he wouldn't be around to be chastised for it.

"You're live, sir," Juliard said.

"Engineering, I want you to ignite engine four on my mark. Give it everything you've got," he ordered, leaning forward and raising a hand even though he knew they couldn't see it. Nolan watched the view screen as the *Johnston* plunged deeper into the asteroid field. Rocks of all sizes flew around them, and it was a testament to Emo's skill that they survived.

The Tigris vessel hadn't broken off, but the gap had widened as the cats struggled to keep up. They were bigger and faster, but less maneuverable.

"Mark," Nolan said, dropping his hand. The ship surged as the fourth engine came back online. "Emo, use that large asteroid as cover, then bring us about."

"Acknowledged, sir," Emo said, pouring on the speed. Nolan's stomach lurched as the vessel passed under the largest asteroid they'd yet seen. He couldn't actually feel the inertia, but his eyes tricked his body into thinking it could.

They passed under the asteroid and, as soon as it screened

them from the Tigris, Emo flipped the vessel. The ship came

about, its nose aimed in the direction from which the Tigris

would appear.

"Ezana, warm up the main cannon," Nolan ordered.

"Target, sir?" the chief asked, a sheen of sweat covering

his forehead.

"Use the turrets to soften up that depression at the base

of the asteroid. Fire the main cannon into the rift that opens

up," Nolan ordered, studying the asteroid. "Hold your fire until

the moment the Tigris vessel comes into view."

The next eight seconds were the most tense of Nolan's life.

He'd never been in a real ship-to-ship combat, and he had that

eternity to contemplate the consequences of his plan. If it

didn't work, they'd be helpless.

"Fire," Nolan roared, the instant the sleek body of the

enemy ship appeared below them.

The gauss cannons began their staccato, sending slug after

slug into the asteroid. A deep hum built within the bowels of

the ship, then rose to a high-pitched whine. The *Johnston*'s main

gun--the most powerful weapon humanity had ever developed--fired

a tank-sized hunk of depleted uranium into the asteroid with the

force of a many-megaton bomb.

The shot sent a magnetic ripple from the barrel, as the

cannon dispersed the excess energy. The rift they'd fired into became a canyon; a quarter of the massive asteroid peeled off as the explosion flung it straight into the Tigris vessel. The ship was tough, its tritanium hull strong enough to deal with the stresses of entering a star. But it wasn't tough enough to deal with the impact of thousands of tons of dense rock.

The Tigris vessel exploded in a brilliant shower of debris, and the bridge crew began to cheer.

Chapter 5- Egg Breath

Nolan's chest was heaving, more from adrenaline than true exertion. The clapping died down and he was left staring at Captain Dryker, who was still spooning eggs into his mouth. Dryker stared back, unperturbed.

"What the hell were you thinking?" Nolan demanded, something hot slithering into his vision. "We could have all been killed. You abandoned your command during combat."

"What the hell were you thinking, *sir*," Dryker corrected mildly. He set his now-empty plate on top of a nearby monitor, then turned back to Nolan. "You came to us from Fleet Command, did you not?"

"Yes, but I don't see what that has to do with anything," Nolan said. He was aware of the heat in his voice, aware that he was addressing a superior officer.

"It has everything to do with the situation," Dryker said, narrowing his eyes. "I wanted to see what you were made of, Commander. You have precisely zero combat experience. You were too young to fight in the Tigris war, and your resumé says you're an analyst."

"That's why I have such an issue with your behavior," Nolan

shot back, rising from the captain's chair. "If I'd frozen up, we'd all be dead. You were reckless, *sir*."

"Was I?" Dryker said, rolling the words around as if he were trying to decide if he liked the way they tasted. "I won't have an officer on my ship who can't fight, Commander. You're green, and you need experience. Guess how you get that experience?"

Nolan was silent for a moment as he considered his reply. He didn't have time before the captain plunged ahead.

"You know who I am. You know what I did in the war," Dryker said, folding his arms as he speared Nolan with his gaze. "I needed to know that you were competent, and that you could think on your feet. I was close enough to resume command if you couldn't handle it."

"I still disagree with the decision," Nolan protested. He wasn't quite ready to let it go, but didn't know what he could accomplish by pushing the issue.

"I know. I disagree with me being posted here in the first place, but we're the 14th. We haven't seen new equipment since before the Tigris war. We work with what little Fleet gives us," Dryker said. He gave a heavy sigh. "I've read your dossier, Commander. I know what they say about you. That you can't keep it in your pants, and getting caught with the wrong admiral's daughter is how you lost your cushy Fleet gig and ended up here."

"Respectfully, you can go frag yourself, sir."

"Well, you've got some fire at least," the captain said. He turned to Juliard. "Lieutenant, have Hannan's squad head to the shuttle bay. The commander will be joining them for a little jaunt to the planet."

"Jaunt to the planet?" Nolan found himself asking. He clenched both fists, willing himself to take deep breaths.

"That's right," Dryker said, turning back to him. His brown eyes bored into Nolan. "You're on a combat vessel now, Nolan. You don't get to push paper and chase skirts. We work for a living out there. You've been trained as an OFI field agent, so this should be a cake walk. We were called here to investigate the sudden silence of the Mar Kona colony. It's high time we were about that, wouldn't you say?"

"Sir, is it wise to have command personnel leave the vessel?" Nolan said, in one last attempt to get the captain to see reason.

"We do things differently out there, Commander," Dryker said, leaning in close. Now his breath smelled of fake eggs and coffee. "You're going planet side, because we want someone with command authority in a position to react quickly. We don't know what to expect down there. Now get your ass off my bridge and down to the shuttle bay."

"Yes, sir."

"Oh, and Commander?" Dryker said as Nolan moved for the hatch.

Nolan paused.

"Nice work. You've got a real head for tactics."

Chapter 6- Meet the Marines

Nolan wasn't sure what the hell to think as he made his way below decks. The ship wasn't massive, but corridors were tight and it took several minutes to reach the shuttle bay. During that time, he alternated between being pleased that he'd commanded his first combat and being angry at the Captain's actions.

Dryker was a hero. He'd been one of the last five people to survive the Tigris attack on the Elbas station, and it had been that battle that led to the Tigris offering a truce. Dryker was a legend.

Of course, Dryker had also been exiled to the 14th fleet while all four of his contemporaries had moved into the admiralty. After today, Nolan was pretty sure he understood why.

Nolan ducked through the final hatch and into the single largest room on the *Johnston*. It was about fifty feet across and thirty feet wide, with the vast majority of the space taken up by a sleek black shuttle. Four people were already clustered outside of it, and as Nolan approached he heard a booming laugh.

It came from a man roughly the size and shape of a brick wall. His beard was even the right shade for the comparison. The

man had a bandage around his neck--and he wasn't the only
wounded member of the group. Another Marine, this one still in
his teens, was drenched in blood. It covered the back of his
TX-11 armor, and a hasty patch had been applied to what looked
to be Tigris slug hole in the front.

"Attention," barked a third figure, the shortest of the
lot. She was pretty, in a severe sort of way. Her scalp looked
recently shaved, and her armor was dented and scarred from
repeated use.

Both wounded Marines snapped to attention, as did the woman
who'd spoken. The last figure, a man with corporal's stars, sat
calmly on an ammo crate, carefully using a rag to clean the
inside of the barrel of a sniper rifle. He looked up and nodded
at Nolan, but didn't rise or salute.

"Is there a problem, Corporal...?" Nolan said, folding his
arms.

"Mills," the man said, looking up from his rifle. "Yeah,
there's a problem. Word is you're a womanizing paper pusher
who's never seen combat."

"Since this is our first meeting, I'm going to let your
insubordination slide," Nolan said, staring Mills down. "You
don't know anything about me, Corporal. Don't judge me until
your own morality has been tested. You have no idea what

happened, or what I was asked to do."

"Mills, I've had about enough of this shit," the short woman said, her voice calm. She took two steps forward, then wound up and clocked the seated Marine in the jaw. He crashed to the deck, then scrambled to his feet.

Mills's face tightened in anger as he regained his feet, but he looked apologetically at the woman who'd knocked him on his ass. "Sorry, Sarge."

"What's our motto, Mills?" the woman asked, leaning forward to stare directly into the sniper's face.

"Be polite, be professional, but have a plan to kill everyone you meet," Mills replied, looking up at her with icy blue eyes.

"You just broke the 'polite, professional' part of that," she said. "Don't let it happen again."

"I recognize the quote," Nolan said. "Major General James Mattis."

"That's right," the woman said. She eyed him curiously. "Listen, I know this first meeting crap is awkward, so let's move past it. I'm Sergeant Hannan. That's Mills, obviously. The young one is Duncan. The big one is Edwards."

Nolan nodded at each of them in turn.

"There's only one thing you need to know if you're going to

ride with us," Hannan continued. "You're strategy. You tell us the objective. We're tactics. We achieve that objective. I know you have operational authority, but I expect to be given charge of my unit. You want us to keep you alive, you stay out of our way and let us do our jobs. That work for you?"

Nolan could see from the squad's expression exactly what was happening here. If he exerted authority, it would make him look like an arrogant officer. If he caved, then he'd effectively be ceding authority to Sergeant Hannan.

"I'll leave you to conduct basic operations, Sergeant," Nolan said.

Hannan's smile grew predatory.

"But make no mistake," he said. "I'm the Command Officer here. You will follow any orders I give without question. Is that clear?"

"Crystal. Sir," Hannan said, a scowl replacing her smile.

Chapter 7- Gone

"Mills, take us down over there. Land on the south pad,"
Hannan ordered, gesturing at the wide plasteel pad the local
police on Mar Kona used. It was curiously empty, as was the
entirety of the Mar Kona colony. No ships flitted between
skyscrapers. No pedestrians clogged the pristine streets. Hannan
didn't like it, not one bit.

"Sarge, where did everyone get to?" Edwards asked, leaning
forward over Mills to peer through the shuttle's view screen.
Mills gave Edwards an annoyed glance, but didn't say anything.
He guided the shuttle down until it bumped gently against the
pad.

"That's what we're here to find out," Commander Nolan said,
before Hannan could offer a reply.

Her jaw clicked shut, and she suppressed the urge to deck
the smug bastard.

"Sergeant," Nolan said, "scan for communications, please."

"Yes, sir," Hannan replied, nodding to Mills.

Mills tapped a series of commands on the shuttle's console,
and a green light began to blink slowly. After a moment it
turned yellow, then a solid red. Text scrolled across the

screen, and Mills turned to face her. "Looks like there's a single distress beacon about two clicks into the jungle south of us, near some old ruins."

"Ruins?" Edwards said, still looming over Mills. "I thought this was a human colony."

"It is," Nolan said. He'd already risen, and was walking to the back of the shuttle. He pulled a tactical vest from the wall, fitting it over his simple grey body armor. The vest carried everything from spare clips of universal rounds to a couple of compressed MREs. "This place didn't always belong to humans, though. The Primo empire was much larger, once upon a time. The ruins belonged to them at some point."

"Edwards, stow the chatter. Get focused," Hannan said, rising from the co-pilot's chair. She grabbed a tactical vest as well. "Duncan, you with us?"

The wide-eyed kid was even more wide-eyed than usual, probably from the cocktail his suit was feeding him--or maybe from the remorse of getting another soldier killed. He blinked up at her. "Present, Sarge. Ready to kick some ass."

"Mills, I want you roaming. Stay within two hundred meters," she ordered, slapping the large red button next to the shuttle's deployment ramp. It whined as it descended, hissing as the shuttle's atmosphere normalized with Mar Kona's. The place smelled like flowers, and she could hear birds and monkeys chattering in the background. It was damned unnerving after a lifetime spent in space.

"You won't see me, but I'll be there," Mills said, snatching up his rifle as he passed. He leapt off the ramp and started trotting south.

"Duncan, I want you on point. Edwards, take the rear. I'll be in the middle with our esteemed commander," she said, walking down the ramp. Edwards and Duncan moved into their assigned positions and they all began moving south, away from the city. Nolan moved into step next to Hannan.

"You don't like me, do you?" the commander asked, low enough that only she could hear.

The question caught her off guard. She *didn't* like him, but it was rare for an officer to be direct. That was a small mark in his favor.

"No, I don't," she said, deciding that honesty was best. She scanned the jungle before her, an intimidating mass of trees and flowers. Anything could be hiding in there.

"Why?" Nolan asked. He'd drawn his sidearm, and cradled the weapon in both hands. At least he'd been trained to shoot, though she doubted the low-caliber pistol would be much use against Tigris. Not unless he got a head shot.

"Because Mills was right. You're a paper pusher," Hannan said, quickening her pace. Both Duncan and Edwards matched it automatically, and after a moment Nolan did too. "You were exiled to the 14th because you pissed someone off. Scuttlebutt is that you slept with the wrong woman, but I don't give a shit about that. I care about your ability to command in combat. If you mess up, my men pay the price. We can't afford to have a paper pusher giving orders. That's how people die."

"That's fair," Nolan said, nodding. He already wore a thin sheen of sweat, and his breathing was a little ragged. Too much time behind a desk. "I'm not trained to be a Marine. Hell I'm not trained to be a Fleet Commander. I worked in tactical, and my whole goal was to work up the OFI command structure."

"Oh," Hannan said, grimacing. The OFI was a dirty word to enlisted personnel. The Office of Fleet Intelligence existed to make life difficult for every other branch of service, and acted like they were the sole reason humanity had held its own against the Tigris.

"That said, since I'm here, I'm going to do my best to be a good officer," Nolan continued.

Hannan, studying the jungle as they approached the trees, didn't answer that. "Shut up, sir," she said, dropping to one knee behind a giant root that snaked from one of the trunks. She held up a fist, and both Edwards and Duncan took cover. Nolan did the same a moment later, but she wasn't watching him.

"What is it?" Nolan hissed.

"Mills," she said, nodding to a tree about fifty meters into the tree line. Somehow Mills had scaled one of the massive trunks, and was using a mirror to reflect sunlight back in her direction. "He's spotted something."

"Contact," Edwards yelled.

Something was sprinting through the trees. Hannan couldn't make out much; the figure was using some sort of stealth tech and, except for a faint ripple, it blended almost perfectly with the foliage around it. The only reason she was able to track it was the swaying of the bushes as it passed.

The figure paused, and two head-sized balls of blue energy shot in their direction. The first obliterated the root she'd been hiding behind, and Hannan dove out of the way. She rolled through mud and leaves, coming up behind a thick tree trunk.

She risked a glance around the trunk, then darted back into cover. "It's at six o'clock. Edwards, Duncan, move to flank that thing. Now."

"What about me?" Nolan asked. He was crouched behind a trunk, peering around it. Damned fool was going to get his head shot off.

"Keep out of sight," she snapped, darting forward a few feet and diving behind another root. Three more balls of energy flashed, sending up a spray of debris as the area she'd just occupied exploded. "They're using plasma weapons, so keep moving. Cover won't save you."

"Mills," she barked into her comm. "End that thing."

"Acknowledged," Mills murmured back.

There was a sharp crack from the tree where Mills was crouched, and the insubstantial figure suddenly stumbled forward. Whatever cloaking tech it was using failed, giving her the first look at the alien. It was tall--maybe two meters--and bipedal, with some sort of rifle clutched in one hand. Its armor was a smooth blue alloy, like nothing she'd ever seen. Its chest tapered down into a waist far narrower than a human's. The legs were just as thin, though clearly still powerful.

For a moment, she thought it was a robot of some type, but Mill's shot had cored the thing through the chest and orange blood had spattered the ground all around it. The creature turned, and blurred back into the jungle.

"Holy crap," Edwards called. "That thing is moving fifty clicks an hour."

Chapter 8- Ambush

Nolan rose slowly from behind the tree trunk, scanning the area where the strange armored figure had been shot. Orange blood splattered the leaves, and a trail of it led into the jungle.

Hannan spoke into her mic. ""Mills, get back to the jungle floor and track that thing. It's moving in the direction of the distress beacon."

"Belay that," Nolan ordered, holstering his as-yet-unfired pistol. He moved to stand next to Hannan, who was glaring up at him as if awaiting an explanation. Was he making the right move? "Sergeant Hannan, have your squad take up defensive positions, and get ready for incoming."

"What makes you think we're about to have incoming? We ran across a single scout, which is wounded and probably making for its unit," Hannan protested. She was much shorter, but still managed to intimidate the hell out of Nolan. "We need to move, and move quickly. These things could already have reached the beacon."

Nolan considered for a long moment. He was an inexperienced paper pusher, as Hannan had pointed out. But he'd also been through officer training, and had been the top analyst in his division. Something about this situation didn't sit well. Where were all the people? Even the Marines guarding Mar Kona had been taken.

In the end the captain's words decided it for him. If he was going to be a part of this crew, then he needed to act like a leader. That might mean making mistakes, but even mistakes were better than inaction.

"Just do it, Sergeant," he said. "This is strategy, not tactics. Your disagreement is noted, and I encourage you to include it in your report to the captain." He glanced around the clearing. "Tactical placement is your call, but get these men into a defensive perimeter."

"Fine," Hannan snapped. She turned to face the tree where they'd last seen Mills. He might still be there, but there was no sign of him. "Mills, keep a look-out for approaching hostiles. Edwards, use that V between those two large roots for cover. That should give you a good firing lane. Duncan, you're watching our rear."

Nolan watched the Marines move, impressed by their precision. Within a few moments they'd followed orders, and all four of them had overlapping fields of fire. Nolan drew his pistol again, though he knew he wouldn't be much more than a bystander if it did come to combat. He was a good shot, but he'd brought the wrong weapon for prolonged fire fights.

Several minutes passed, and Nolan began to sweat. Not just because he was overly warm, but also because he was starting to doubt himself. Were these unknown assailants already at the beacon? Had his decision to fortify their position, instead of pursue the aliens, cost whomever set the beacon their life?

"Contact," Mills whispered over the radio. "At least three hostiles, moving through the jungle in your direction. None of them are leaking blood, so I don't think it's the same one we ran into."

"Paint the lead target," Hannan whispered back, her voice amplified by Nolan's earpiece. "The second it's in range, Edwards and I will light it up. Mills, you'll shift to targets of opportunity. Duncan, keep your eyes on our northern flank."

The next few minutes were agonizing. Nolan stayed low behind a tree trunk, most of his body concealed by tall ferns. He darted glances in the direction Mills had said the hostiles were coming from, but occasionally looked back in Duncan's direction, too.

Then all hell broke loose. Something shimmered in the distance. Nolan wouldn't have thought much of it, except that a red laser appeared on the thing's chest. Then Edwards's TM-601 filled the jungle with thunder as slugs tore into the target. A second stream of slugs, belched at a higher pitch, shot from Hannan's position, and the shimmering target lost its stealth tech. It faded back into view, its entire body riddled with holes, and was flung backwards to land in a heap at the base of a large tree.

Cracks sounded from Mills's tree, presumably more shots from his sniper rifle. Nolan leaned up from cover, just a few inches, but couldn't see what Mills was firing at.

"Help!" Duncan yelled, not more than a dozen feet behind him. Nolan spun to see a figure shimmer into existence next to Duncan. Three glowing blades extended from one of its wrists-- some sort of plasma weapon, crackling with blue energy.

Nolan brought his pistol up, but it was like moving through molasses. The hostile was just too fast. It brought its blades down in a tight arc, plunging them into Duncan's chest. They sank into the Marine's heart as if his armor were cloth. The teen twitched once, then toppled to the ground.

Nolan squeezed the trigger as fast as he could, and the alien's head jerked backwards as a shot ricocheted off its faceplate. That got its attention. It darted forward, gliding across the jungle floor like a hunting cat. It was clearly fixed on Nolan, and he knew there was no way he'd be able to run.

A crack sounded behind him, and the thing's head ceased to exist. Its body toppled to the ground near Duncan's.

"You're welcome," came Mills's voice over the comm.

"Thank you," Nolan mumbled, the adrenaline spiking. He stared at the body, wanting to approach but somehow convinced the thing was still dangerous.

"Clear," Hannan yelled across the clearing. She came striding up to him, a stream of smoke still rising from the barrel of her rifle. "You all right? You look a little shaken."

"Yeah, I'm fine," Nolan said, though he did feel a little ill.

A boom shook the jungle, much more powerful than any of the gunshots. It was almost enough to knock Nolan from his feet, and he stumbled back into a tree. Then a second boom sounded, and a third. With a sickening feeling, Nolan realized what was happening.

"Get down," he roared, sprinting toward Hannan. He tackled her into the underbrush just as a fourth boom sounded from only a dozen feet away. It picked him and Hannan up, flinging them into a wide puddle in a spray of muddy water.

Chapter 9- Ruins

The ringing drowned out all other sound. Nolan shook his head, staggering from the muddy water to the shore where Hannan was already recovering. A detached part of his mind remembered that her armor would pump her full of stims. He wished he had something similar, but his more generic armor didn't come with the same load-out.

"How did you know?" Hannan asked.

Her voice was muffled. Distant. Nolan shook his head again.

"I heard the first three explosions. Back at the OFI training academy, we studied insurgents. Boobytrapping weapons and armor that they were forced to leave behind was common," he said. His voice sounded strange in his own ears, but the sharp ringing was fading.

Edwards had already approached, but there was no sign of Mills. In the trees, probably. There were signs of Duncan, all over the jungle. Nolan fought back the nausea. He stumbled over to the most recognizable part, and picked up the private's dog tags. Nolan tucked them into a pocket, aware that Hannan was watching him.

"That's not what I meant. How did you know that they'd come

for us?" Hannan asked, cocking her head. "If we hadn't set up a defensive perimeter we'd all be dead now." She offered Nolan a hand. "We owe you, commander."

"Thanks," Nolan said, accepting her hand. She had a firm grip. He released it, and sat heavily on a fallen log. "I just need a minute, then I'm ready to head to the beacon. You asked how I knew? Look around us. Every last person in Mar Kona is gone, and that includes the Marines. Whoever or whatever these things are, they're tough enough to overwhelm everything. I didn't think they'd be terribly impressed by one more Marine squad, and saw no reason they wouldn't try to take us, too."

"That makes a lot of sense," Hannan conceded, with a nod. "If they're gathering people, then they'd want to gather us too. As soon as they knew we were here, they sent a group to overwhelm us."

"Exactly," Nolan said, standing up. "I think I'm ready to move now. Shall we head to the beacon and see what's what?"

"That's up to you, sir," Hannan said, giving him a respectful nod. "You're in charge. You proved that."

"All right then, disperse your squad as you see fit, and let's see if whoever set that beacon is still around to be rescued," Nolan said.

He was dimly aware of Hannan barking orders over the comm.

Edwards marched in the jungle behind them, while Hannan led them
in the direction of the beacon. Mills was no doubt lurking
somewhere above, and it was somehow reassuring that Nolan
couldn't see him. Maybe that meant these strange aliens couldn't
either.

"Commander?" Hannan asked, her eyes ceaselessly scanning
the jungle as they advanced.

"Yeah?" Nolan asked, trying with limited success to mimic
the way she moved.

"I've never seen aliens like this, never even heard of
them. You're OFI, or were anyway. Do the spooks know anything
they're not saying?" Hannan asked. Her voice was pitched low,
and her attention never wavered from the jungle ahead of them.

"We've never seen anything like this, at least not that I
know of," Nolan said, keeping pace. "Their technology is clearly
advanced. I've never seen handheld plasma weapons this small, or
any weapons with that kind of punch."

"I thought only Primos used plasma weapons," Hannan said.

"That's what I thought, too. They've never let the tech get
out," Nolan replied. Something about this made him uneasy. "The
weapons we saw were both smaller and more powerful than anything
I've seen the Primos use. I'd hate to see what kind of ship
these things arrived in."

They were silent for the rest of the trek and, fifteen minutes later, finally reached a ridge that looked down on a jungle-filled valley. In the center of the valley stood magnificent ruins cut from some sort of white stone, ringed by a large wall that was broken in several places. Two huge statues, worn smooth by the millennia, stood atop the gate leading in.

"Looks empty," Hannan said, though her tone was dubious.

"One way to find out," Nolan said, starting down the trail that led into the valley.

"Hold on," came a voice from behind them. "We can make this a lot faster," . Mills stepped from the jungle not more than ten feet away. Nolan had had no idea the man was there until he spoke.

Mills began fitting attachments onto his rifle. He stuck what appeared to be a harpoon in the barrel, added a spool of thick wire to the side, and took aim at the wall below. Then he fired, and the harpoon sank into the wall, leaving the wire in its wake, which Mills affixed to a nearby tree, taking up the slack and pulling it tight before tying it off.

"A zipline?" Nolan asked, impressed.

"Yeah, should shave a few hours off our time," Mills said. He hooked a carabiner over the line, then slid down into the valley.

Chapter 10- Lena

Ziplining was a new experience for Nolan, but there was something exhilarating about sailing over the strange jungle. He landed at the base of the wall next to the others--and if his landing wasn't as graceful as Hannan's, at least he wasn't embarrassed.

"The beacon is sixty meters past the wall, outside whatever that structure is," Hannan said, peering around the wall and into the courtyard.

"Movement?" Edwards asked. The big man had been quiet since Duncan's death.

"None. The beacon is just sitting there. I don't see any movement. It's possible whoever set that thing has already been taken," Hannan said. She turned to Mills, who was crouched on the other side of the gateway leading into the courtyard. "Get high, Mills. See what you can see."

Mills nodded, then trotted down the wall until he reached a broken section. The speed with which he ascended shocked Nolan. Sure, their armor gave them an advantage, but these people were incredibly skilled. Given the 14th's reputation, that shouldn't have been the case.

"Edwards, advance inside. Follow the wall and keep a bead on that beacon," Hannan ordered. She stepped inside the courtyard, sinking to one knee behind a fallen column. "That leaves the beacon for you, Commander."

Nolan took a deep breath and walked into the courtyard. Part of him expected to be disintegrated, but nothing stirred as he approached the little metal ball. He stopped next to it, peering down at the flashing red light on the side. He reached down and picked it up.

"It's Tigris make," he yelled over his shoulder. "I'm guessing it belonged to a science team, given the debris we found when we first arrived in system."

"You're correct, human," came a feminine voice from behind him. Nolan whirled to see a figure crouched in the shadows. He couldn't make out much, but he spotted a golden tail swishing around her shoulder. Her accent was clipped and polished, something like human British. "I set the beacon, and I was a member of a science team dispatched to these ruins."

"You were using us as bait," Hannan yelled, rising from cover and stalking toward the figure.

"You're more perceptive than I was led to believe Marines of the 14th fleet could be," she said, finally stepping into the light. She had thick, golden fur and a well-muscled frame.

Leonis Pride nobility, Nolan was certain. "I apologize for the deception, but it was a necessary one. The rest of my team has already been taken and, unless someone capable of rescue showed up, I was planning on hiding indefinitely."

"How long have you been here?" Nolan asked. He re-holstered the pistol he'd unconsciously drawn when she'd first spoken.

"Four days," the Tigris said, holding up a four-fingered paw. She approached slowly, her nose twitching as she crept closer. "We were researching until yesterday night, when the strangers arrived. They had three ships, and began loading in anyone they could catch. They had teams of...well, invisible soldiers. Those soldiers gathered everyone, and took them into the ships."

"How did you escape? They seemed pretty thorough," Hannan asked, eyes narrowed. Nolan noticed she was still gripping her rifle, as if ready to fire.

"I was blessed by Tigana," the Tigris said. She blushed. "My team was documenting the surface ruins, and I was the only person below. We came because this place began emitting a signal just a few months ago--a signal older than should be possible, as it predates the Primo empire. We wanted to discover the source."

"How did being underground help? Didn't these things go

inside?" Nolan asked. He knew he wasn't getting the whole truth, though he accepted what she had said so far.

"They did," the Tigris said. She glanced at the entrance to the structure dominating the compound. "I discovered the source of the signal. It was coming from a communications array deep inside, and it appeared to be powered by a stabilized singularity. That's tech we've only seen in the Helios Gates, and I realized that it would probably mask other signals. I hid near the generator, and they never came for me. I guess it worked."

"Do you have a name?" Nolan asked.

"Lena of Pride Leonis," the Tigris said.

"Lena, there's no way to soften this. Your vessel has been destroyed. We can give you a lift off this rock, if you'll give us a full report about everything you encountered here," Nolan offered. He didn't really have the authority to transport her anywhere but, as she was the only viable lead, a white lie seemed acceptable.

"I'd expected as much," she said, ears drooping. "The *Revelation* wasn't built for war. I'm willing to tell you everything I know. I had a lot of friends on that vessel. I'll do whatever I can to see that whoever is behind these attacks is brought to justice."

"Lena," Hannan asked, drawing the Tigris's attention. "Did these things take anything but people?"

"Not that I saw, though they did search the ruins. I got the sense they were looking for something, though I don't know what. I couldn't understand their language," Lena said, shrugging apologetically. "It's possible they were seeking something in the ruins but, whatever it was, they didn't find it."

"Thanks for your candor," Nolan said, reaching for his comm. He thumbed it. "*Johnston*, this is away group one. We've recovered a single refugee. We're returning to the ship."

"Holy shit," Edwards said, drawing Nolan's attention.

A ship broke the jungle cover in the distance. It was unlike anything Nolan had ever seen.

Chapter 11- Void Wraith

Nolan snapped down his visor and set it to *Record*. What he was seeing was surreal. A ship easily twice the size of the *Johnston* hovered over the jungle, its metallic blue surface different from anything Nolan had encountered. The ship was curved, with two pincher-like wings extending from a central body, in a sort of stylized V.

"Uh, what is that thing doing?" Hannan asked. No one answered.

A deep thrum passed over them, something powerful just beyond the edge of hearing. Then a small blue light formed between the wings. The ball grew larger until it began to crackle and spark, then the weapon discharged. The ball shot into the jungle, vaporizing another section of the ruins. Nothing remained but a smoking crater.

"Let's move," Nolan said. He didn't pause, just broke into a full sprint. The others followed, including Lena. No one needed to ask why.

The thrumming grew more powerful, and Nolan realized why. The ship was approaching.

"Pick up the pace, people," Hannan yelled. She broke past

Nolan, sprinting for the tree line. Nolan willed his exhausted muscles to work faster, but both Edwards and Mills burst past him.

Lena matched his pace, and she seemed just as winded as he was. They kept moving, adrenaline and fear motivating them forward. The thrumming grew louder still, but Nolan didn't risk a glance over his shoulder. He saved everything for the run ahead of him, giving a sigh of relief when they finally reached the jungle.

He slid to a halt next to a massive tree with a million roots, and finally risked a glance back the way they'd come. The strange ship was now hovering directly over the ruins they'd just left. A ball of energy had already begun to grow, and Nolan winced when he realized the kind of destruction it would leave.

The ship fired, and the resulting explosion vaporized the ruins. The wave of destruction continued outward, expanding toward the jungle. Nolan took a deep breath, and made his peace. He watched the energy approach, then finally stop a dozen paces from the tree line. When it was done, another crater had been created. The ruins were gone, and so was the surrounding valley.

"It's leaving," Hannan said, pointing skyward. Nolan followed her finger.

The ship was breaking orbit, and heading directly toward

the sun.

"Should we warn the *Johnston*?" Edwards asked.

"No," Nolan said, absently. He was still staring at the retreating ship. "It will take several minutes for our transmission to reach them, and by that time it'll be too late to plot an intercept course. After what we just saw, I do *not* want to reveal our location. We'll wait for these things to leave, then shuttle back to the *Johnston*. Dryker can decide what to do with all this."

Chapter 12- Report

Captain Dryker entered his quarters in a foul mood. He closed and sealed the hatch behind him, then sat heavily on his bunk. What the hell had he just gotten mixed up in? The ship that had left Mar Kona had been unlike anything recorded in mankind's brief sojourn as a spacefaring race. It was possible that the Tigris or the Primos might know more about them, but he wouldn't be allowed to contact them outside diplomatic channels. Especially given that they'd just destroyed a Tigris warship.

New races didn't just suddenly appear, especially new races with technology that rivaled or exceeded the Primos. It was a conundrum, and one he simply didn't have enough data to analyze. So he gave up for the time being. Dryker laid down, fluffing the flat, shapeless pillow as much as possible.

"Captain, this is CIC," Juliard said, her voice coming from his comm.

"If we're not under attack, it can wait," he said, pulling off one of his boots and tossing it in the corner.

"Admiral Mendez would like to speak to you, sir." Juliard's tone conveyed a great deal about the urgency.

Damn it. Dryker had served under Mendez in the last war,

and he still owed the old man.

"Put it through," Dryker said, picking up the tablet from his desk and routing the call there. The green and white logo for the Quantum Network appeared, and a moment later the Admiral's face sprung into existence. His dark hair now sported a few patches of grey, especially in his thick beard.

"Ahh, Jim. I'm so glad I was able to reach you." The admiral gave him a warm smile. He snipped the end off a cigar, holding it between his thumb and forefinger rather than lighting it.

"What's this about, Manny?" Dryker asked. He pulled off his other boot and tossed it in the corner.

"Why don't you tell me, Jim?" the admiral replied, raising a thick eyebrow. "I've got a report from your XO claiming he was pushed into a combat situation that could have wiped out everyone aboard the *Johnston*."

"You were the one who told me he was some kind of prodigy," Dryker said. He tugged off his Fleet jacket and dropped it on the floor. "You and I both know he'd never have been busted to the 14th if he hadn't been sleeping with your daughter. Nolan's spent the last four years learning to fight Tigris and Primo alike. He knows their vessels, their tactics, and our capabilities better than anyone. He also performed extremely well during officer testing, ranking in the top 3% of his class.

He's OFI material, through and through. I needed to see if all

that was bullshit, or if he was as good as you claimed."

"And if you'd been wrong? If he'd frozen up?" Mendez shot

back. His gaze hardened. "The kid's right, Dryker. It was

reckless."

"We play by different rules out here. Even if we didn't,

the vessel I had Nolan engage was a privateer, not the *Claw of*

Tigrana," Dryker countered. He stopped undressing and faced the

tablet. "The 14th isn't given anything in the way of resources,

and you know it. Our only prayer is making the best use of the

little we're provided. I'm getting ready to retire, Manny. This

kid will likely replace me in the next year. I either need to

get him up to speed, or wash him out. I'm tired, and I don't

have a lot of options. Besides, I'm not falling for your

bullshit. I know you too well."

"What do you mean?" the admiral said, leaning back in his

chair. He was focused on his unlit cigar, and didn't meet

Dryker's gaze. That told Dryker everything he needed to know.

Manny was playing games.

"I just reported the wreckage of two Tigris ships in human

space. I've included data about new technology, and potentially

a new race," Dryker said. He waited until Manny met his gaze before continuing. "One of the vessels destroyed was science class, which means the Leonis pride is going to be pissed. When they find out we have one of their royal family on board, they'll be even more pissed. Yet you haven't brought up any of that. You're grilling me about a routine command decision concerning my XO. What the hell, Manny? Stop playing games. Why did you really call?"

"All right, if you want to play it that way," Mendez replied. He withdrew a silver lighter, lit his cigar, and took two experimental puffs. "The Tigris have lobbied our embassy to turn over the UFC *Johnston*. Since the admiralty knew that would mean the deaths of the entire crew, we sought another option. Apparently, the Primo are willing to intercede. They'll provide a neutral meeting ground, and will render judgement once both parties have presented their findings. You're to report to Theras Prime and turn yourself over to the Primo."

"What?" Dryker said, blinking. "Are you serious, Manny? We just encountered a new race, one that appears to be wiping out human colonies. Mar Kona was *gone*. Every last person. And you want me to waste time playing politics?"

"You're damn right I do," Mendez snarled. He leaned closer to the screen. "Do you have any idea how dangerous the Primo are? You've tangled with the Tigris, and you know how outclassed we were in the last war. Go back three more centuries. Have you

ever heard of the Seraphinium?"

"No," Nolan said, unsure where the admiral was going with

this.

"Exactly. No one has heard of them, because the Primo wiped

them out. They destroyed an entire race, because that race broke

a treaty with the Tigris," Mendez explained. He paused to take

another puff, and seemed calmer when he spoke again. "The Tigris

are claiming you broke the treaty. Do you see where that puts

us?"

"Okay, I see why you're concerned," Dryker allowed. "But

what about the evidence we can present? Surely the Primo will

realize that there's a new player."

"Evidence?" Mendez scoffed. He shook his head. "There is *no*

hard evidence, just a grainy video of a ship lifting off. You

claim these aliens self-destructed, and can't bring back so much

as a single one of these alleged plasma weapons."

"It may not be hard evidence, but you've got the word of my

CO, and of my Marines," Dryker countered. "The kind of plasma

weaponry they saw doesn't exist anywhere, that we know of. It's

more advanced than the Primos. You can't tell me that doesn't

alarm you."

"What I think doesn't matter. Evidence *does*," the admiral

said. "Someone's going to pay for this, Dryker. I don't want it to be you."

"Give me time to find harder evidence. Just a week. Then we can kowtow to the Primo. They're a patient species. Embassy can keep them occupied for a little while," Dryker pleaded. He hated that he was doing it.

"I can't," Mendez said, looking genuinely regretful. He tapped the ash off the end of his cigar. "You know I'd like nothing better, Jim. I just can't do it."

"Manny, OFI sent me to Mar Kona to investigate for a reason," Dryker said, wishing he had a glass of brandy and eight hours of sleep. "You had to know something was out there."

"All we knew was that the colony hadn't reported in for three days," the admiral said. He leaned closer to the screen, spearing Dryker with his gaze. "You still can't tell me what happened to those colonists."

"I can't get answers if I turn myself over for prosecution," Dryker shot back. He tried to keep his tone even, but it wasn't easy. He knew he had a bad temper. That was what had landed him in the 14th, after all.

Mendez sat up straight. Manny was gone, replaced by The Admiral.

"You are required to take your vessel to Primo space. I'm

giving you a direct order," Mendez said. He paused, letting his words sink in. "I can't protect you on this one, Jim. Get to the coordinates provided, and get there quickly. Maybe we can salvage something out of this disaster."

"Of course," Dryker said, nodding. "We'll head to Theras Prime with best speed."

"Oh, and one more thing," the admiral asked, leaning back and making his next words just a little too casual. "Did you recover any artifacts from the ruins?"

"I told you, the ruins were destroyed by whatever this vessel was," Dryker said. Why would Manny be interested in the ruins?

"Fair enough. Get here soonest, and I'll do what I can to protect you." Then the admiral terminated the connection.

Dryker had no intention of heading to Primo space. He'd already been a scapegoat once. This time, he was going to get to the bottom of this, whatever it took.

Chapter 13- Kathryn

Kathryn paused before Admiral Mendez's door, waiting for the retinal scanner to identify her. Its green beam passed over her eye, then chimed as it went dark. She waited for several tense heartbeats as her arrival was relayed to the Admiral. Mendez was her direct superior, and he was notoriously hard to please. More than one career had been ended by a visit just like this one, and the fact that he was her father didn't mean that she'd be spared. She'd seen, with Nolan, exactly how harsh he could be.

"Enter," called a voice from within. The doors slid open of their own accord, and Kathryn was admitted to the admiral's office. She gave the place the kind of once-over every OFI agent was trained to do, looking for anything out of place, anything that had changed.

Her father sat behind a wide mahogany desk flanked by massive bookshelves. Those shelves contained real books, mostly classic literary pieces. The titles ranged from *Moby Dick* to *War and Peace*, though there were also more than a few tactical volumes like Sun Tzu's *The Art of War* and Michael Ragan's *Tactics & Strategy Unchained*.

"Do you know why I've called you here, Lieutenant Commander?" Mendez asked. *Lieutenant Commander*, not Kathryn. Her father stared impassively at her, perching behind his thick black beard like an assassin about to ambush prey.

"No, sir," she said, clasping her hands behind her back. Using as few words as possible until she knew more seemed like the most prudent course.

"When was the last time you spoke to Commander Nolan?" Mendez asked, his gaze searching.

"I don't remember, exactly. At least a few weeks," she said, resisting the urge to shrug. It was a useless, half-hearted gesture, one she'd used entirely too often as a self-conscious teen.

"Good." Mendez opened a drawer in his desk and withdrew a cigar. He rolled it between his fingers. "What happened with him was bad business, and I'm hoping we can put it behind us."

"I'm hoping to, sir. I was told those records were sealed," she said, keeping her tone carefully neutral. She suspected that "sealed" didn't really mean anything, and this was confirmation. The whole situation was an open book to any admiral with the curiosity to look, and her father had entirely too much self-interest in the whole sordid affair. A fresh wave of guilt washed through her. If Nolan hadn't shielded her, not even her father would have been able to save her. She'd been in command, after all.

"They are sealed," Mendez said. He continued to roll the cigar between a thumb and forefinger, but made no move to light it. "Your own promotion was contingent upon your silence, and I understand that. Nevertheless, I expect you to be forthcoming in this matter. I have questions about Nolan's character."

"Of course, sir," she said. What else could she say?

"Why was Nolan exiled to the 14th?" Mendez asked.

She knew that the admiral already knew the answer. He knew it better than anyone, since he'd orchestrated the event. So why was he asking? "He was demoted for conduct unbefitting an officer of the fleet."

"In your opinion, was that judgement fair?" Mendez asked. Her father was watching her carefully, and she knew her career likely rode on her answer here. It killed her, but she took the safe route, just like she had when Nolan had been demoted.

"Yes, sir," she said. "His judgement was questionable."

"Questionable enough that he might spread unfounded rumors about a new alien race? Rumors designed to exaggerate his own importance?"

She was silent for as she mentally backpedaled, trying to find a way out of giving the answer she knew Mendez was after.

There wasn't one. There was no way to avoid throwing Nolan to the wolves without destroying her career.

"It's possible sir," Kathryn replied. Part of her died as she uttered the next words. "I didn't know him well, but after losing his command in OFI he might do something crazy to get it back."

"Would you be willing to testify to that fact?" her father said. It wasn't really a question.

Kathryn suddenly realized why she was here. Her father wasn't content with exiling Nolan. He was preparing to set him up to be a scapegoat for something, though she had no idea what or why.

"Yes, sir." Her voice was small.

"Thank you, lieutenant commander. That will be all."

Kathryn turned smoothly on her heel and headed for the door. None of this made sense. What did her father hope to gain from all this? The *Johnston* was all the way on the edge of space, away from anything that mattered. It was time to do a little digging.

Chapter 14- Suspicious

Nolan ducked into the *Johnston*'s brig, shocked at how tiny
it was. There were two cells, both three feet wide and about six
feet long. Each contained a toilet, and a long steel bench.
Nothing more. The cells were cordoned off with the sort of thick
steel bars he'd have expected in a 20th century prison. Crude,
but effective.

Lena sat regally on the bench in her cell, back pressed
against one wall. Her tail began flicking the moment she looked
up and saw Nolan, and he wondered if she was irritated or eager.
Tigris facial expressions were hard to read.

"Sir?" the Marine on duty asked. Nolan gave a start when he
realized it was Edwards.

"At ease, private," Nolan said. He ignored the lack of a
salute. "Captain Dryker ordered me to interrogate the prisoner."

Edwards nodded, relaxing slightly. He still gripped his
assault rifle with both hands, but no longer looked like he was
going to shoot Lena if she twitched the wrong way. Nolan turned
back to the cell, moving to stand within a foot of the bars.
Lena didn't move, though she was watching him warily. The
silence stretched as Nolan struggled to begin.

"Do you have any idea what the Leonis Pride will do when they realize I'm being held as a prisoner?" Lena said in that clipped, British accent.

"We'll get you back to your people," Nolan promised. He dragged a chromed stool closer to the bars and sat. "I apologize for your detainment. The captain has authorized me to have you moved to proper quarters, provided you're willing to cooperate."

"Cooperate how?" Lena asked, her ears twitching.

"You were at Mar Kona for four days. Down on the surface you told us you'd come because of a signal, but that doesn't wash," Nolan said, crossing his arms. He studied her closely, but she didn't react. "There's no way you could have known the signal existed until you reached the planet. Even you admitted that it was weak enough that you didn't pick it up until you reached the ruins."

"You're very astute for a human, commander. Two of our colonies disappeared. Both were near Mar Kona, and both had Primo ruins," Lena explained, extending a single claw to scratch at her neck. "Your colony had those same ruins, and we feared that it would be the next target. I was there because I was testing a theory."

"It looks like you were right," Nolan conceded. Something still didn't sit right. "Why were you there alone? Your vessel--

the *Revelation,* I think you called it?--should have had a large
military escort."

"Indeed," Lena said, cocking her head to the side. "You
seem to know a great deal about our military protocol. Science
vessels like the *Revelation* are always escorted. In this
instance, we were alone because our escort refused to enter the
Mar Kona system."

"Why would they refuse?" Nolan asked.

"That's an excellent question, and I went there in hopes of
learning the answer," Lena said, giving an irritated growl. "Our
people are bold. We are aggressive. The idea that we won't
investigate the disappearance of our own colonies is
unfathomable. I can think of no reason why we'd avoid such a
thing. The Tigris should be livid, and every fleet vessel should
have been mobilized. Yet that didn't happen. Not only did they
not investigate, they forbade *me* to investigate."

"That explains why you were there, but not what you were
hoping to learn. Who do you think is after Primo ruins, and
why?" Nolan asked.

"I tire of your questions." Lena's expression darkened. "I
lost a lot of friends, a lot of brilliant minds, when the
Revelation was destroyed. We didn't find out who was attacking,
or why. I have no idea what they want with the ruins."

"What about the colonists? Were they missing from the Tigris worlds as well?" Nolan asked.

"We couldn't locate even a single survivor on either colony. Everyone was gone, and there were few signs of battle," Lena said. She leaned a bit closer to the bars. "We're a warrior race, as you know. There should have been more blast marks, more blood. Whoever did this surprised our people--no easy feat."

"Given the cloaking technology we encountered, that seems likely," Nolan said. He stifled the urge to scoot his stool further from the bars. "How large were the colonies you lost?"

"The first had over seventy-five thousand people, the second nearly a hundred and twenty-five thousand," Lena said, watching him intently.

"Mar Kona had a little under five thousand people. The numbers at your colonies would have required a lot of manpower to subdue, which means there have to be a lot more of those ships out there," Nolan said, thinking aloud. Edwards shifted behind him, but said nothing.

"The question, Commander, is what will the OFI do about it? Will your vessel investigate?" Lena asked.

Nolan didn't answer immediately, but decided that there was no harm in theorizing about fleet response, especially since it seemed like they had a common enemy. "Why do you ask?" he finally said.

"Because of my own government's anemic response," Lena said. Her eyes flashed. "If they'd sent warships, my friends might still be alive. We might have had enough time to find out why the ruins are so important."

Her anger seemed genuine, and Nolan couldn't blame her. Why would the Tigris turn a blind eye to an aggressive new foe?

"I imagine OFI will be very interested in this. We're seeing a new race with advanced technology. My government can't ignore that," Nolan said. He reached for his communicator. "I'll speak to Captain Dryker, but after he hears my report I'm sure he'll relay it to OFI. We'll probably be sent to investigate further."

"If that's the case, then you're going to need to know which world to investigate," Lena said, straightening. "I can tell you which worlds they're likely to hit, if you stop treating me like a prisoner. I need a place to bathe, and some proper food."

"I'll forward your request to the captain," Nolan said. He turned for the doorway, but paused. "I have one more question. How do you know so much about the Primo ruins?"

"I'm an archeologist, captain. My life's work is studying the empires that rose and fell before recorded history. How much do you know about the Primos?" she asked, rising to stand near the bars.

"As much as any human, I guess. Primo is short for Primo Genitus, the first race," he said, wondering where she was taking this.

"That name is a misnomer. The Primos are not the first species to inhabit this sector of space, at least not in their current incarnation. Something came before them, and I've made it my life's work to find out what," Lena said.

Chapter 15- Change Course

Nolan raised his hand to rap on the Captain's door, and was surprised when it opened before he had a chance to touch it. Dryker's head poked out, his beard even more unkempt, and his hair mussed from sleep.

"Come in, Commander," he said, pushing open the hatch. Nolan ducked through, taking a moment to inspect the captain's quarters. They were spartan: just a narrow bed, a nightstand, a desk, and a tiny couch. It wasn't much bigger than Nolan's own room. "Go ahead and have a seat."

Nolan sat on the couch, and the captain took the desk chair. He scrubbed his fingers through his beard, then looked expectantly at Nolan.

"I've met with the prisoner, sir," Nolan began. He was still learning about Dryker, and wasn't sure how best to give reports. Short and honest seemed best. "I'm not sure she should even be a prisoner. She's demanding her release, and threatening retaliation from the Tigris government."

"She was in OFI controlled space without permission. That gives us the right to hold her," Dryker countered. He reached for a packet of powered coffee and dumped it into a plastic cup of water. It began to steam and hiss as the chemical reaction turned the recycled water into something that might pass for coffee.

"True, but we have more in common than I'd have thought. Lena's ship was there investigating whoever our new hostiles are," Nolan offered, relaxing into the couch. It was small, but surprisingly comfortable. "She claims that two Tigris colonies have been wiped out. They showed up at Mar Kona because they thought it was about to be hit."

"Interesting. I'm guessing these other worlds had Primo ruins?" the Captain asked.

"How did you know?" Nolan didn't bother to hide his surprise.

"I had a conversation with the admiralty. Let's just say they were a little too interested in those ruins, which suggests that there is a common thread here," Dryker said. He scowled. "I don't know what's going on, and I don't like not knowing. OFI knows more than they're telling."

"That corresponds to something odd Lena said," Nolan offered. He smoothed his uniform, then met Dryker's gaze. "She claims the Tigris were unwilling to investigate these attacks, and she wants to know what Fleet plans to do about them."

"This crap just keeps getting deeper," Dryker said, sipping

his coffee. He grimaced. "Ugh, that's terrible. So the Tigris won't look into entire colonies going dark, and--surprise, surprise--OFI isn't interested either. We've been ordered to report to Primo space. I'm to turn myself over."

"Primo space?" Nolan said, floored by the news. "The Primo haven't intervened directly since the end of the Tigris-Human war. Why now?"

"I don't know, and the admiralty wasn't saying. What I *do* know is that OFI needs a scapegoat. Two Tigris vessels were destroyed in human space, and forensics will prove that we destroyed at least one of them. What's easier to believe: that we destroyed both, or that some mysterious new alien race showed up?" Dryker asked.

"We have proof," Nolan protested. "Footage of the alien vessels. Eyewitness testimony."

"That isn't proof," Dryker said, shaking his head. "That's footage, which could have been doctored. We don't have proof, and if we want to get to the bottom of this we need to find it."

"What do you have in mind, sir?" Nolan asked, relaxing back into the couch again.

"We're not going to Primo space. I'm going to get to the bottom of these attacks, and we're going to find proof that OFI can't ignore."

"How are you planning to do that, sir?" Nolan asked.

"That's a great question. Lena was able to identify Mar Kona as the next likely target. What does she have to say about other likely targets?"

"I'll speak to her about drawing up a list, but she's been clear that she'll only cooperate if we stop treating her like a prisoner," Nolan said, rising to his feet.

"That's fair," Dryker said, nodding. "Get her some quarters. The guards stay, but they'll give her some space. Tell her I want the three closest targets these hostiles are likely to hit. We need to get to a set of these ruins before they do, so we can find out what makes them so important."

"Yes, sir," Nolan said, starting for the door.

"One more thing, Nolan," Dryker said. He stood, facing Nolan. "If we do this, we're disobeying OFI orders. I can claim it was my idea, but they'll likely come after you too. They'll say you should have relieved me of command."

"I'm prepared for that sir," Nolan said. "OFI ruined my career, and tarnished my reputation. What we're doing out here is the right thing, and it could save lives. I'm with you on this, regardless of the price."

Chapter 16- In System

"We're entering the Helios Gate now, sir," Emo's southern drawl brought Nolan back to the present. It was the first time he'd commanded the *Johnston* while transversing a Helios Gate. Dryker had been giving him more and more bridge shifts.

They slid from the star's ultra-dense core into an area of completely blackness. There was no extra matter, no light or heat from the sun. The only illumination came from the Gate itself. The immense structure appeared to be one solid piece of gold, constructed in a wide triangle. Each corner of the triangle was set with a sapphire-colored gem larger than the *Johnston*. The gems glowed with their own inner light, a clean brilliance similar to Primo weaponry. The center of the Gate was a circular gap; flows of the bright energy shot into the center, forming a shimmering globe of crackling power.

"Broadcasting destination," Emo said, tapping in several commands. The sphere brightened as more energy was fed by the Gate, then it flared as brilliantly as the star they'd passed through. Emo turned back to Nolan. "Wormhole established."

"Take us in, Ensign Gaden," Nolan ordered, shifting in the

captain's chair. He needed the experience, but he wondered why
Dryker was ceding so much command time. He'd barely emerged from
his quarters over the past twenty-four hours.

The *Johnston* drifted closer to the sphere and, as they
closed, it became clear just how large the Helios Gate was.
Bright light flickered off its golden surface, and it seemed to
take forever to reach the Gate itself. Nolan gripped both arms
of the chair as their vessel entered the Gate. There was a brief
moment of vertigo, then they were passing out the other side of
the sphere.

There was nothing to distinguish their destination from the
origin Gate. It was a perfect mirror, identical in every
respect. Only their Helios charts let them know they were
somewhere else. Those charts would guide them through the sun,
helping them orient in the correct direction. Otherwise they
might emerge at the wrong point and have to circle the star
until they could reach their destination, which could add hours
or even days to transit times.

"Limiter engaged," Juliard said. "Wormhole closing."

The gate's limiter shunted energy back into the surrounding
star, rather than letting it feed the wormhole. If the limiter
weren't engaged, the wormhole would exist until the stars
creating it burned out. They were one of the few vulnerable

parts of a Helios Gate, and there was a reason why galactic law forbade damaging them.

"We've begun our acceleration toward Purito," Emo said. "We'll emerge from the sun's corona in four minutes."

The inductive shield flared around the ship, painting everything on the view screen white. It used the energy of the star to power itself, protecting them from the heat and pressure in the heart of the star. The *Johnston* vibrated as it picked up speed, inching its way closer to the surface. Nolan hated this part. They were blind, their sensors utterly useless. Anything could exist outside the star, but until they cleared the corona they'd have no idea it was there.

He shifted uncomfortably until the *Johnston* finally cleared the photosphere. The view screen changed, showing a towering inferno of red and orange flares. They shot into space around them, burning both hotter and brighter than the yellow star they'd emerged from at Mar Kona.

"Any ships detected?" Nolan asked. He rose from the captain's chair, eyes fixed on the view screen.

"The star's coronal loop could be blocking our scans, but we haven't detected anything yet, sir," Juliard said. She didn't even glance up from her terminal.

"There's every likelihood at least one Tigris vessel is

already here," Lena said. She'd been standing silently on the other side of the captain's chair, so quiet he'd forgotten she was even there. "This space is controlled by my pride, the Leonis. They're aware of my research, and it's possible they could be patrolling."

"I thought you said this place was sparsely populated?" Nolan said, turning to Lena. The Tigris eyed him distastefully.

"I *did* say that, but you have to understand the circumstances. We've lost a science vessel, a grave affront to my people," Lena countered. "It's very possible they're taking the threat more seriously now. Even if they aren't, they'll be looking for the *Johnston*."

"No need to borrow trouble yet," Nolan said. "We may see a Tigris vessel, but until we do we proceed. We need to get in and out of here as quickly as possible. Juliard, wake the captain and let him know we've arrived at Purito."

"Yes, sir," Juliard said. She spoke quietly to her console, then turned back to him. "The captain would like a word, Commander."

Nolan walked to Juliard's console, leaning over the screen. The captain was bleary-eyed, his hair mussed from sleep. He stifled a colossal yawn. "Nolan, I want you to take a team to the surface. Get to the ruins, and see what you can find. We need to know why these ruins are so important. Juliard, are you

picking up any communications from the planet?"

"Yes, sir," Juliard confirmed. "All normal chatter. There

isn't very much of it, but what I'm picking up is recent. Unless

something happened in the last twenty minutes, everything is

normal on the surface,"

"I'll get to the shuttle," Nolan said, starting to the

hatch. "Lena, you're with me."

Chapter 17- Away Party

Nolan peered through the doorway into the shuttle's cockpit. Sergeant Hannan was in the co-pilot chair, with Mills guiding the shuttle towards the planet. Purito was similar to earth, but instead of a bluish tint its atmosphere was green. Eighty percent of its surface was covered in water, with small subcontinents dotting the surface. Its image grew larger and larger, dominating the entire view screen as the shuttle approached.

"Make for that continent," Nolan said, pointing at one of the largest islands below the equator.

"We've got the coordinates, Commander," Hannan said, giving him a quizzical look.

"Sorry, Hannan. I'll stop micromanaging," Nolan said, returning to the rear of the shuttle. Edwards sat on one side, cleaning the massive TM-601 he'd used in their last encounter.

Lena sat opposite him, face buried in a tablet. Her eyes scanned back and forth, and Nolan wondered what she was reading. Something about the ruins, no doubt.

"Commander Nolan," a voice crackled over his comm. "This is *Johnston* actual."

"Go ahead, sir," Nolan said, activating the display. Dryker's face peered back at him.

"We've got company. A Tigris warship just exited the Helios Gate," the Captain explained. "They're clearing the sun's corona, and they're definitely making for the planet. Odds are good they'll deploy a surface team, so be ready for some company."

"Acknowledged," Nolan replied. "We'll get down there and get out before they arrive."

"Godspeed, Commander," Dryker replied, then the feed went dark.

Nolan rose and headed back to the cockpit. "Hannan, we're going to have company when we get down there."

"Thanks for the heads up," Hannan said, nodding. She unbuckled herself from the copilot's seat, and ducked past him into the hold. "Edwards, did you bring that special ordinance I requested?"

"Yes, sir," Edwards said. The private shot a wide grin at Hannan. "If we make some new friends, we'll be able to give them a warm welcome."

"Excellent," Hannan said, slapping the shoulder of Edwards's armor.

"Everybody buckle up," Mills called from the cockpit.

"We're hitting atmosphere."

Nolan moved to the bench were Lena was sitting and buckled in next to her. "Do you really think you can figure out why the ruins are important?"

"Do you really think you can stop a Tigris war party while we get answers?" Lena shot back, her tail flicking behind her. "You do your part, and I'll do mine."

"Couldn't you reason with them?" Nolan replied. "I thought scientists were revered."

"Revered, not obeyed," Lena said, giving a deep sigh. "If they realize I'm there, they will take me back to their ship and see that I'm turned over to the pride leaders. We'll never get answers."

The shuttle bucked, then bucked again. The turbulence increased, and Nolan found himself clutching at the safety straps attached to his seat. In theory, he shouldn't have had anything to worry about, but he knew that this shuttle only had two inches of armor.

The cabin grew warmer, and he could see heat ripples shimmering around the edges of the view screen in the cockpit. Purito's atmosphere was thicker than Earth's, and that meant more turbulence on the way down.

The next several minutes were tense, but eventually they

broke through the cloud cover. The view screen revealed a calm, green sky and, below the shuttle, a series of tiny islands.

"ETA three minutes," Mills said, banking the shuttle. The view shifted, showing more of the water below as they lost altitude.

In the distance, Nolan saw the reason they'd come to the world: the Primo ruins. A little spur shot out from the main island, and the northern shore was dominated by the remains of what appeared to be an entire city. Ivory spires stabbed up into the sky, reminding Nolan uncomfortably of a skeletal hand.

As they flew closer he picked up more detail. The ruins were empty, as expected. They were also massive.

Searching this place was going to take forever.

Chapter 18- Company

"Where am I setting this thing down?" Mills called from the cockpit. His tone was more than a little annoyed, but that was typical--and he'd been even more testy when told they were taking Lena along.

"Lena?" Nolan asked.

"I'm unsure," she said, blinking. "It took us two days to locate the signal at Mar Kona."

"So what do you suggest? We've got closer to two hours before company arrives," Nolan replied. He knew people didn't do their best work under pressure, but they didn't have much choice in this instance.

"Allow me to observe the city, and I'll see if I can locate what we're seeking," Lena said. She unbuckled herself, then moved for the cockpit. Her balance was enviable, and she seemed unfazed as Mills banked the shuttle.

Nolan resisted the urge to follow, instead letting the Tigris peer through the view screen. She'd proven capable so far, and if he let her be she might come through again.

"There," she called, pointing at a large temple that was nearly covered in moss. "That structure appears to be a larger

version of the temple on Mar Kona where we found the generator.
It might not be connected, but that's the best starting point
I've got."

"Sarge?" Mills asked, looking to Hannan. Nolan understood
that Mills wouldn't be insubordinate, but neither was he taking
orders from a Tigris.

"Do as the lady asked, Corporal," Hannan said.

Mills said nothing, and the shuttle began its final
descent. Less than two minutes later, they were settling into a
smooth landing on the wide stone street outside the temple.
Stones cracked under the shuttle's weight, and the ship tilted
forward as it finally came to a halt.

"You're slipping," Hannan said, giving Mills a look.

"I can only work with what I've got. These stones are older
than...well, dirt," Mills said, a bit defensively.

"Come on, people; we've got work to do," Nolan said,
unbuckling. He grabbed a tactical vest, then tossed one to Lena.
"Let's get out there and see what we can find."

Nolan slapped the red button next to the ramp, and it began
to extend. He trotted outside, almost immediately winded. The
gravity was definitely stronger than Earth's, though not enough
to keep him from functioning.

"What's next, Lena?" he asked.

"Mmm," Lena said, walking down the ramp and peering around her. She licked her chops, spending a long minute studying their surroundings. "I believe the temple is the best place to explore. Do you have any sort of scanning device? Something that will pick up low-level signals? Specifically, ELF."

"E-L-F?" Edwards asked, scratching at his bushy red beard.

"Extremely low-frequency waves," Nolan supplied. "Yes, my comm device will do that. It's got very limited range though. We'll have to explore the inside of the structure."

"Then that's exactly what I'd suggest doing." Lena had pulled on her tactical vest. She looked around at each of them. "Does someone have a weapon I can use?"

"Give her your sidearm, Edwards," Hannan ordered.

Edwards unclipped a large pistol from his side and offered it grip first to Lena. "It's got one hell of a kick, but I'm sure you can handle it. Sorry I don't have a holster you can use."

"This will suffice," Lena said, studying the pistol's action. "It's lighter than Tigris weapons."

"Heads up, commander," Hannan said, pointing at the sky above.

"Shit," was all Nolan could muster. A fat bronze shuttle had just broken the cloud cover and was descending their way.

"Lena, any idea what kind of complement that thing carries?"

"I'd guess a dozen Tigris warriors. There might be fewer, but I tend to doubt it," Lena said. She shaded her eyes, staring hard at the shuttle. "Commander, do you see the sigil near the prow? These are our most elite warriors, the Claws of Tigrana."

Nolan gave Hannan a worried look. The Claws had savaged countless human forces during the war.

Hannan shot back a confident smile. "Get your ass inside that temple, Commander. We'll hold off the cats. They won't be here for several minutes, and that gives us plenty of time to get into position."

Chapter 19- Tigris

Dryker sipped his coffee, waiting for the Tigris vessel to close. He already knew who it was, whom the Leonis pride would have sent.

"Holy shit," Emo murmured. The bridge was silent enough that it carried.

"Did you have something you wanted to say, Ensign Gaden?" Dryker asked.

"Uhh," Emo replied. "That orange and black sigil on the prow. That's the *Claw of Tigrana,* sir."

"I'm well aware of that, Ensign," Dryker confirmed. He rubbed his temple with his free hand. Some days he wished he could have just stayed in bed.

"Captain, we're being hailed," Juliard said. Dryker waited a moment before replying.

"Put it onscreen," he ordered, suppressing a sigh.

The view changed from the approaching Tigris vessel to a shot of its bridge. Most of that view was taken up by a large bronze chair piled high with scarlet cushions. The Tigris sitting upon it was the most intimidating he'd ever seen. Her golden fur had faded in places, though the orange around her ears was still bright. One of her top fangs had been replaced with a silver implant--recently, if Dryker was any judge. She looked even more lethal these days, which was saying something given how lethal she'd looked the last time he'd seen her.

"Hello, Dryker," the enemy commander said, a low growl rolling from her throat as she finished the last word. Her feline eyes narrowed. "I should have known it would be you."

"Hello, Fizgig," Dryker replied. He sat up straighter, and tried to hide his discomfort. Of all the ships the Tigris could have sent, the *Claw of Tigrana* was the worst. "I don't suppose you'd be willing to listen to an explanation? This isn't what it looks like."

"I'll listen for--" She glanced off screen, then back at him. "Two more minutes. That's the time it will take us to close with you. After that, I will board your vessel. Your crew will die screaming, and you will linger in agony for days. Whatever trick you used at Mar Kona won't work here. We are no helpless science vessel, or incompetent privateer. We are Claws of Tigrana."

"I know better than anyone who you are, Fizgig. We're on the same side. You've lost two colonies, and are about to lose a third," Dryker offered. Fizgig didn't look impressed, but he continued anyway. "A new player is wiping them out, not us. You know humanity. Would it be possible for us to wipe out an entire Tigris colony without leaving a trace? Would we be able to take all the bodies?"

"No," Fizgig said, pausing to consider. Then she growled again, low and threatening. "Your species is too weak; we both know that. But it doesn't change the fact that you're in Tigris space without authorization, or that you've destroyed at least one of our vessels. That's an act of war, Captain, and I'm well within my rights to destroy you."

"You are," Dryker agreed, rising from his chair and approaching the view screen. "But before you attack I want you to think about this. There is a new player, one Fleet Command is pretending doesn't exist. Why would my government ignore that kind of threat? You're wasting your time on us. One of your own scientists led us here. Give her time to find what she needs."

"You've kidnapped one of our scientists?" Fizgig roared. Her tail swished dangerously, and Dryker knew he'd made a mistake. "I will scatter your atoms across this sector. Prepare yourself, Dryker. This time you will not be spared. There are no Primo to shelter you. The Leonis will have justice."

Chapter 20- Dig In

Hannan keyed in the shuttle's auto defense sequence, then leapt from the ramp as it began to close. She sprinted across the uneven flagstones, making her way up the steps toward the temple.

"Mills, are you in position?" she said, chest heaving from exertion. The heavier gravity was painful, but it would affect the Tigris just as much.

"Affirmative," Mills whispered. She didn't ask where he was, not even over an encrypted channel. There was too much chance the enemy would hear. "Their shuttle just touched down a half-click from here. Better get into position quickly."

"Crap," Hannan said, increasing her pace. She ran the last dozen feet into the temple's wide entrance. The corridor disappeared into darkness ahead of her, in the same direction that the Commander and his pet cat had gone. "Edwards?"

"Here," Edwards called, standing up from where he'd been hiding. He was using a fallen column as cover. The thick stone was almost as tall as a person, and would stop most forms of ordinance. Perfect cover. "Sounds like hostiles are inbound?"

"That they are," Hannan said, skidding to a halt behind a

section of an inner wall that had caved in. The large stone

blocks shielded her profile from anyone advancing up the

hallway. She tried to calm her breathing, but the brief run had

left her ragged. She hated high-gravity worlds. "You've got that

special ordinance?"

"Yeah, though I'm a little worried about using it here,"

Edwards said, glancing up at the ceiling. "This whole place

could come down if we're not careful."

"We? If *you're* not careful, you mean," Hannan said, her

breath slowing to a more manageable pace. "Don't use it unless

you have to--and, if you do, fire it straight up the middle of

that hallway. It has to detonate outside the tunnel's main

supports."

"Sure thing, Sarge," Edwards said, patting his pack

affectionately.

"Contact," Mills whispered over the comm.

There was a sharp crack from outside, the report echoing

across the empty city. That was good; it would make it difficult

for the Tigris to spot Mills's position.

"Target down. Nine more inbound," Mills whispered.

"Crap," Hannan said, breath still a little ragged. "Be

careful, Mills."

There was no acknowledgment, but she hadn't expected there

to be. Mills would stay out of sight, and only take sure shots.
He might get two or three more kills in, but that still meant an
awful lot of inbound targets.

"One more thing," Mills whispered over the comm. "They're
definitely wearing orange and black armor."

"Shit," Edwards breathed.

He met Hannan's gaze, but she kept her expression neutral.

"Lena was right," he said. "We don't have a prayer."

"Stow it, private. I don't care who's coming; we still have
a job to do," Hannan said. "These ones aren't going to go down
like the dreck that boarded the *Johnston*. These ones will come
in smart. That doesn't mean we can't take them down, though.
We've got a clear line of fire, and the advantage of heavy
cover."

Edwards didn't reply, but she could tell from his
expression he was terrified. She couldn't blame him. Very few
Marines had met the Claws of Tigrana and lived to tell about it.

They lapsed into silence while they waited. Almost a full
minute went by, then there was another crack. Hannan knew it
must be from a different location, but that was impossible to
verify with the wild echoes across the city.

"Target down," Mills whispered. "Heads up, Sarge. Four cats
inbound on the tunnel. Looks like the second squad is holding

back."

Hannan sank into cover, slowing raising the muzzle of her
weapon. She scanned the tunnel entrance, ready to react as soon
as she saw anything.

Two figures rushed up the stairs, both carrying wide,
tritanium shields. She recognized the material immediately. It
was the same thing the Tigris coated their ships in, and it was
all but impervious to small arms fire. Those shields had to be
monstrously heavy in the higher gravity--but if the Tigris felt
the extra weight, they certainly didn't show it.

"Fire," Hannan yelled. She opened up with her TM-30, aiming
for exposed feet. Her target stumbled forward with a curse,
planting his shield against the ground. She'd hit him, but not
fatally.

The deeper report of Edwards's TM-601 was deafening in
close quarters, each round belching a foot of flame from the
muzzle, as he sent a stream of rounds into the shield on the
other side of the entryway. The Tigris carrying it was knocked
backwards a step, and nearly toppled. Then another pair of
Tigris leaped into the hall, a light-furred male helping to
stabilize the shield. Edwards's fire rang off it like a hammer
hitting a gong. The bastards had brought portable cover tough
enough to take a tank round.

"Cease fire," she roared, but her voice was completely drowned out. Edwards stopped firing a moment later.

Hannan stared hard at those shields. Four Tigris huddled behind them. For now, they were at an impasse. She knew it wouldn't last. The Claws would begin their big push soon.

Chapter 21- Ancient

Nolan adjusted his visor, tapping the third button on the right to engage low-light vision. It amplified the ambient light leaking in through the tunnel, and lit the place like it was day. The walls, where they weren't caved in, were covered in fantastic murals.

"How are these still here?" he asked, glancing at a particularly vibrant one on the wall next to them.

"The ancient Primo built their cities to last," Lena said, advancing confidently up the corridor. She wasn't wearing a visor, but then she didn't need one. The Tigris were renowned for their night vision, which was part of why their boarding parties cut power in the vessels they attacked. "One of their techniques involved molecularly bonding ink to stone. It's effectively part of the rock, sort of like the tattoos you humans use to mar your skin."

"Interesting," Nolan said. He kept pace with her, noticing the air was more stale now that they were further from the surface.

They passed under a wide domed roof, then into another narrow tunnel. Lena stopped abruptly, and Nolan bumped into her from behind. He took a step back, drawing his pistol from its holster. "Why did you stop?"

"Do you feel that?" Lena asked, barely above a whisper.

"No," he said, straining to hear. Tigris had better hearing than humans, so he knew it was unlikely he'd detect whatever it was.

"There's a low hum, just like I heard in the ruins on Mar Kona," she explained, ears twitching atop her head.

"If it's the same hum, then you think there's an active power core down here?" Nolan asked.

"Possibly. We'll have to explore to know for sure," Lena started cautiously up the tunnel, and he followed with his pistol gripped in both hands. It was unlikely that anything threatening was down here, but it was best to be prepared.

"I do think there's a power core. I'm almost certain of it," Lena finally said. The tunnel continued to narrow until it was just four feet across. "I find that troubling. There's no way the power source could have been on very long."

"How do you figure?" Nolan asked. "This place is pretty remote. It's deep inside a temple. Isn't it possible that it's just been overlooked?"

"No, it would definitely have been found. This world is inhabited, and these ruins are often explored. My graduate class came here as part of a class project," Lena said, stepping over several stone blocks that had caved in and spilled across the floor. "Our teachers were quite clear. This place has long since been picked clean, by scavengers if no one else. If this power core had been powered someone would have located it."

"Well, that's more than a little terrifying," Nolan said, piecing ideas together.

"Why do you say that?" Lena asked.

"Because if it came on recently, then something triggered it," he theorized. "That same something must have triggered the ruins at Mar Kona. It may have triggered all the ruins that are being attacked by these new hostiles."

The floor sloped down, and they walked in silence for a short distance.

"You're probably right, and I see why that's terrifying," Lena finally said. The floor was leveling off, and it opened up to a wide chamber. "Look, over there."

Nolan toggled the second button on his visor, which shone a soft red light in a wide beam across the room. It was dark enough here that even ambient light wasn't enough to allow his goggles to show detail, but the addition of a little light made a huge difference. He could suddenly see the entire room, and what he saw was breathtaking.

The walls were carved with sigils, and reminded him of a trip he'd taken to ancient Egypt as a kid. He still remembered the Pyramids and temples he'd seen, and it staggered him to think that this place was five or six times as old.

"What's this?" Nolan asked, walking over to a pair of wide, white doors. They were unmarked.

"A transportation device of some kind?" Lena asked, stretching out a hand to touch the doors. As her fingertips brushed them, they slid open with a soft hiss. Inside was a narrow box with unmarked walls.

"I think it's an elevator," Nolan said, stepping inside. Sure enough, there was a panel near the door with a series of symbols. "Can you read these?"

"They're ancient Primo, of a dialect I'm not familiar with. They look a lot like symbols I've studied, but there are significant differences. I think they're numbers," Lena said, squatting next to the panel to study it closely.

Nolan leaned down and pressed the symbol at the bottom. The doors began to slide shut, and Lena took a step back. "Are you sure that was wise?"

"No, but we know we're short on time," Nolan said. He put a hand against the wall to stabilize himself as the doors slid shut and the car began to descend. "We have no idea how long it will be until the Tigris arrive, so we need to get in and out."

"True, but we have no idea where this thing is taking us,
or if the shaft below us is obstructed," Lena said.

The elevator car jerked sharply, and there was a groan from
the mechanism above. Nolan holstered his pistol, using his free
hand for more balance. "Okay, maybe that button wasn't the
brightest idea."

The car continued to descend for long seconds, then finally
slowed. It lurched to a stop, and the doors slid open.

Chapter 22- Hannan's fight

"Edwards, it's time for that special present," Hannan
yelled, emerging from cover just long enough to fire off a short
burst. Answering bursts came from the Tigris, pinging off the
stone near her head. Damn, they were quick.

"On it, Sarge," Edwards called. He disappeared behind his
column for several seconds.

Hannan used that time to lay down covering fire, this time
from the opposite side of the stone block. The Tigris were
waiting, and a burst of fire cut into the stone next to her
face. A piece of shrapnel ripped into her cheek, and she fell
back with a cry. That was more than a little too close.

"Fire in the hole," Edwards roared, rising just far enough
to aim a long bulky launcher at their foes.

There was a loud *whump* as the missile left the tube. It
hurled towards the Tigris, who had almost no time to react. They
ducked behind the tritanium shields, which was probably the best
of a limited set of options. Hannan did the same, pulling behind
cover. It was a wise decision.

A deafening explosion echoed through the corridor, drowning
out all sound and popping one of her eardrums. It was like an

ice pick through the skull. A wave of fire and heat passed over her a split second later, and had it not been for the stone block between her and that explosion she was sure she'd have been cooked.

Warmth spread through Hannan's system as her armor gave her a dose of whatever chemical cocktail it thought would make her the best soldier. The pain from the shattered eardrum receded, and she rose into a half-crouch so she could peer over the stone block.

Judging from the tangle of bodies and the twisted wreckage of shields, the missile had detonated right between the two Tigris who'd first entered the tunnel. Neither was moving, and their shields were bent and deformed from the blast. The other two Tigris, the ones who'd entered after, seemed to have fared better. They were stumbling out of the tunnel, back to their own ranks.

"Oh, no, you don't," Hannan said, snapping her assault rifle up to her shoulder. She sighted for a moment, then cut down the closest Tigris. It went down in a spray of blood, giving a choked feline cry as it fell.

She was pivoting to take down the second Tigris when its chest burst out its back. The Tigris collapsed where it stood, unmoving.

"Nice shot, Mills," she panted into the comm, light-headed. The chemicals were masking the fatigue for now, but she knew that wouldn't last forever. This higher gravity was a real bitch, and she wasn't sure how much longer she and her squad could keep fighting.

"Sarge, think that will drive them off?" Edwards asked. He was leaning against the fallen pillar, chest heaving as he panted out the words.

"No," she said, planting her back against the block as she slid back into cover. "They're Claws. They'll keep coming until they're dead, or we are. They never retreat."

"What are we going to do?" Edwards asked.

"They don't know that we just used our only missile," Hannan said. She shook her head to clear it. The chemicals were helping, but not enough. Something warm and sticky was leaking from her ear. "Hopefully they'll be cautious. That might buy us a little time."

"I wish we had more missiles," Edwards lamented.

She gave him a sharp look. "You realize there's a reason we're called the underfunded 14th, right? We're lucky we had the one," she said, more crossly than she'd intended. Pain made her irritable.

"You think we should warn the commander?" Edwards asked.

"Nah," Hannan replied. She propped her rifle against the stone next to her and withdrew her canteen. "Warning him won't help. He'll be in and out as fast as he can. Let's just hope the cat he brought can figure out whatever they need figured out."

Chapter 23- VI

Nolan stood in the elevator for several long seconds. All
he could do was stare, and from Lena's slack jawed expression
she felt the same way. The room before them was a stark contrast
to the level above. The white stone was pristine, the murals as
vibrant as if they'd been painted yesterday. The high, vaulted
ceiling was covered in stars, each glowing with enough
illumination that his visor was no longer needed.

"This is everything I've ever hoped to find," Lena said,
stepping from the elevator. "Look at the shelves along those
walls--those little square boxes? Those are Primo data cubes.
This temple is beyond priceless."

"How old is this place? And how did it survive?" Nolan
asked, entering the room. He peered up at the ceiling, then down
at a structure in the middle of the room. It was a small
metallic pedestal, different from the rest of the room. This
metal was a deep sapphire blue, with black prongs jutting from
the top. He had no idea what it might be used for.

"I'm not entirely sure," Lena said distractedly. She was
standing next to one of the shelves, peering closely at the
strange glittering cubes. "I'd guess at least twenty-six

thousand years based on the ruins above. As to how it survived,
I'd imagine this place was sealed until the moment we activated
the elevator. Without a power core, this place just lay
here...dormant. Not even air got in or out."

"Wouldn't that make the air here poisonous?" Nolan asked,
recalling tales of ancient Egyptian tombs.

"Not if they had some sort of atmospheric scrubbers," Lena
said. She turned to face him. "They must have kicked on as soon
as we started down the elevator."

"That's all great, and I know this place is important, but
we need to find the proof the captain is after, and get the hell
out of here," Nolan said. As if to punctuate his words the room
shook, and he heard a distant, muffled explosion. "We're out of
time, Lena. Whatever you're going to do, do it."

"Give me a little room to breathe," Lena said. She paced
back and forth for a moment, muttering in Tigris. Then she
approached the pedestal and crouched next to it, fiddling with
several gemstones set into the side. "This reminds me a great
deal of the virtual intelligences I've seen in Primo libraries.
The architecture is a little different, but the basic structure
is the same."

"This is a primitive version?" Nolan asked.

"No, just the opposite. This thing is far more advanced,"

she said. A moment later the pedestal began to hum and she
backed away.

Nolan drew his pistol, moving between Lena and the
pedestal. The top began to glow with a clean, blue brilliance.
Then a holographic figure sprang to life. The translucent being
was familiar. Nolan had never met a Primo face to face, but he'd
seen enough of them on vid to know what he was looking at. This
thing was dressed oddly, but those too large eyes and elongated
fingers were unmistakable. Like all Primos, the hologram had a
tiny mouth and no nose.

"*Du ka son ta ke,*" the figure said, giving a low bow.

"What's that?" Nolan lowered his pistol, but didn't holster
it.

"This is a VI--a Virtual Intelligence," Lena said,
approaching the figure. "The Primos still use them today, for
informational purposes. This one is older than any I've ever run
across. It shouldn't exist."

"What's it saying?" he asked.

"I'm not quite sure," she said. "I think that was a
greeting. It's very similar to archaic Primo. *Du kat sona* means
'good morning.' I can't quite understand this thing."

"*Mumba con ka?*" the creature asked, blinking its large
holographic eyes.

Lena didn't answer. Nolan just watched, hoping she could figure out something useful from her conversation with the thing. He glanced at the elevator. That explosion could have been anything, but odds were good Hannan was involved. She hadn't said anything over the comm, which he hoped was a good sign.

Nolan considered contacting her, but worried about distracting her if she was in combat with the Tigris.

"*Ooka don. Vuka Spectra ballas*," the hologram said.

"Commander?" Lena said. Her tone was urgent.

"What is it?" Nolan asked, glancing between Lena and the hologram.

"I can't make out everything, but those last words were unmistakable," Lena replied, her ears twitching. She fixed him with those feline eyes. "*Vuka Spectra* translates directly as Void Wraith."

"What's a Void Wraith?" Nolan asked, raising an eyebrow.

"It's an ancient Primo legend, something they use to frighten children," Lena said. She turned back to the hologram. "*Soko con Vuka Spectra?*"

The hologram nodded, then extended a hand. Another hologram appeared next to the Primo, this one terrifyingly familiar. It showed a familiar vessel, its curved hull the same color as the base of the pedestal.

"It's the ship we saw lift off from Mar Kona," Lena breathed. "This VI claims that's the Void Wraith."

"At least we have a name," Nolan said. He circled the pedestal, thinking. "Lena, you said this place is 26,000 years old right?"

"At least that old. I see where you're going with this. If this thing hasn't been disturbed in at least that long--"

"Then the Void Wraith are at least that old," Nolan finished for her. "Whatever we're seeing predates all known galactic cultures, even the Primos. Is there a way you can remove this VI and take it with us?"

"I think so," Lena said, crouching next to the pedestal again. "It looks like this thing is housed in a Primo data cube. I can remove it, but we won't be able to power it or access the data on our own."

"Do it. We'll figure out how we can use it later," Nolan said.

Chapter 24- Slug Fest

"The Tigris vessel is coming about," Emo said. Dryker detected a note of urgency in his normally relaxed drawl. "Should we run, sir?"

"Negative. Lieutenant Ezana, warm up the main cannon. Bring all turrets to a forward-facing position," Dryker ordered. He gripped both arms of his chair, settling into the relaxed readiness that long exposure to combat had bred in him. "Emo, bring us about to match the Tigris attitude. Get ready for a forward attack run."

The *Johnston* pivoted smoothly in space until it faced the Tigris vessel. The Tigris were accelerating toward them, but Dryker was ready for that. They'd attempt to grapple the *Johnston*. If they succeeded, the fight was over before it began. If they failed, the *Johnston* was still at an enormous disadvantage. They were playing a losing game, but he had to try.

"Lieutenant Ezana, target their aft launch tube," Dryker commanded, keeping his tone smooth and even. Showing stress before the crew would be devastating to morale, and that was as dangerous as the Tigris themselves.

The *Johnston* began to accelerate, the ship shuddering as the engines heated up to maximum thrust. The Tigris vessel grew larger and larger on the view screen, until Dryker could see the trio of large black ports that made the Tigris so feared--the ones that fired the dart fighters that allowed the Tigris to land boarding parties in the middle of combat. The *Johnston* was still damaged from the last pair of dart hits they'd taken, back in the Mar Kona system, and the last thing they needed was another pair of holes. Not to mention a swarm of angry Tigris warriors prowling the corridors of the ship.

The two vessels were close now, or close when measured across the vast distances of space. A deep hum built in the bowels of the ship, then the gauss cannon fired. It was a devastating weapon, the pinnacle of mankind's arsenal. Humanity had learned quickly that lasers were all but useless against ships that had been designed to withstand the stresses of a star's internals--but those same defenses didn't do much against a huge hunk of irradiated metal.

"Shot away, sir," Mr. Ezana said, in a thick accent. A moment later an explosion bloomed on the Tigris vessel, sending a cheer up from the crew. The starboard launch tube was obliterated by the gauss cannon, and the attack sent a spray of golden debris into space.

"Sir, they're launching cables," Juliard said.

"Evasive maneuvers, Emo," Dryker called, leaning forward in his chair.

The *Johnston* fired its aft thrusters, juking left as three harpoons shot from the Tigris vessel. If even one landed, the *Johnston* was doomed.

Two went wide, but the third was aimed directly at their starboard side. Fortunately, the pair of turrets on that side of the ship were working overtime. They belched a volley of high velocity rounds, their twin streams of metal converging on the harpoon. It was knocked wide by the shots, and passed harmlessly underneath them.

"Best speed, Emo. Get us some room," Dryker ordered.

The *Johnston* accelerated away from their opponents. The Tigris were going the opposite direction, which meant they had to bleed off their momentum before they could pursue. That bought at least a little time.

"The Tigris are coming about again," Emo called.

"Juliard, plot me their intercept course. How long do we have?" Dryker asked, as calmly as he could manage.

"Three minutes to intercept, sir," Juliard replied.

"Damn it," Dryker cursed. The Tigris had been spacefaring when mankind still thought the world was flat. Their technology

was just *better*. There was no way the *Johnston* could outrun
them.

What should he do? Turn about and attack again? It might
work, but it was unlikely. The Tigris adapted quickly, and
Fizgig was by far and away their most cunning commander. She'd
terrified humanity during the last war, and had single-handedly
destroyed most of the 1st fleet. If he used the same tactic,
she'd be ready.

"Full burn, Emo. Keep them at range as long as possible,"
Dryker ordered.

That would give them a few minutes at least. He stared
tensely at the view screen, which now showed the view from the
rear of the ship. The Tigris vessel had already grown from a
speck into a full-sized warship. They were closing, and fast.

Dryker leaned back in his chair, rubbing his temples. There
were no good decisions here. He watched helplessly as the Tigris
grew closer, then closer still.

"Why aren't they firing darts at us?" Juliard asked in a
quiet voice.

"Because firing would slow them down," Dryker replied,
still focused on the view screen. "Fizgig knows we can't escape,
so she's going to run us down."

"Captain, they'll be in harpoon range in twenty seconds,"

Emo called.

"Acknowledged," Dryker said, considering. "Emo, evasive maneuvers the second they fire."

Four seconds later the Tigris launched a volley of harpoons. This time the shots were wide of each other. There was one central shot that would definitely hit the *Johnston*, and three that would go wide if the *Johnston* held course. Moving in any direction would put them in the path of another harpoon. Clever.

Emo tilted the stick, and they moved out of the path of the incoming harpoon. Sure enough, that put them into the path of another harpoon. A loud boom echoed through the ship as the harpoon punched through the rear starboard wing. The ship lurched as its speed was reduced, and Dryker winced at the size of the Tigris vessel now directly behind them.

"Sir, we've lost atmosphere in parts of A, B, and C decks," Juliard informed him.

"Lieutenant Ezana, if you can sever that cable there's a bottle of brandy in it for you," Dryker said, adrenaline making his voice waver.

"Aye, sir," Ezana said, as the Tigris vessel loomed closer, reeling them in with the cable attached to the harpoon.

The turrets on the starboard side of the ship began to

fire, converging on the cable holding them in place. They were answered by turrets on the Tigris vessel, which fired a steady stream of high velocity rounds into the *Johnston*. One of the starboard turrets exploded, but the other continued to fire at the cable.

"Captain," Juliard called, "we're receiving damage reports from all over the ship. We're taking a beating, sir."

"Have fire support teams move to that side of the ship. Seal all affected areas," Dryker ordered, staring hard at the view screen. "Come on...come on."

Then the remaining starboard turret finally did its job. The cable holding them in place took a direct hit, snapping away from the *Johnston* and rebounding off the Tigris vessel. The harpoon was still embedded in the *Johnston*, but fortunately it had missed their engines.

"Emo, get us to maximum speed. Use the planet to sling shot us," Dryker barked, rising from his chair.

"Aye, sir," Emo called. The *Johnston* pulled away from the Tigris, gaining a little distance.

"Sir," Juliard called. "They'll be on us again in forty-seven seconds."

"Blast it," Dryker snapped. There just wasn't any way to escape. They were outclassed.

"Sir," Juliard called, tentatively. "The Tigris have broken off their pursuit."

"On screen," he called. The view screen shifted to show the Tigris vessel, which was hovering above the planet. It wasn't pursuing.

There was no way Fizgig would let him escape, not when he was so close. It just didn't make any sense.

"Open a channel, Juliard," Dryker ordered. The screen shifted to reveal the Tigris bridge. Fizgig glared at him with those terrible feline eyes, tail thrashing angrily.

"The void watches over you this day, Captain Dryker," she snarled, looming closer to the screen. Her fangs flashed. "Tomorrow is another matter. Run, because I *will* hunt you."

Then the communication was cut.

Chapter 25- Escape

Hannan took another sip of water before speaking into the comm. "Do you have eyes on the enemy, Mills?"

"They're sticking to the area around their shuttle," Mills whispered back. "They aren't making a move to attack. I don't have a clear shot yet, but I'm maneuvering into position."

"Keep us posted," Hannan said. She picked up her rifle and used it to help her get to her feet. The drugs were beginning to wear off, and the exhaustion was getting heavier.

"Sarge," Edwards called, a note of warning in his voice. He spun to face the corridor leading into the temple, and she did the same.

"Hold your fire," the commander called, his voice unmistakable. "We're coming out."

"About time," Hannan yelled back, lowering her rifle. She kept behind cover, darting a glance at the tunnel where the charred cats still lay. She'd never get the smell of burnt fur off her armor.

"Sit rep," the commander said, dropping down into cover next to her. He was panting from exertion but, given how she felt, she couldn't really chide him for it.

"Five hostiles down, five remaining. We can't exit this place without taking fire," Hannan said. "No casualties yet, but we're pretty beat. Not sure it would be wise to launch a frontal assault."

"Why haven't they tried attacking again?" Lena asked.

Hannan assumed the question was rhetorical, but she answered anyway. "No idea, but I'm thankful they haven't. We can't repel them a second time."

"Sarge?" Mills whispered over the comm.

"Go ahead, Mills," she said, leaning against the block again. It was cool against the back of her head.

"The cats are pulling back. They've just boarded their shuttle, and it looks like they're lifting off."

"That doesn't make any sense," Hannan said, shaking her head. "They've got us dead to rights--and, even if they didn't, the Claws never retreat."

"Never," Lena agreed. "Unless they've received new orders."

The sound of a shuttle's engines rumbling to life echoed through the dead city. A spray of gravel washed past the front of the tunnel, then the shuttle lifted skyward. The sound of its engines began to recede.

"Commander Nolan, this is *Johnston* actual," Dryker's voice crackled over the comm. "Please tell me you've got what we came for."

"I'm not sure, sir," the commander said. He scrubbed a hand
through his beard and peered down at something that Lena was
carrying--some sort of cube. "I think so."

"Get your ass back to the ship. We'll wait in low orbit for
your shuttle. *Johnston* out," Dryker said.

"You heard the man," the commander replied. He rose to his
feet again, and began moving up the corridor toward their
shuttle. "Let's get the hell off this rock before the Tigris
change their mind."

Chapter 26- Fizgig

Fizgig was not pleased. She rose from the plush velvet cushions of her chair, her tail flicking back and forth behind her. It was a clear sign of her displeasure, and none of the other bridge officers met her gaze. They knew better than to risk her ire. She licked her paw, then used it to smooth an errant lock of fur on her neck. Grooming calmed her, and if ever she needed to be calm it was now.

"Are we really letting them go?" Khar asked, growling low in his throat to show what he thought of the notion.

"You heard the same communique I did, prideless," she asked, whirling on Khar. The burly male stood near the weapons panel, his mane askew from a noted lack of grooming. It was his responsibility to attack, and Fizgig knew his pride had been wounded when they'd pulled away from the human vessel.

"We had them," Khar said, a low growl rumbling from his chest. His tail rose over his shoulder, a subtle insult. "One more pass, one more pursuit, and we'd have boarded them. The *Johnston* destroyed the *Revelation*. They wiped out scientists. There must be retribution. To do otherwise is pure cowardice."

Fizgig pounced. Her claws slid from their sheaths, and she

raked them across Khar's face. He stumbled backwards, reaching for his pistol. She didn't give him a chance. Fizgig balled her paw into a fist, then slammed it into Khar's sensitive belly with all the force she could muster. Khar collapsed to the deck, mewling pitifully and trying to crawl away. Spots of blood dotted the patch of white fur on his nose.

"You are a fool, blinded by pride," Fizgig said, seizing Khar by the scruff of his neck. She hauled him to his feet, meeting his gaze. "Our kits are in danger. The old and the young are being attacked. *They* are our priority. The humans will be dealt with--but when we receive word that our homes are being defiled we respond. Our honor does not matter. Only the lives of those in our pride matter."

She dropped Khar and returned to the command chair. Fizgig forced herself to sit, though she allowed her tail to flick wildly. "Izzy, is the shuttle aboard?"

"It's docking now, mighty Fizgig," the white-furred pilot replied, with a deferential nod.

"Get us to the Helios Gate. Make for the Panthrine system, as quickly as possible." This command was the opposite of the one Fizgig wished to give, but her own words rang in her head. They had a responsibility.

"Yes, mighty Fizgig," Izzy said, her tail swishing eagerly.

She tapped in a series of commands, and the *Claw of Tigrana* accelerated toward the sun.

Fizgig's eyes automatically narrowed, though the view screen cut out nearly all of the sun's incredible brilliance. They plunged into it, waves of flame washing over the sides of the ship. Then the vessel began to slow. Making their way through the photosphere was easy, but by the time they reached the sun's core movement took incredible energy. It was the densest material in the known galaxy, and displacing that mass wasn't easy.

Fortunately, energy was all around them. Every Helios-capable-vessel could channel solar mass, and theirs was no exception. The *Claw* forged deeper into the star, finally reaching the artificial bubble at the center. The Helios Gate's titanic structure dominated the darkness, its harnessed singularity hovering in the center.

"Take us through," she ordered, flexing her claws. This part always made her nervous, though she couldn't say why.

"Connection established," Izzy said, the fur on her tail standing up until it resembled the odd trees humans used to celebrate their winter festival.

Their vessel plunged into the singularity, and there was a moment of weightlessness. Then they were elsewhere, outside another Helios Gate, in another star. That was impossible to tell just by looking, of course; the center of every star she'd been in appeared identical, and the Helios Gates themselves were indistinguishable.

"We're pushing through the core now," Izzy called from her communication station. Her white fur was painted orange by the sunlight dominating the view screen.

They pushed through the star's mass, long minutes going by until they finally emerged into the corona. She waited until they'd cleared it before issuing orders.

"Play back the latest signals from Panthrine," Fizgig commanded, digging her claws into the cushions.

"Yes, mighty Fizgig," Izzy answered.

"--under attack. Everyone is being taken. They've destroyed our warships, like they were kindling. If anyone is receiving this, get away from here. Save yourself." The voice crackled over their communications system, echoing across the bridge.

Low growls came from several of the crew around her-- herself included, she realized. "Get me a scan of the planet. Is anyone still fighting?"

"Scanning now," Rowler said. The lean male was the only scientist aboard, and he was a mere acolyte. "These signals are six minutes old, but it doesn't look like any units are still up. They've been wiped out, or taken."

"Get us to that planet. Now," Fizgig ordered. She resisted the urge to hiss at Izzy, knowing that her pilot would get them there as quickly as she could.

"Mighty Fizgig," Izzy said, tapping a button on her console. The view screen shifted. "A vessel is rising from the planet. It's clearing the atmosphere now."

"What is that thing?" Fizgig asked, rising from her chair and approaching the view screen.

The vessel was larger than the *Claw*, nearly the full size of a Primo carrier. It was made from similar material--the unmistakable blue-black alloy of the first race-- and had two long, curved wings that extended before the main body. The thing looked deadly.

"Can we get into position to intercept?" Fizgig demanded.

"Yes," Izzy answered, tapping another series of commands. "They'll have to pass by us to reach the sun."

"Now these furless will find out how the Leonis pride defends their territory," Fizgig said. This time she did growl, low and deep in her throat.

Then something impossible happened. The strange ship shimmered, then faded. It disappeared entirely, leaving a patch of empty black space in its wake.

"Can we still detect it? Is it giving off any signals?" she demanded, rounding on Rowler.

"No, mighty Fizgig," Rowler said, apologetically. His tail drooped. "They've vanished from our sensors. They're completely cloaked."

Not even the Primo had full cloaking technology. What the hell were these things? Fizgig thought back to the *Johnston*, and to Captain Dryker's words. Perhaps there was more to them than she'd first thought. Perhaps a new player *had* entered the game, but if that was the case it raised an interesting question. Why wasn't Fleet Command more interested in finding out who or what these things were?

It didn't matter. Like it or not, she'd been tasked with bringing the *Johnston* to justice. The humans had destroyed one of their vessels, and would need to pay in blood. After that, then she could learn more about this new enemy.

Chapter 27- What Now?

Nolan was the last to enter the Captain's ready room. It was an offshoot of the CIC--just a big chrome table set into the floor, and six chairs. Two of those chairs were occupied, one by Captain Dryker and the other by Lena.

"Sit down, Commander," the Captain ordered, gesturing at the chair across from him. "Show me what you've got, and let's hope it was worth pissing off the top commander in the Leonis Pride."

Nolan slid into the chair, resting his arms on the table. He nodded to Lena, who produced the data cube they'd liberated. She set it on the table in front of the captain, who picked it up and examined it.

"What am I looking at?" Dryker asked, still studying the device.

"Lena?" Nolan said, knowing she was more qualified to explain.

"That's a Primo data cube, Captain," Lena began. She leaned closer, pointing at a rune on one of the faces. "These are archaic, and predate the Primo empire--well, the *existing* Primo Empire anyway. The technology is unmistakable, though."

"What does that mean? How can this thing be useful?" the captain asked, eyeing Lena sharply.

"It's a Virtual Intelligence, sir," Nolan offered, knowing the captain was after tactical data. "This VI contains records of whatever this ancient empire is. Lena dates that empire from at least 26,000 years ago--and here's the part you'll be most interested in. The VI showed us a ship. The same ship we saw back on Mar Kona."

"So, whatever these things are, they've existed a long time," the captain said. He handed the cube back to Lena. "Is that all you recovered?"

"The only artifact, yes. But we have a name now," Nolan said. "The VI called these things the Void Wraith."

"Are you serious?" the captain asked, raising a skeptical eyebrow. Nolan suppressed a spike of anger.

"Quite serious, captain," Lena said, bristling. Her tail swished haughtily. "I realize how this must sound, but--"

"Do you?" the captain broke in. "Let me tell you how it will sound to OFI. You want me to tell them that a Primo fairy tale has returned after 26,000 years, and is now wiping out colonies. Don't worry though, because we have a magic cube...that we can't actually understand or use in any way. Is that about the length of it, Commander?"

"Sir, that's not fair," Nolan said, fists clenching under the table.

"I didn't say it was fair, but we need proof, Nolan. Hard evidence, or we have no chance of convincing either the Primo or OFI that there is a real threat out there." The captain steepled his fingers, staring hard at Nolan.

"What we need is a way to translate this cube," Nolan offered. "I'll reach out to a friend of mine at OFI and see what she can recommend."

"That friend of yours wouldn't happen to be named Lieutenant Commander Mendez, would she?" the captain asked, voice reproachful.

"She would, sir, though I'm not sure why that should matter."

"Because she's the reason you were exiled to the 14th," Dryker growled.

"Does that mean you're ordering me not to speak to her?" Nolan asked, as neutrally as he could. Kathryn was bad news, but she was the only option he could think of.

"There might be another way," Lena offered. "It's possible that a Primo library could translate the cube. I think they're our best shot."

The captain glanced at her, seeming to consider her words.

"We're due in Primo space today. When we don't show up, they'll be hunting us, too. I'm not sure that making for one of their libraries is a good idea," Dryker said, shaking his head.

"Clearly, you're uneducated where the Primo are concerned," Lena said, even more primly than before. "Primo libraries are considered holy repositories of knowledge. They are neutral ground. If we visit one, they cannot apprehend or harm us while we are on the premises."

Captain Dryker stared hard at Lena, then finally broke eye contact. He heaved a deep sigh.

"Very well, then we'll take both courses. Lena, see if you can arrange a visit to a library. Make it as close to human space as possible." He turned to Nolan. "Commander, reach out to your 'friend.' See what she can tell us, but don't take any risks, and don't divulge anything beyond our need for a translator."

"Yes, sir," Nolan said. He dreaded talking to Kathryn again.

Chapter 28- Old Flame

Nolan made the call from his quarters, after finally

deciding a direct quantum call was better than an electronic

message. He didn't want to talk to her; if he was going to have

to, then the best way to do it would be all at once. Like

ripping off a bandage.

Waiting for the call to connect was brutal. After several

moments, the comm panel flashed green and the screen lit up. It

showed a face he wished he could forget: Kathryn's beautiful

eyes and her addictive smile. Her long dark curls spilled down

the shoulders of her uniform.

"Nolan," she said, blinking. "This is a surprise. After how

we left things...well, I didn't expect to talk to you again."

"Hi, Kathryn," Nolan said, clearing his throat. "Listen,

this isn't a social call. I need your help. Given circumstances

between us, I'd say you owe me."

"That's true," Kathryn said, biting her lip. Her eyes shone

with emotion, but after a moment the mask descended and she was

all business. "What do you need?"

"If I needed to translate something from ancient Primo, is

there anywhere in Fleet space I could do that?" he asked, trying to give her as little as he could.

"I'm not sure, but I could find out. What do you have?" she asked.

"I can't talk about that," he countered, shaking his head.

"Nolan, listen. I know you don't trust me, but I need you to try," Kathryn said, leaning closer to the screen. She stared searchingly at him, and for a moment he wished he was close enough to touch her. "OFI is acting awfully strange. They've shrugged off Dryker's reports of new technology, which seems really out of character. I'd have expected them to leap at the chance to learn about a new race, especially an advanced one."

"Maybe they want to avoid pissing off the Primos? We did destroy a Tigris warship."

"True, but there's more to it than that. They could have smoothed over that incident, and still investigated Dryker's report," Kathryn said. "Admiral Mendez has been making a lot of off-log calls, and OFI has been sharing a lot of intel about the *Johnston* with both the Primo and the Tigris. It sounds like they're working on a joint task force to hunt you down."

Nolan suddenly realized what that meant for Kathryn. Even talking to him could end her career, not to mention causing a rift with her father. Part of him wanted that to happen, but the rest was grateful for her taking the risk.

"There's more. Nolan, you're into something deep. I've seen the Tigris call for blood, we expect that. But the Primos? They don't get involved. For them to want to hunt you down...there's something we're missing. Something big. Big enough to hang you out to dry. Don't expect any help from OFI. In fact, consider them hostile."

"I already do," Nolan replied. He touched the screen with his palm. "Thanks for the info, Kathryn. Find out what you can about translating, and get back to me. If you learn anything you're willing to share, you can use the usual drops."

"I'll do that. Take care of yourself, Nolan." She sighed quietly, and brushed her bangs out of her face. "I wish I'd made different choices."

"You and me both," Nolan said, and cut the connection.

He needed to get some sleep before they reached the library in Primo space.

Chapter 29- Planatos

"Commander, we're in communications range," Juliard said, rousing Nolan from his thoughts. He straightened in the Captain's chair, stifling a yawn.

It was late, a little after 2 a.m. ship's time. They'd just arrived in system to Planatos, one of the oldest Primo systems-- so old, in fact, that the star had gone from a red dwarf to a blue. It burned hotter to retain equilibrium, painting everything in the system with a different brush than Nolan was used to.

There were no planetary bodies here, just a single orbiting station. Like all Primo structures, the station bore fluted columns and had plasma funnels built in at regular intervals. It was breathtaking, and the star's sapphire illumination made it even more so. The Primos had no doubt designed it here for that reason, as they were obsessed with aesthetics. Form was just as important as function, even in their weaponry.

The station bristled with particle cannons, each capable of ripping the *Johnston* to shreds. The cannons were designed to fire beams of ionized particles that tore through armor, and were powerful enough to cook anything close. The place was a veritable fortress.

"UFC *Johnston*, this is Planatos station. State your
intended business, or be destroyed," a metallic voice echoed
over the comm.

"Planatos, this is UFC *Johnston*," Nolan said, shifting in
the command chair. "We'd like to request a meeting with a
librarian. We've recovered something we think you'll want to
take a look at." He knew that the libraries were supposed to be
neutral, but part of him still wondered if the Primo station was
about to blast them into atoms.

Long moments went by with no answer, and the *Johnston* held
its location. Then the voice finally spoke again. "Approach
docking port seven. Keep your weapons powered down, and do not
deviate from your course, or you will be destroyed."

"Acknowledged," Nolan said, nodding to Juliard. She gave
him a thumbs-up when the connection had been severed.

"Touchy bunch, aren't they?" Emo said, glancing over his
shoulder with a raised eyebrow.

"They're not overly fond of 'lesser' races," Lena said. She
sat cross-legged on the floor, a few feet to the right of the
captain's chair.

"If they're willing to help us, I'll happily put up with a
little arrogance," Nolan said. He rose from the captain's chair

and moved over to Juliard's station. "Can you get me the captain on the line?"

"Sure," Juliard said, keying in a sequence on her terminal. A blue light began flashing, then the screen resolved to the captain's sleepy face.

"Captain, we've arrived in system at Planatos. We're docking now," Nolan explained.

"Good," the captain said, rubbing blearily at his eyes. He gave a cavernous yawn. "I'll be in the CIC by the time we dock. Once you've been relieved, I want you to take Lena aboard that monster to see what the Primo can tell us about this cube of yours."

"Are you certain they won't alert the Primo government, sir?" Nolan asked.

"No," Dryker admitted. The camera shifted to show him sitting on his bed. He began pulling on his boots. "They could rat us out, and we need to be ready for that. I'll have Hannan standing by to extract you if things go south."

Chapter 30- Library

Nolan shifted back and forth nervously as Hannan spun the metal wheel to unlock the hatch. It opened with a hiss, revealing the Primo docking tube. The walls were made of blue-black metal, reinforcing the troubling connection between the Void Wraith vessel and the Primo.

"Let's complete our business swiftly," Lena said, stepping into the tube. Her ears twitched in a way Nolan linked to nervousness, not that he could blame her. He stepped in with her, and they crossed the dozen paces to a black iris-style door on the far side.

The iris slid open at their approach, revealing two imposing figures in blue-black armor. Nolan recognized the staves they carried, though he'd never seen an arbiter before. Arbiters were the elite Primo guards, widely feared across every culture in known space. Each held a six-foot staff that crackled with blue plasma at either end. Their shock staves could knock a man unconscious with the simplest brush.

The weapons were made still more intimidating by the aliens that held them. They were personifications of the hologram Nolan and Lena had found: tall, thin aliens with no nose and a tiny

mouth. Their eyes were the same--a bright red, unbroken by iris
or pupil--but their skin was different. The one on the right had
dark blue skin that blended well with his armor. The one on the
left had black skin that contrasted with its eyes and made them
stand out demonically.

"You will accompany us to the library proper," the black-
skinned arbiter said. Its voice was flat, yet still carried a
note of disdain. It turned on its heel and started walking back
to the library. Its legs bent oddly as it moved, in the opposite
direction than a human's, or even a Tigris's. This made for an
awkward gait, but did nothing to diminish the Primo's imposing
demeanor.

"Lead the way," Nolan said. He and Lena fell into step
behind the arbiters, who led them through a wide corridor and
deeper into the library. Tiny floating pedestals with brightly
glowing flames lit the corridor at even intervals, an odd
contrast to the incredible technology around them.

They entered a huge chamber, easily hundreds of feet tall.
Above them, Nolan could see floor after floor, each containing
near-endless rows of shelves. Those shelves didn't contain
books, as he'd expected. They looked a lot more like the shelves
in the Primo ruins, and were lined with data cubes. The entire
library was silent, not a single voice raised. There was no

clink of armor, no occasional sneeze or cough. This place felt

as empty as the dead city on Purito, even though he could see

Primo scholars dotting the floors above.

There weren't many, maybe a dozen in total. That seemed

tragic somehow, especially given the sheer size of the library.

Given the tables around them, hundreds or even thousands of

scholars could have worked here without making the place feel

crowded.

A few scholars looked up as they passed, but most ignored

them. They had different skin color, ranging from light blue to

deep purple. Those last received a low bow from the arbiters as

they passed. Nolan didn't know what their skin color signified,

but clearly it was important in their culture.

"Wait here," the lead arbiter finally said, pausing next to

a large table with four chairs. The chairs were awkward affairs,

designed for the Primo's very different legs. Nolan chose to

stand, though Lena sat as gracefully as she could manage.

The arbiter who'd spoken turned on his heel and strode off

into the library, leaving them with a single guard. Nolan took

the opportunity to sit, and Lena sat next to him.

"I've always wanted to see one of the original libraries,"

she said, gazing around her in wonder. "There's more knowledge

here than everything gathered by your culture and mine, put

together. It's been here longer than either of our races have been spacefaring."

"Let's hope they're willing to share that knowledge," Nolan said, gazing up at the levels above them. The place was impressive, though being here unnerved him. If the Primo decided they wanted the cube, or wanted to detain them, there wasn't much he'd be able to do about it.

Several minutes later, the arbiter returned with a robed Primo. This Primo had dark blue skin and studied them impassively as he approached. He stopped before their table, and looked from Nolan to Lena.

"One of you is a scholar?" the Primo asked in a flat, emotionless voice. It still managed to imbue the question with an unflattering amount of skepticism.

"I'm an anthropologist, specializing in early Primo ruins. Pre-dynastic mostly," Lena offered, ears twitching.

"I see," the Primo said, with a little distaste. It folded its spindly arms under voluminous sleeves. "Why have you come to library alpha seven two?"

"We wish to invoke *safecall*. I've brought an artifact we'd like examined," Lena offered. She reached into her satchel, pulled out the data cube, and set it on the table. "This came from ruins that pre-date the Primo empire. I've estimated the age at twenty-six thousand years."

"Clearly, the academy on Tigrana is as ignorant as we feared," the acolyte scoffed. "I mean no insult--you cannot be blamed for your race's lack of knowledge, of course--but data cubes weren't created until post-dynastic times. They first appeared in the third dynasty, and were not properly refined until the seventh."

"Why don't you verify the cube's age?" Nolan said, trying to keep his tone even. "Maybe you can enlighten us about it."

"And what does this 'ancient data cube' contain that would make it worth our time?" the acolyte asked, cocking its slender head to the side.

"It's a VI, but one that speaks a dialect that seems to predate all Primo culture," Lena explained. She seemed hesitant, but then forged ahead. "The syntactic guides are very similar, but I can't quite place most of the words it used."

"I see," the Primo said, its mouth becoming a flat line. It stared hard at Lena, then bent to pick up the data cube, inspecting the runes. "I can have this examined. If it's what you claim it to be, then the library will be grateful for its return."

"Return?" Nolan asked, rising to his feet. Out of the corner of his eye he saw both arbiters tense, ready for combat.

He moved his hand away from his sidearm. "That cube belongs to us. You can study it, but it's leaving with us."

"I see," the acolyte said, this time with more than a little distaste. "If you wish to deny us possession of the artifact we will not stop you, of course. Unlike both humanity and the Tigris we hold our traditions in high regard. Please wait here. We'll study it, and attempt to verify your 'findings'."

The acolyte strode away with the cube, and both arbiters followed. Lena and Nolan were left alone at the table.

"Cheerful bunch," Nolan said darkly.

"I understand their hesitation. They don't respect younger races, because they have almost ten thousand years more experience than we do," Lena said, sighing heavily. Her tail swished back and forth behind her.

"You seem as well-versed as they are," Nolan said, shrugging.

"I doubt that. Primo universities are renowned across the galaxy. They spend two decades training. My own studies only lasted three years," Lena said. She rested her elbows on the table, staring around her in awe.

"So how did you get into all this?" Nolan asked. He propped his feet up on the table, partly because he knew that would annoy the Primo. "Scientists are rare among the Tigris, right?"

"Extremely," Lena said, meeting Nolan's gaze. "I was a very curious child, even more so than my siblings. My parents encouraged that. I started asking hard questions at a young age, so they enrolled me in the academy on Tigrana."

"What kind of questions?" Nolan asked.

"Things like why every sentient race in the quadrant is bipedal," Lena said, her gaze taking on a feverish glint. "That just shouldn't be possible. Surely at least one other type of sentient life would have developed. Why not an amorphous blob, or something with three legs? Or six? I also wonder why most races can reproduce with one another. Primo don't like to admit it, but their DNA is compatible with both humans and Tigris. If we evolved separately, how is that possible? We should be radically different, yet we share over ninety-five percent of our DNA across all three races."

"I'm no anthropologist, but that definitely raises some interesting questions," Nolan admitted. "So what's your theory?"

"I don't have one. At least not yet. But that's why I began studying ancient Primo culture. They're the earliest known race. It's even reflected in their name. Primo Genitus. First race," Lena explained. "If answers exist, they're in the roots of Primo culture."

"Commander?" Nolan's comm crackled. At the sound of the captain's voice, several Primo glanced their way in annoyance.

"Yes, sir?" Nolan asked.

"Let's finish this up quickly," the captain said. "We've just received word that two more colonies have been hit."

Chapter 31- The Admiralty

Kathryn hesitated as she entered the conference room. Seven

men sat around the table, each of them one of the most

influential admirals in the OFI. There was more collective power

in this room than anywhere else in human space. She moved to

stand behind her father, placing her hands behind her back.

There were two other aides in the room, each adopting a similar

pose.

"You all know why we're here," her father said, his dark

eyes roaming the assembled admiralty. "The *Johnston* has gone

rogue. It should have reported to Primo space two days ago, and

we've had no direct report since."

"The *Johnston* is your responsibility, Mendez," Admiral

Kelley said. He was an older man, with deep white hair and a

face like granite. "It's unclear to me why you think it

necessary to call this gathering to deal with one AWOL captain."

"I'll tell you why it's necessary," Mendez shot back,

pounding the table with a fist. "We're not the only ones looking

for the *Johnston*. The Tigris are mobilizing--and that isn't even

what should really concern us. The Primo are moving, gentlemen."

That caused a stir. Everyone began murmuring at once, and

several admirals began typing furiously on data pads. Kathryn's

father was, ever the master showman, let the tension build, then

spoke again.

"The question," he yelled, silencing the room, "is what we

choose to do about it."

"Should we do anything at all?" Admiral Chu asked. He was

the youngest man at the table, in his early fifties. "If the

Tigris or Primo find the *Johnston* first, what do we really lose?

We simply disavow them, and sanction any action either

government wants to take."

"That ignores a critical factor," Kelley said, jumping in

just before Mendez could reply. "What if the *Johnston* is right?

I've seen the footage they forwarded. The vessel shown is unlike

anything we've ever seen, and the fact remains that colonies are

disappearing. Two more went dark this morning. Two, at the same

time. Are none of you alarmed by this?"

Kathryn expected a show of support, from Admiral Stiegman

at the very least. Stiegman was responsible for one of the two

colonies that had disappeared that very morning, yet he sat

there impassively. What the hell was going on?

"No one?" Kelley asked, his gaze roaming the assembled

faces.

"The disappearance of those colonies is alarming,

certainly," her father finally said, his tone placating. "I've dispatched several vessels to investigate, and I know that Admiral Chu has done the same. If there is any substance to these claims, then we'll find it. I find that unlikely, however."

"Unlikely?" Kelley roared, half-rising to his feet. "I can't believe what I'm hearing. We have circumstantial evidence showing a new race of very hostile aliens. We're losing colonies at an ever-growing rate. What will it take to convince you that there's a problem?"

"Real evidence," her father delivered smoothly. "I'm not saying there isn't a problem, but we can't afford to go off half-cocked. Not when the Primo are interested in this. Are you willing to risk offending them?"

Kelley's jaw clicked shut, and his eyes narrowed. He sank back into his seat, scanning the assembled faces again before speaking. "No one wants a war with the Primo. We all know how that would end for humanity. But, at the same time, I don't want to see one of our vessels turned over as a sacrifice--not even one from the 14th. This whole thing leaves a sour taste."

"You're right," Mendez said. He said no more for a few moments, gathering the attention of the room before continuing.

"I move that we dispatch a division of the 1st fleet to hunt down the *Johnston*. If we find them first, then we can choose how to deal with this. That way we avoid a diplomatic incident, and keep the *Johnston* from being turned over. We can likely get away with just offering Captain Dryker to the Primos."

"Is there a second?" Admiral Chu asked, looking around the room.

"I'll second," Stiegman said.

"All in favor?" Chu asked.

Everyone but Kelley raised their hand.

"Vote passes, six to one," Chu said, rapping a gavel on the table. "Admiral Mendez, you called this meeting. Did you have anything further to discuss?"

"Not at the moment," her father replied, giving a plastic smile as he rose to his feet.

Something about the entire situation chilled Kathryn to the core. The horrified look on Admiral Kelley's face spoke volumes. To her mind, he was the only one talking sense, yet the others had simply brushed him off. She knew better than anyone that everything her father did was calculated. She was missing something vital.

Chapter 32- Confirmation

Nolan had very little to do while they waited for the Primo
to return. Lena had buried herself in a data cube she claimed
couldn't be found anywhere else, which left him alone with his
thoughts. He found himself chasing around the events of the last
several days, from the first attack on Mar Kona to the recent
disappearances. There were patterns there, but so many pieces
were missing.

It felt like hours had passed by the time the blue-skinned
acolyte returned, this time with four arbiters in tow. That
alarmed Nolan, and his hand slid unconsciously to the grip of
his pistol--not that the weapon would do anything here. If
they'd considered it a threat, the Primo would have confiscated
it. The fact that they had let him keep it underscored how
outclassed he'd be in a fight here.

There would be no physical resistance on his part. Hannan
wasn't going to break in and save them if something went wrong,
regardless of the captain's assurances.

"We've examined the data cube," the acolyte said.

That drew Lena's attention, and she finally looked up from
the data screen she'd been studying.

"It seems the cube is 26,092 years old. This predates the Primo dynastic culture, making it the oldest data cube on record. It's quite a find."

The way the acolyte stated the facts--as if it had been the one to discover them--rankled, but Nolan held his tongue.

"We've copied the cube into our local archives, and will begin a full study of its contents," the acolyte continued. "If you'd like a copy of our findings, we will arrange to have it forwarded to your ship."

"How long will that take?" Nolan asked.

"Between seven and nine hours," the acolyte said.

"What about the cube? Where is it?" Lena asked. She rose from her seat, stepping around the table to stand next to the acolyte. "If you've copied it there's no reason to keep the original."

"Are you certain you can't be persuaded to turn it over to the library? It is a Primo artifact, and belongs with us," the acolyte said. It stuck a hand inside its robe, probably to clutch the cube.

"Quite certain," Nolan said, rising to his feet. "We'll take it back. Now, if you please."

"Very well," the acolyte said, extending the cube to Lena. She took it, and dropped it back into her satchel. "We've made a

slight modification to the programming of the original code.
This modification includes several modern languages, so that you
can communicate with the VI. No payment is necessary for this
service."

"Commander Nolan, this is *Johnston* actual," the captain's
voice came over the comm. The acolyte seemed startled by the
sudden voice. "Return to the *Johnston* immediately. Run,
Commander."

"Sir?" Nolan said, switching his comm to internal so only
he could hear it.

"We've got three Primo warships emerging from the Helios
Gate. They don't look friendly, and they're headed our way. It
might be coincidence, but I seriously doubt it." The Captain
sounded tired.

"You son of a bitch," Nolan said, turning to the acolyte.
"Who did you tell we were here?"

"Our organization is neutral, but of course we passed your
arrival along to the proper authorities. If they choose to
detain known fugitives, it's none of our business," the acolyte
said. It wore a very smug smile, and Nolan resisted the urge to
punch it in its tiny mouth.

"Let's go," Nolan said, seizing Lena's hand. Then they ran
for the *Johnston*.

Chapter 33- Blockade

"Commander Nolan is aboard, sir," Juliard said.

Captain Dryker relaxed into his chair, his attention focused on the view screen. "Time until intercept?"

"It's too late, sir. The Primo carriers are nearly here," Emo said, glancing nervously up at Dryker.

These were Primo ships of the line, which not even he had ever faced. The Primo mostly kept out of galactic squabbles, and had for several centuries. The few exceptions had ended in the total annihilation of whichever group had been foolish enough to anger the Primo.

"Juliard, call Nolan up here," Dryker said. Then he turned back to Emo. "Keep the engines hot, and get ready for full burn on my command."

"Should I ready the weapons, sir?" Ezana asked from the gunnery station.

"Negative," Dryker said. "If we do they might take that as hostile."

"The commander is inbound," Juliard called.

Dryker's knuckles turned white as he gripped the arms of his chair. The three carriers grew larger on the screen, each blue-black vessel larger than either a Tigris or human flagship. They were pretty, all curves and artfully-placed weaponry.

Pretty, but no less deadly for it.

"Sir?" Nolan asked, plunging breathlessly through the hatch.

"About time," Dryker said, shooting to his feet. "Commander, you've studied the Primo, yes?"

"I'm familiar with all the data the OFI accumulated," Nolan allowed. He glanced at the screen, going white before turning back to Dryker. "What do you need to know, sir?"

"How do we fight them?" Dryker asked.

"We don't," Nolan said, moving to stand next to the captain's chair. His eyes were focused on the view screen again. "The Primo use four particle beam weapons. They're extremely accurate at short range, and will melt our hull to slag in seconds. If they use maximum charge, they can even short out electronics in the areas hit by the weapon. Their hulls are a composite armor we've never successfully identified. We have no idea what its composition is, or where they manufacture it."

"But it is vulnerable to our weaponry?" Dryker asked. The carriers grew larger on the screen, silhouetted against the backdrop of the blue dwarf.

"Yes, sir," Nolan nodded. "There's an account of a gauss

cannon being fired at a carrier. The carrier took significant
damage, though it immediately wiped out the vessel that fired
on it."

The carriers were close now, relatively speaking. There
would be no getting past them--not without a fight, anyway.

"Recommendations?" Dryker asked.

"Our only choice is to stay docked," Nolan said, scratching
at his newly grown beard. "In theory, we're in neutral
territory. The carriers can't apprehend us unless we leave the
library."

"We can't stay here forever," Dryker snapped. He rose from
his chair and approached the monitor.

"We could make a run for it," Emo said, his voice
quavering.

The three carriers were now close enough to make out the
sigils on their hulls, each colossal vessel fanning out in a
different direction. Dryker stared at them helplessly, trying to
find an option that didn't end with the deaths of everyone on
the *Johnston*.

A bright blue beam shot from the first carrier. Dryker
winced, but there was no impact.

"What are they attacking?" he demanded, rounding on
Juliard.

"Sir, that shot hit the library," Juliard replied, her surprise evident. "The library is firing back."

There was an exchange of particle weapons, beams flashing from all three carriers. The library shuddered, and the ship's connection to the docking tube cause it to shake as well.

"Sir, all three carriers are launching drones," Juliard said, her voice more steady now.

Hundreds of tiny fighters drifted from the carriers. They began coordinated strafing runs at the library. The library wasn't undefended, and dozens of particle beams picked off fighters. It was a terrifying display of ferocity, on both sides.

"Emo, decouple us from the station. We're making a run for it," Dryker said, walking as calmly as he could back to his chair. He sat, gripping the arms again.

The *Johnston* pulled away from the library, accelerating rapidly toward the star. One of the carriers adjusted its course toward them, and several dozen drones moved to intercept.

"Incoming, sir," Juliard warned.

"Full burn, Emo. Ezana, pick off as many bogies as you can," Dryker ordered. He was aware of the quaver in his voice, and of Nolan watching him with concern. For a moment Dryker considered turning over command, but knew this wasn't the right time. He needed to get them through this.

The whole bridge rocked as a pair of particle beams hit. Sparks flew from several panels, and the lights flickered.

"We've lost power to the aft side of B deck," Juliard called. "Compiling damage reports now."

A blue-black fighter whipped by the view screen, firing tiny blue plasma pulses into them. Dozens of its companions joined in, and the *Johnston* shuddered under the furious assault.

"Sir, we can't take much more of this," Juliard said, giving him a sober look. "Engine two just took a hit. We've lost pressure in the aft wing. We're sealing what we can, but the damage is spreading faster than we can contain."

The turrets began to fire and, one after another, the fighters exploded. For every one destroyed, three more continued the attack. The *Johnston* was gaining distance from the library, but at this rate it wouldn't matter.

"Is the carrier pursuing?" Dryker demanded.

"Negative, sir," Emo said.

"Fire on A deck, sir," Juliard said. "It's spreading quickly."

"Order damage containment teams to deal with that first," Dryker said, lurching as the *Johnston* jerked from another impact.

"Sir, the fighters are breaking off," Emo said, giving Dryker a wide-eyed look. "It looks like they're moving back to the library."

"They're letting us go?" Dryker said, relaxing a hair as they pulled further away. The ship had sustained heavy damage, but the shuddering stopped. The turrets went quiet, and it appeared they had a clear path to the star.

"Oh, my God," Nolan said, his eyes widening. He turned to Dryker. "They're destroying the library to prevent the data cube from reaching Primo command."

Chapter 34- Reveal

Nolan rapped on the hatch to Lena's temporary quarters. There was no answer, so he rapped again. The wheel on the hatch spun, and it opened to reveal Lena's rumpled face. She licked her chops in a very alarming way. "Nolan! Come in. I was just going to go find you."

Nolan ducked through the hatch and into the cramped quarters. Lena had been given a room with a single bunk and nothing more. There wasn't even another place to sit. She was using the bed as a research station, and had a tablet with wires running to the cube. She returned to her position, tapping the tablet screen then studying the data feed.

"It's the first chance I've had to break away from repairs," Nolan said, rubbing the back of his neck. "Engine two is offline, our hull looks like Swiss cheese, and we lost two turrets on the aft side. We need six months in dry dock to get back into fighting shape."

"We're alive," Lena said. "Also, I've been able to converse with the cube. It contains far more information than I'd have guessed. I've only done a cursory examination, but I'm already learning some disturbing things."

"Don't keep me in suspense," Nolan said, leaning against the wall. "Tell me what you've found. Is it the kind of proof that might get our respective governments to take some action?"

"If we can get this in front of the right people they won't be able to ignore it.," Lena said, finally looking up. "How much do you know about early Primo history?"

"Pretty much nothing," Nolan admitted.

"The Primo empire didn't hit their stride until about nineteen thousand years ago. Before that is the period they refer to as their pre-dynastic times. For nearly six millennia they were nothing more than scattered tribes, and many of those tribes weren't even capable of space travel," Lena explained. "This cube predates those dark ages by at least a thousand years."

"I know that the library said the same thing, but how are you substantiating that date?" Nolan countered. "That will be important if we're presenting this as evidence."

"Stellar drift," Lena said, giving an excited smile. "This data cube contains star charts from the time it was made. I cross referenced those charts with our current astrological charts. Our galaxy has a rotation, just like a solar system or even a planet. That rotation takes approximately twenty-six thousand years, and the chart in the cube lines up with ours almost perfectly."

"Okay, so what is this thing?"

"As near as I can tell, it's a record of something they called the Eradication. It seems to have been a final war, one that was wiping out their empire," Lena explained. "The implications are staggering. It means that the Primo empire we know isn't the first. It's the second incarnation. The first was wiped out twenty-six thousand years ago, and it took them nearly seven millennia to rebuild something close to what they'd had before."

"Wiped out by what is the question. These Void Wraith?" Nolan asked, remembering the term from their brief encounter with the VI in the cube.

"That's the implication. The Void Wraith used technology very similar to the Primo, and there were some theories that they were an offshoot of the Primo empire. Those theories were never substantiated, because the Void Wraith wiped out most resistance. They eradicated world after world, taking all citizens they encountered. Just like we're seeing with the colonies that are disappearing."

"Okay," Nolan said, exhaling as he considered. "So why did these Void Wraith leave the job unfinished? And why return now?"

"I don't know. It may have something to do with the

galactic cycle. Every 26,000 years our galaxy completes a full

rotation," Lena said. She used her tail to hold the tablet and

picked up the cube with both hands. "My research is slow going.

I wish we had a Primo cube reader. Then we could plug in the VI

and ask it directly. I'll have to see if I can create a

makeshift one. May I have access to your machine shop?"

"I'll arrange that," Nolan said, nodding. "If you could

compile all footage of the Void Wraith, and any information

about their vessels and weaponry that would be helpful. We're

going to need that if we want to convince our respective

governments to do something about this."

"I'll compile a data dump of the footage from the last war.

It won't be comprehensive, but I can have something workable in

a few hours," Lena offered.

"Do that," Nolan said. "I'm going to go fill in Captain

Dryker."

Chapter 35- Eavesdropping

"I cannot believe I'm this stupid," Kathryn muttered. She inched along the ventilation duct, using her hands to pull her along.

She'd been in here for over twenty minutes, all to cross fifty feet. Doing so put her above her father's office, and she could hear his voice drifting up through the grate in the ventilation duct a few feet ahead of her. Kathryn pulled herself slowly forward, until she could smell the heady scent of tobacco.

A quick scan of the room showed that Mendez wasn't alone. He was sitting behind his mahogany desk, and across from him sat a figure she couldn't quite make out. They were speaking in low tones, but a quick adjustment to her headset amplified the microphone gain enough to pick up their words.

"Kelley is a problem," said the man across the table. "He'll need to be eliminated."

"Already taken care of," her father shot back, his annoyance evident both by his sneer and the tone of voice. "Kelley's housekeeper will stumble upon his body tomorrow morning. The admiral tragically died of a heart attack, a common problem in his family."

"Others will suspect," the man on the far side of the desk said. He leaned forward, and she caught a shock of blonde hair. "This cannot be allowed to draw attention to our special project. If they learn of the Ghantan system before we are ready--"

"That won't happen," her father said. He opened his desk drawer and removed a cigar, rolling it between his fingers as he stared at the unidentified man.

"How can you be so sure?" the man asked. "Every lie has an expiration date, Admiral. Sooner or later the wrong people will find out."

"This is OFI command, Bruce." The admiral used a pocket knife to snip the end of the cigar, then smelled it before placing one end in his mouth. "We have the best countermeasures in human space. Every signal is tracked here. Everything. There are no bugs, and the only personnel who know are with us. We can keep a lid on this, until we're ready to move in force."

Kathryn smiled grimly. Her OFI training had been very thorough, and she knew that her father was right. Anything capable of transmitting a signal would be immediately picked up. If someone had dispatched a drone to crawl through the ventilation system, alarms would have gone off at every security terminal.

Even someone doing so manually, like she was, was nearly impossible. There were scanners between every level, which meant that someone could only move around the ventilation system on the level where they entered it. Since her office was only two away from her father's, she was able to exploit that loophole.

"If you say so, I'll take your word for it," Bruce said. "It's a pity we couldn't reach Kelley. He'd have made an excellent ally."

"Too much risk," her father said, flicking a silver lighter. He puffed at the cigar. "Kelley is--was--paranoid. Reaching him with a larva presented too many chances for failure. Discovery or, worse, the destruction of a larva."

"You're right," Bruce said. "Any word from our Tigris counterparts?"

"They've kept the Leonis pride focused on the *Johnston*, and away from Ghantan. That's worked for now, but you know how difficult the cats are to control," her father said. He took a long draw from his cigar.

"True," Bruce replied. He waved a hand in front his face, as if warding off the pungent smoke. "What about the Primos?"

"Our Primo allies have had much better luck, though there is a wrinkle. That's why I called you," the admiral said. A note of discomfort entered his expression.

"Wrinkle?" Bruce asked. The word was emotionless, but the color drained from Mendez's face.

"The *Johnston* docked at a Primo library," Mendez admitted. He paused, setting the cigar in an ashtray. "They had an artifact with them. A VI extracted from the ruins on Purito."

"They have a VI?" Bruce roared. "How could you let this happen, Mendez? You assured me the *Johnston* wouldn't be a problem."

"And it won't," Mendez said, raising both hands placatingly. "The *Johnston* took severe damage fleeing the Primo system. They're being hunted by the Tigris, and they can't return to our space or they'll be picked up immediately. It doesn't matter what they find. If they pause to tell anyone they'll be shot down. The library was destroyed before it could transmit the data cube to Theras Prime."

"You'd better hope that's the case, Mendez," Bruce growled. He rose to his feet, positively looming over the admiral, and placed both hands on Mendez's desk. "Our masters are not forgiving. Deal with this wrinkle, or they will deal with you. Do you understand?"

"I understand," her father said, weakly.

"Good," Bruce said. Then he turned on his heel and headed

for the door.

Kathryn leaned forward, trying to peer through the ventilation grate. She couldn't quite make out the man's face. Her movement caused the panel under her midsection to buckle slightly, and the noise caught her father's attention. The admiral looked up, face knotted with suspicion.

Kathryn shrank back against the grate, holding her breath. It felt like the admiral was looking right at her, but after a moment he returned his attention to his desk. He picked up his cigar, taking another puff. Kathryn relaxed a hair.

This was big. Too big. Kelley was about to be assassinated. Multiple admirals were working for an outside force. Apparently, parts of the Tigris government and the Primo government had been compromised as well. What the hell was a larva?

She had to get word to Nolan.

Chapter 36- Licking Wounds

"Show me this VI, and make it quick. I've got about four hundred other things to deal with," Captain Dryker said as he ducked under a bundle of exposed wiring, and into what passed for a conference room aboard the *Johnston*.

Nolan was seated at the far side of the table, staring intently at the crazy contraption Lena was working on. She'd constructed a small black box, with a number of wires extending from the side. Those wires wrapped around the cube they'd liberated from Purito.

"I just need one more minute," Lena said, without looking up from her work. She connected a final wire to one of the cube's facets, then soldered it into place. "There we go. I can turn it on whenever." Lena blinked up at him, using a paw to smooth her golden fur.

"Do it," Dryker said, settling a hand on the grip of his sidearm. There wasn't any threat here, but turning on an alien artifact didn't seem like a good idea, no matter how badly they needed the information.

Lena pressed a button on the side of the black box, and it began to hum. A moment later multicolored light burst from the

top of the device. It coalesced into a holographic figure,
roughly two feet tall. The figure was dressed strangely, but it
was undeniably Primo.

"Welcome to installation 419," the figure said, bowing. "I
am Ducit Alba. How may I be of assistance?"

"Do you know where you are?" Dryker asked. He released his
weapon, crossing his arms.

"I do not," the hologram said. It looked around the
conference room. "This architecture is strange. Have I been
removed from installation 419?"

"Yes," Nolan said. He met Dryker's gaze, then raised a
questioning eyebrow. Dryker nodded, and Nolan continued. "You're
aboard a human vessel. Roughly twenty-six millennia have passed
since you were left in installation 419."

"Calculating," the hologram said. It flickered briefly. "A
complete galactic rotation has occurred. If our theories were
correct, the Eradication has begun."

"Eradication?" Dryker asked. He dragged a chair to the side
of the table closest to the VI, then sat down.

"I was created during the final war, along with many others
like me, to serve as a record. When victory became impossible,
we shifted the focus of our efforts. If we could not defeat the
Void Wraith, we hoped to ensure that our offspring would have

the necessary tools to do so when they came again," the VI explained.

Dryker was silent for a long moment as he considered. "What can you tell us about this final war?"

"Prior to the war, our civilization spanned the bulk of this galaxy. We'd colonized over four hundred worlds, and used our Helios Gates to travel between them. Our empire existed for over ten millennia." The VI flickered again, and the room began to smell of ozone. Lena knelt next to the box and began fiddling with it. "Then the Void Wraith arrived. First, they came in secret. They built fleets in the corners of our empire, and used stealth to grow in strength. Colonies were attacked without warning, disappearing without a trace.

"Our government was slow in responding. We could not agree on the source of the attacks, and by the time we learned the true nature of our adversary it was too late," the VI said. "Hundreds of fleets had been built, and they roamed our space at will. We won battles, but no matter how many Void Wraith we stopped...there were always more."

"Where did these Void Wraith come from?" Nolan asked.

"Unknown," the VI replied.

"Why did they take your colonists?" Dryker asked.

"Unknown," the VI replied.

"Okay," Dryker said, heaving a sigh. "What can you tell us about the Void Wraith technology? Do you possess weapon schematics?"

"Yes," the VI said. "We identified several models. We named their shock troops Judicators. They appear to be independent cybernetic units that answer to some sort of collective intelligence. They use high-yield particle weapons, and self-destruct if captured or incapacitated."

"And their vessels?" Nolan asked.

"We named their ships Harvesters, as those vessels harvested our colonies," the VI explained. "We never captured one, so our knowledge was limited."

"Can you tell us anything else about the Void Wraith?" Dryker asked.

"I can tell you a great deal, but without refining your query I do not think you will find the information useful," the VI said.

"Okay, turn it off," Dryker ordered.

Lena flicked a switch on the black box and the VI disappeared. Dryker rubbed his temples as he considered his options.

"What now, sir?" Nolan asked quietly.

"Now," Dryker said, looking up to meet Nolan's questioning

gaze, "we decide how to fight back. We know that the Void Wraith
are a threat. If they're operating like they did 26,000 years
ago, then their top priority is building a fleet. Perhaps
they're using our colonists as slave labor to do that.
Regardless, we need to find that fleet."

"Even if you find it, what will that do?" Lena asked.

"On its own, nothing," Dryker admitted. "But it's the next
step. If we can find the fleet, we have hard evidence. Evidence
the OFI can't ignore."

"So how do we find that fleet?" Nolan asked.

"That's the real question," Dryker said, rising from the
table. "I'm leaving you two to do that. Lena, I want you to
interrogate the hell out of that VI. Find out everything you can
about the Void Wraith. How did they build their fleets last
time? Nolan, I need you to contact Lieutenant Commander Mendez.
She's high enough in the OFI command structure that if they know
anything about a possible staging area for these Void Wraith she
might be able to find it. It's possible OFI already has the data
they need, and just don't know what they're seeing. Get her
working on a solution."

Nolan grimaced, but nodded. That pleased Dryker. He knew
Nolan's history with the Lieutenant Commander had left a scar,
but it said a lot that Nolan was able to compartmentalize his

feelings. The commander understood that his duty came first, and that was a rare thing in the officers who generally found their way to the 14th.

"What about you, sir?" Nolan asked.

"We took one hell of a beating in that last fight," Dryker said, patting the wall. "The *Johnston* is tough, but she's hurting. I don't much like hiding out in an asteroid field, but I don't see much choice. We need time in dry dock, and since that isn't going to happen I'm going to see what we can do on our own. You two will have twelve hours to work. That's the length of time I'm giving our techs to get the *Johnston* back on her feet. After that, we'll reconvene and decide what to do next."

Chapter 37- Reconciliation

In his quarters, Nolan picked up his tablet, took a deep breath, and dialed Kathryn. It wasn't as hard as it had been the last time, though his pulse still quickened when the connecting icon flashed. Then her face appeared.

"Nolan," Kathryn said, blinking. She glanced over her shoulder, then back at the tablet. "Give me a second."

The line went staticky for a moment, a sure sign that she'd engaged additional countermeasures. OFI calls were hard to track anyway, but almost every former operative had cooked up their own additional encryption. It wasn't just smart; it was a survival mechanism.

"I'm glad you called," Kathryn finally said. Her expression softened. "We haven't really had a chance to talk."

"Now isn't the time, Kathryn. Hopefully that time is soon, but we've got bigger concerns right now," Nolan said. It was only partially to dodge dealing with his feelings. "Listen, I need to know if anything hush-hush is going on with the brass."

"You have no idea," she said, glancing down at her wrist. "We've only got about two more minutes before the line isn't safe. My encryption should hold that long. I'm going to have to

report this call to the admiralty, but I don't have to tell them
what was said."

"They're watching you?"

"Closely," Kathryn replied. She reached out to touch the
screen with her fingertips. "I'm sorry about how all this went
down, Nolan. I wish I could change it."

"Two minutes?" Nolan said, raising an eyebrow. Kathryn
wasn't normally sentimental, and it surprised him that she was
so distracted.

"I'll give it to you straight. The admiralty has been
infiltrated somehow. My father is working for someone, a man I
don't recognize," she explained, glancing furtively over her
shoulder again. "They're hanging you out to dry, which I know
you're already aware of. It goes deeper, though. They're trying
to keep attention off something they called 'Ghantan.' I think
that's the name of a system, but I couldn't find a record of it
anywhere. I don't know what they're hiding there."

"How do you know they've been infiltrated?" Nolan asked.
He'd gone cold. This confirmed suspicions he already had, and
raised new ones.

"They were open about it. It's worse, though. Admiral
Kelley's body was found this morning. Heart attack."

"Shit," Nolan said. Admiral Kelly had been a good man, and

heart attacks were a signature of OFI assassins. "You're sure this line is secure? What's to stop them from coming after you?"

"It's secure, but there's nothing to protect me, Nolan," she said, wrapping a lock of hair absently around one finger. "Like I said, I'll report the call. I think my father expects you to contact me."

"Probably a good plan. Tell him we're trying to hide from the Primo and the Tigris while we repair the ship. It's the truth," Nolan suggested.

"I'll do that," Kathryn said. Her eyes widened. "Oh, one more thing I thought you'd want to know. My father talked about agents among the Tigris, and among the Primo. Whatever this conspiracy is, it's bigger than just the OFI."

"Jeez," Nolan said, leaning back in his chair. The news hit him like a hammer. "Thanks, Kathryn. If you find anything else, use one of our drops. I'll do the same, and I won't contact you directly again."

"Be careful, Adam." Kathryn's expression was somber. She stabbed the disconnect button, and the screen went black.

Kathryn had only used his first name once before, and he knew why she'd done it now: it was as close as she could get to expressing her feelings. Nolan shook his head, suppressing that part of the conversation. He had more important things to deal with.

Chapter 38- Aha

Nolan waited for the tech to finish with his welder before stepping around the man and into the conference room. The Captain and Lena were already seated. Lena's strange contraption was scattered all over the table, but the VI was off at the moment.

"Come in, Commander," Dryker called, gesturing to the seat opposite him. Nolan dropped into it, setting his coffee on the table next to him. It was all that was keeping him going.

"Did you learn anything useful?" Nolan asked Lena.

"Not really. I've compiled all the data I could glean into a directory on the *Johnston*'s main drive. I've sent you a link," Lena explained. Her fur was unkempt, and her normally alert gaze was vacant. Not surprising, since the entire crew had spent the last twelve hours working feverishly.

"What about you, Nolan?" the Captain asked. He looked more awake than Nolan felt. Maybe the Captain had found time for a nap.

Nolan certainly hadn't.

"I spoke to Kathryn, and she's given me one hell of a revelation," Nolan explained. He sipped his coffee, and

considered how best to explain. "The admiralty has been
infiltrated somehow. What's more, she believes that both the
Tigris and Primo have been infiltrated as well."

"I expected as much," the Captain said. He scrubbed his
fingers through his hair, and gave a deep sigh.

"You knew?" Nolan asked.

"Suspected," Dryker said. He shook his head. "It makes too
much sense. We've been yanked around, and the admiralty has made
no move to solve this problem. I first suspected something the
last time I spoke to Mendez. He's changed, and not in a good
way. Hanging out a Fleet captain as a scapegoat? That never
would have flown with him a few years ago. The final
confirmation was the Primo blowing up their own library. Someone
high in their command structure wants to cover up what we've
found."

""Something the VI said got me thinking." Nolan looked from
Lena to the Captain. "Remember when it said that the Void Wraith
were careful to keep hidden until it was too late? What's the
best way to keep hidden?"

"Hiding in plain sight," Lena said, blinking.

"Exactly," Dryker confirmed. "If you plant agents within
any government capable of reacting, you can ensure that your
activities remain unnoticed until you no longer care about their

discovery."

"So what do we do about it?" Lena asked.

"I have another piece of information that might give us an answer," Nolan said. "I probably should have led with it. The admiralty is trying to keep attention off something they call 'Ghantan.' Kathryn ran a search, but couldn't find a reference to it. She guesses it might be a system."

"I haven't heard of it," Dryker said.

"Neither have I," Lena said.

"What about the VI?" Nolan asked.

"Good point," Dryker said, smiling grimly. "If you're a long vanished race, what's the best code? Terms from an empire that no longer exists."

Lena pressed a button on the side of the black box, and a moment later the holographic display flickered to life. The Primo VI appeared, giving them a bow as it resolved. "How may I serve?"

"Are you familiar with the Ghantan system?" Dryker asked.

"The Ghantan system is the largest producer of varentium ore," the VI explained. "It supplied Fleet operations for nearly two centuries, until the final war."

"How do we cross reference the location with modern star charts?" Nolan asked.

"I have an idea for that," Lena said. She picked up a silicon chip, and inserted it into the side of the black box. "This will link the VI to the *Johnston*'s mainframe."

"Is that a good idea?" asked Dryker. "What if this thing tries to take over the ship?"

"It can't," Lena said. "The data bandwidth from this connection is minimal, and I can terminate it at any time."

"Ahh, so much data," the VI said. It flickered briefly. "I've accessed your star charts, and have overlaid our own. Given the stellar drift, the most likely location of the Ghantan system is here."

A star map shimmered into existence above the black box, replacing the VI.

"That's in Primo space," Nolan said, leaning closer. "We can be there in three Gates."

"Emo, this is the captain," Dryker said, speaking into his communicator. "What's the status of repairs?"

"We're a mess, Captain, but engine two is back on line. We're missing a lot of armor, and down two turrets on starboard," Emo said.

"It will have to do. I'm forwarding a course to you now. Fire up the engines, and make for the Helios Gate," Captain Dryker commanded.

Chapter 39- Scout

"You have the bridge, Commander," Captain Dryker said. The words caught Nolan off guard, and he didn't react immediately. He glanced at the view screen, then back at the captain.

"Are you sure, sir?" Nolan asked. The view screen was a mass of red, showing the undulating layers of the star's core as they pressed through to the surface. In a few minutes they'd emerge into the Ghantan system.

"I'm sure," Dryker replied, rising from the Captain's chair. "I'm tired, son. You're capable of handling this, and part of being in command is knowing when to delegate."

Nolan watched as the Captain ducked through the hatch and out of the CIC. The bridge crew shared looks, and Nolan could tell they were concerned. They placed their collective faith in the Captain, and that faith had just been shaken. The Captain had revealed weakness, and at a critical time.

"Juliard, how long until we breach the photosphere?" Nolan asked, moving to the captain's chair.

"Three minutes, sir. It will be another six until we're free of the corona," Juliard said. She glanced at the hatch where the captain had disappeared, then back at her console.

"Alert me as soon as we've reached the corona," Nolan said. He lapsed into silence, watching the screen as they pushed through the sun.

The very idea that they could travel through a star still awed him. The tremendous pressure and heat were unlike anything else in the galaxy, and the fact that various races had harnessed technology that allowed them to circumvent those pressures was a testament to just how much could be accomplished.

Minutes passed, and no one spoke. The crew had been through a lot in the last week, a wholly separate set of pressures. They were cut off from their government. Cut off from family, friends, and any other type of support. They were being hunted. Their ship was severely damaged. They were low on ordinance.

"We're breaching the photosphere and entering the corona, sir," Juliard said, her voice breaking the near silence. The only other sound came from beeping monitors, and the background hum of the computers.

"Orders, sir?" Emo asked as the *Johnston* burst from the dense, roiling mass of flame and plasma.

"Make for that solar storm," Nolan commanded. He rose from the captain's chair and moved to stand next to Emo. "Keep us under cover."

"Are you certain, sir?" Emo asked. The waif-like pilot shifted in his chair. "That storm could tear our engines apart if we aren't careful. The rear inductive field won't function while we're under thrust."

"Dryker claims you're the best pilot in the 14th," Nolan said, folding his arms. "Is he lying?"

"No, sir," Emo said. He guided the *Johnston* toward the storm, a mass of flares bursting and twisting from the sun's surface.

"I know I'm new here," Nolan said, straightening. He looked around the bridge, making sure that each and every person was paying attention. "I know I'm not the captain. But I'm what we have right now. My father had a saying: "On your death bed, you're visited by the person you could have been." What we're doing is dangerous. We could die. But if we don't do this--if we sit by--then the entire galaxy could pay the price."

No one replied. There was no applause. But everyone stood a little straighter; they bent to their stations with a little more pride. Nolan suppressed a smile, returning to the captain's chair. He wasn't a great commander, but he'd just taken a step toward being a good one.

The *Johnston* bucked wildly as a solar flare shot up from the sun's photosphere. It knocked them to starboard, and Nolan would have fallen if he hadn't caught himself on the captain's chair. A few gasps came from the crew, but no one panicked. Emo guided them around the flare, into the tip of the storm.

"We're about two hundred miles above the surface, sir," Emo said, guiding them smoothly around another flare.

"Juliard, begin scans," Nolan ordered.

"Yes, sir," she said. The view screen flickered, providing a visual of the area she was scanning.

The Ghantan system didn't contain planets, but it did contain a vast asteroid belt circling the star. There had to be billions of rocks, and Nolan wondered idly why those rocks hadn't formed into a planet.

"Sir," Juliard said after several moments. "We're detecting two objects. I'll put them on screen."

"Look at the size of that thing," Nolan said, studying the larger of the two objects on the screen. It was massive, almost a planet in its own right. "That's a factory. See along the rear section? Those are dry docks. This thing is building ships out of those asteroids."

Nolan counted seven vessels docked in the berths on the bottom of the factory, and it was possible there were more on the side they couldn't see. Each of the vessels--complete, or close to it, as far as Nolan could tell--was constructed of the now-familiar blue-black alloy, in the strange pincher-winged V-shape that he'd first seen on Mar Kona...was it really only a week ago?

The factory itself resembled one of the Primo's carriers, but far larger and far more lethal; it bristled with weaponry unlike anything Nolan had ever seen. Clearly, any approach would result in swift death. It would take an entire fleet to take that thing down, and that fleet would likely suffer heavy casualties.

"What do you make of the second object, Lieutenant?" Nolan asked Juliard. He stared at the odd spherical structure floating a short distance from the factory.

"I'm not sure, sir," she replied, pursing her lips. "It's giving off massive amounts of radiation of a type we've never seen. That thing has almost as much mass as a small star. Those ports on the bottom appear to be thrusters, so whatever it is...it's probably mobile."

"Complete your scans, then get us the hell out of here," Nolan said, barely above a whisper. They'd found the Void Wraith, but now what the hell were they supposed to do? They'd need an army to deal with them...and they didn't have one.

Chapter 40- Leak

Nolan shielded his eyes from the approaching flashlight,
lowering his own so as not to blind the other crewman.

"Sorry, sir," said a tech he didn't recognize, lowering his
flashlight. He ducked past Nolan, hurrying down the corridor
toward C deck.

Even in the darkness, Nolan could see the man was tired.
They all were. Every last crew member had been drafted into
repairs, and even with all their hard work the *Johnston* was in
bad shape. That wasn't as apparent right now, because they'd
gone dark. Only life support and gravity had power. Everything
else, anything that broadcast a signal, was dark.

He continued up the corridor, stepping over a thick conduit
along the floor then ducking under a ladder. He finally reached
the captain's ready room, which had a small portable lantern
near the center of the table. Captain Dryker and Lena were
already there, each nursing a cup of coffee--probably the only
thing keeping them conscious.

Nolan scratched at his chin as he sat down. The stubble was
starting to itch, and was threatening to become a full beard
unless he found a razor today. Maybe he should just leave it.

Maybe that was how the captain had first grown his beard. Not shaving meant one less thing to worry about daily; when you had the pressures of command, every worry added to the pile.

"All right. Let's recap what we know," the captain said, rubbing at his eyes. He looked more haggard than usual, his uniform rumpled and beard unkempt. The same coffee stain from the day before was still on his right cuff.

"You've read the initial report about the two structures. The first is obviously a starship factory," Nolan said. He turned to Lena, who was busy grooming. "I'm hoping Lena might have some theories about the second structure."

"I don't have a theory, but I do have some interesting data," she said, looking up to meet Nolan's gaze. She stopped cleaning herself, folding her hands together. "The second structure contains a heavy element we've never seen before."

"What do you mean by heavy element?" the captain asked.

"Hmm," Lena said, licking her chops in a very unsettling way. "Your people have something called the periodic table of the elements. Are you familiar with it?"

"Yes," Dryker said, nodding.

"The number on each element corresponds to the number of protons and neutrons it contains. Heavier elements have more," Lena explained. She gave a yawn, and her fangs flashed in the low light. "The heaviest element on the table has 120 protons. Enriched Uranium has 235. The element in that structure has over five hundred."

"What does that mean, exactly? What would an element like that be used for?" Nolan asked. He ripped open a packet of aspirin, and ate them dry.

"I can only speculate," Lena said. She cocked her head. "There's more energy in that structure than I've ever seen outside of a star. It could do anything from igniting a new sun to being the largest bomb we've ever seen. We just don't know."

"I guess it doesn't really matter what that thing is. They're building it, so we need to destroy it. And that factory," Nolan said. He straightened. "If we're going to do that we need a whole hell of a lot more firepower than the *Johnston* can bring to bear, especially in her current state."

"Where are you planning to get this army?" Lena asked. Her ears twitched. "If the Void Wraith really have infiltrated every major fleet, then there's no way we can convince anyone to come help."

"It's troubling," Dryker said, giving a sigh. "We have to assume that any attempt to bring an organized force to this system will be blocked."

"What about an unorganized method?" Nolan asked. He gave a

grim smile. "How about we use our notoriety against them?
Everyone is hunting us. The Primo, the Tigris...hell, even OFI
seems to want us dead. We broadcast our location to each group,
basically flash our asses, and then run back here."

"So all three governments send groups to hunt us down, and
those groups end up in this system," Dryker finished. He smiled
for the first time in days. "I like it. Tell me more."

"We could use the Quantum Network to alert Fleet and the
OFI," Nolan said, thinking out loud. "That will be the easiest
part of the plan."

"If you want to bring the Leonis Pride you'd need to jump
into the Tigrana system. It's a sacred place. If a human were to
trespass there, the Tigris would have no choice but to hunt you
down," Lena said, blinking. "That would bring the Leonis
running. It might get other prides to come too."

"What about the Primo?" Dryker asked. He still looked
tired, but some of his strength had returned.

"I can't think of a way to get them to come," Nolan said.
He scratched his stubble again. "We could use the Quantum
Network to broadcast a signal to their space, but I'm not sure
they'd react. They're slow and deliberate--and, even if they do
come, its unlikely to happen before the battle is decided one
way or another."

"We'll make the attempt, at least. It isn't the best plan,
but it will have to do," Dryker said.

Chapter 41- Quantum Lite

Kathryn glanced over her shoulder to ensure she was alone, then sat down at the terminal. It was as public as one could get, a small, blocky box set into one of the tables in the mess hall. Ostensibly it was there for busy officers to use during meal times, but more often than not enlisted personnel used it to play games or chat with their SO across the vast distances bridged by the Quantum Network.

She was alone, which was to be expected at this hour. That was why she'd come, after all. The security cameras would pick her up, but that was a good thing. Anyone observing her would see a tired officer taking a break, not an operative conducting clandestine business.

Kathryn sipped her coffee, then fired up the terminal. There were two security cameras in the room, but she'd deliberately chosen a table whose screen wasn't visible to those cameras. In theory, this was the most private place she could be right now. That was critical, as she'd become increasingly sure that she was being watched. That wasn't uncommon in OFI, but it went deeper than that. Her father suspected her loyalties; she was sure of it. Her only hope was that he believed she wouldn't act on those loyalties, so she needed to be sure not to give him reason to doubt her.

The screen lit up, and she did a quick scan of the local news stories. These updated hourly, pulling data from the entire fleet. That was the beauty of the Quantum Network. With quantum entanglement, distance didn't matter. A line of stories filled her news feed, and she began scanning for anything interesting.

Her heart nearly stopped when she read the third headline: *UFC Johnston Sighted In Ghantan System*.

She clicked the link, and began scanning. The article showed a picture of the *Johnston*, and claimed it had been sighted in the Ghantan system. It even included a star map showing that system.

Kathryn grinned. The move had Nolan's fingerprints all over it. Officers would begin checking their news feeds as they woke up, and too many people would see this. It couldn't be ignored. The OFI would have no choice but to send a fleet to investigate.

"Clever, Nolan," she said, leaning back in her chair and stifling a yawn.

Then the story disappeared. Her screen flickered, and she was back on the news feed. She scrolled up, then down. There was no sign of the story. It was just...gone. Someone was scrubbing the news feed, and doing it close to real time.

Kathryn ran a search for the word 'Ghantan' and found four more stories. That made sense. Nolan was thorough, and wouldn't have left something so important to one story. He'd replicated it many times, to try to secure broader notice. The screen flickered. Now there were three stories.

"Damn it," she said, hitting refresh again. It was down to two.

Kathryn considered the situation. She considered everything on the line, and her own role in things. Nolan had located the system she'd pointed him at. He'd likely learned more about these Void Wraith, and was obviously trying to get help there the only way he knew how. If that help didn't arrive, there was probably no way the *Johnston* could stop the Void Wraith. Nolan needed OFI. He needed *her*.

"This is definitely the stupidest thing I've ever done," she said, closing her eyes for a moment. She owed Nolan. He'd given up a promising career, thanks largely to a mistake she'd made. She had to make this right.

Kathryn opened her eyes, resolved. There were two networks in OFI space. The biggest and best was the Quantum Network, which was controlled by the military. But there was also Quantum Lite, the civilian network. It had less bandwidth, and longer queues, but it was how civilian governments communicated. That network fell under the auspices of OFI but, because it was used by far more people than the military network, it was much more difficult to police. Stories could go viral in an instant.

Kathryn copied the last remaining story about the Ghantan system. She spent several minutes writing a simple computer script, one that would replicate the story and fire it off on a timer. Then she bridged the two networks, and set the script to start firing stories into the Quantum Lite network. Doing so would be considered a breach of security. It would be traced back to her eventually, and she'd be brought up on charges. She might be flushed from the service, or--given what she'd seen of her father lately--might meet an even worse fate.

It didn't matter. This was the right thing to do. She'd ducked morality when she had a chance to save Nolan, and had watched his career be picked apart because she'd stayed silent. This was a chance to atone, even if Nolan never knew it. At least she'd finally be able to sleep again.

She executed the script and watched the story begin to replicate across both networks. Then she turned the terminal off, smiled, and walked back to her quarters.

Chapter 42- Here Kitty Kitty

"I cannot believe we're doing this," Nolan said, grabbing the handle set into the CIC's bulkhead.

"It was your idea," Captain Dryker countered from the captain's chair. He was grinning like a madman, his gaze focused on the view screen.

The *Johnston* had just emerged from the star, a G class star not unlike Earth's sun. They were free of the corona, which meant that their sensors were able to scan the system. It also meant that they were visible to anyone in-system who happened to be scanning.

"Sir," Juliard said, her voice quavering. "I count seventy-three Tigris vessels. At least a third are Leonis pride, and most of those are warships. They're primarily concentrated around Tigrana, but there is some traffic to and from the Gate."

"Excellent," Dryker said. He smiled grimly. Nolan noted that the Captain's uniform had been pressed, and he had apparently found time to trim his beard. "Scan for the *Claw of Tigrana*."

"Yes, sir," Juliard said. She was silent for several moments. "I've located it. They're here, sir."

"Open a channel," Dryker said.

A moment later the view screen changed. It showed the bridge of a Tigris vessel, a view Nolan had never seen before. Its layout roughly mirrored that of the *Johnston*'s own CIC, and several Tigris stood near various consoles. Their captain was terrifyingly similar to a female lion, so much so that Nolan took a step backward. She stared imperiously at Captain Dryker, and Nolan read murder in those bestial eyes. There was history between the captain and this Tigris, of that Nolan was sure-- history that went beyond what had happened in the Purito system.

"Another human might not understand the insult you have offered my race by coming here," the enemy captain said. She growled low in her throat, and her tail thrashed wildly behind her. Each time she spoke, Nolan could see her two-inch fangs. "*You* know better, Dryker. You know what you have done, which means you have done it intentionally. Why have you besmirched our honor? Do you crave death so very much? I assure you, you are about to meet her."

"Hello, Fizgig," Dryker said, calmly, and gestured to Nolan. "My XO, Commander Nolan, would like a few words."

Nolan licked his lips, then stepped forward and looked up at Fizgig. "You've lost colonies. So have the Primo. So have we. We've figured out who's attacking them. It's an ancient race.

The Void Wraith."

"The Void Wraith are nothing but a fairy tale," Fizgig said, her eyes narrowing. "You've come all this way to tell stories?"

"We're broadcasting the data we've accumulated on the Void Wraith," Nolan said, stabbing a button on his tablet. "You don't trust us, and we can't blame you for that. But look objectively at the data. We have a common foe, Fizgig."

"Even were that true, I'm still honor-bound to destroy you. Coming here has ensured your deaths."

"Maybe," Dryker said. He gave a cavernous yawn, and the Tigris captain recoiled as if struck. "First you have to catch me, Fizgig. You couldn't do that back at Purito, and you're not going to do it here. I'll even tell you where I'm going: We're heading to the Ghantan system. I'm broadcasting the location now. If you're warrior enough, then follow us. Bring your fleet. I promise you're going to need all the help you can get."

"You--" Fizgig began, growling low in her throat.

"End transmission," Captain Dryker ordered. The screen went black, then returned to a view of space. "Lieutenant, is the Tigris fleet's posture changing?"

"Negative, sir," Juliard said. She paused, studying her terminal. "It appears that only the *Claw of Tigrana* is moving to engage us. The rest of the ships aren't taking the bait."

"Blast it," Dryker said, slamming a fist down on the arm of his chair. "Juliard, access the battle footage from Mar Kona."

"I have it, sir," Juliard said. The view screen showed the debris field they'd first encountered, the wreckage of the science vessel *Revelation*.

Lena tensed, her tail thrashing as she studied the screen.

Nolan felt for her. She was seeing the remains of the vessel she'd called home. Who knew how many friends and family she'd lost when it was destroyed?

"Broadcast this footage system-wide," Dryker said.

"Yes, sir," Juliard replied. She was silent for several seconds. "It's been sent, sir. Every vessel in the system can see it, plus the data Commander Nolan sent."

"That should do it," Lena said, her voice just above a whisper. "No Tigris will be able to ignore that insult, especially those in the Leonis pride. You've shown that you destroyed one of our science vessels, and you've broadcast it in one of our most holy places."

"Let's hope it worked," Dryker said. He turned to Emo. "Get us out of here, Ensign Gaden."

"Aye, sir," Emo said. The *Johnston* began to turn, then headed back into the star's corona.

"Are we being pursued?" Dryker asked, his voice was tense.

"Negative, sir," Juliard said. "The *Claw of Tigrana* is still the only one pursuing us."

"How is that possible?" Dryker said, rounding on Lena. "I thought you said we'd insulted your entire culture."

"You have," Lena said, growling deep in her chest. Her eyes narrowed, and she flexed her claws. "My people will never forgive this. I don't understand why they aren't pursuing."

"The *Claw* will be here in four minutes," Juliard called.

"Get us out of here," Dryker said.

Nolan watched the view screen. It looked like they'd failed, and there was no point in staying any longer. At least one Tigris vessel was following, though that wasn't going to make any difference unless they received a lot more help from some other quarter.

Chapter 43- Fizgig's Wrath

Fizgig flexed her claws as she paced back and forth. Her vessel was moving toward the *Johnston*, but she knew she'd never reach it before it reached the Helios Gate and fled. She supposed it was *possible* that *Dryker* was telling the truth about this Ghantan system, that the *Johnston* would be there waiting for battle--but it seemed unlikely. Captain Dryker was one of the craftiest humans she'd ever met, and he was far too canny to give himself up so easily.

"What are you planning?" she muttered aloud. She was aware of tails twitching all over the bridge, but her crew wisely remained silent. They could feel her fury. She rounded on Izzy, whose eyes were wide as saucers. "Is the rest of the fleet moving to join us?"

"No, mighty Fizgig," Izzy said, in a small voice. Her tail drooped, and she didn't make eye contact.

"Open a channel to Admiral Mow," Fizgig snarled.

The screen flickered, then revealed a cat even older than Fizgig. The admiral's once-rich fur was now dun and faded, the gold on his cheeks fading to a pale white. He stared impassively at the monitor, meeting Fizgig's barely contained fury with utter disdain.

"Why isn't the fleet moving to intercept the humans?"
Fizgig demanded. She unsheathed her claws, stalking to the
screen so she could stare up at Mow.

"Because I have ordered them not to," Mow said.

"Why?" Fizgig roared. "Our honor has been stained, again.
The humans have come to the holiest of holy places. They have
uttered a challenge, a challenge we cannot refuse. We must
pursue them, and punish them."

"And you will do so," Mow said, licking his paw, then using
the paw to smooth the fur behind his neck. "You have been
accorded much honor, Fizgig. Are you telling me that you don't
believe you can best these humans?"

"Of course I can best them, but that isn't the point. This
isn't about a personal matter anymore. This affects all of us.
We must respond with overwhelming strength," she protested. "If
we do not, the humans will think us weak."

"We would accord the humans much honor by sending our
fleet. That would show that they matter--and this I will not do.
You will deal with them personally. Alone. Hunt them, and do not
return unless it is with word of their deaths," Mow said.

Fizgig watched the admiral. This made no sense. Mow had
always been honorable, and would never have retained his

position without that kind of concern. Yet here he was
advocating something that stained not just his own honor, but
that of all Leonis.

"What if the humans aren't lying about these Void Wraith?"
Fizgig asked. She hoped that they were, but a quiet voice in the
back of her head wondered. What did Dryker gain by coming here
alone? Why would he taunt the Tigris fleet, then broadcast his
true location?

"The Void Wraith are a fairy tale for kits," Mow said,
waving a dismissive paw. "The humans still rankle from their
defeat in the war, even years later. Perhaps they have tailored
an ambush, one that could destroy dozens of our vessels. No, we
will not fall for such base treachery. You will deal with this
matter alone. It is decided."

The admiral cut the connection. Fizgig was left fuming. The
Claw was still powering toward the star, and it seemed they had
no choice but to proceed alone.

"Mighty Fizgig," Izzy said, again in a small voice. "The
Rrrrowlerchan is requesting a channel."

"On screen," Fizgig commanded.

"Mighty Fizgig." Zera, the captain of the Rrrrowlerchan,
appeared onscreen. Her orange striped fur rippled with
displeasure, and her tail sketched a pattern of frustration

behind her. "The fleet has monitored your communication. Admiral

Mow has spoken--but this is not right. Honor demands that we

destroy the humans. Our entire fleet should pursue."

"Yet, as you say, the admiral has spoken," Fizgig said,

growling low. "I do not wish this, but I have no choice. I must

obey."

"Hunt well, mighty Fizgig. Your brethren hunger for blood,

and you carry with us the honor of our pride. We wish we could

go with you," Zera said.

Almost, Fizgig considered asking her to disobey the

admiral. Almost, Fizgig sought the help of the pride against the

wishes of her commander. But doing so would dishonor Mow. It

would cause a rift in their ranks, and force her to challenge

Mow for command.

No, she couldn't fracture her people. Not after the losses

they'd suffered.

Unity was vital. She disagreed with Mow, but she would do

her duty. She would pursue and destroy the humans.

"Zera, I beg a favor," Fizgig asked, blinking.

"Name it, mighty one," Zera said, ears perking up.

"If we fall in battle, gather the fleet and avenge us. I

fear that there is a deeper game here. The humans are

treacherous, but I have seen this enemy with my own eyes,"

Fizgig said. She sat up straighter. "If the humans are telling the truth, the Tigris must unite. Do what you can to ensure that."

"As you will it, mighty Fizgig," Zera said. "Go with the gods, matron. You carry the pride of our race."

Chapter 44- Surrender

"Hold position, Ensign Gaden," Captain Dryker ordered. He could tell by the expressions on the bridge crew that they thought he was crazy. Only Nolan supported him, his unwavering optimism etched on those features. Nolan reminded Dryker so much of himself at that age. He would make one hell of a fleet captain if he survived this, exactly the kind of commander that they'd need in this new war.

War. That word had been the counterpoint of his life, and it was somehow unsurprising that it had come again. For a long time he'd hoped that he would either retire or pass away before seeing it again. Eight long years of peace had passed, but at long last war had come again. A different kind of war, one that might extinguish them all if they couldn't pull together--and do so quickly.

"Lieutenant Juliard, I'd like a full core dump into a personal storage device," the Captain ordered. "Make sure it contains all sensor data, all footage of the Void Wraith, and everything we've recovered from the Primo VI."

"Yes, sir," Juliard said, bending over her terminal. Her fingers flew across the screen. "It's being sent to your PSD now, sir."

"Excellent. Send a copy to Commander Nolan, and broadcast
another over the Quantum Network," Dryker ordered. If they died
here, the data needed to live on. If they survived, he wanted a
copy on his person. He had no idea what would happen in the
coming battle, but that evidence *must* survive.

"Captain, I'm detecting a vessel beneath us," Juliard said.

"On screen," Dryker ordered.

Juliard punched the image up, and it showed exactly what
Dryker expected: the *Claw of Tigrana* was approaching from below,
narrowing the distance between them.

"They're hailing us, sir," Juliard said softly.

"Open a channel," Dryker ordered. He sat back in his chair,
and readied himself for the unpleasant encounter.

"Why?" Fizigig growled the moment her golden-furred face
filled the view screen.

"Why, what?" Dryker asked, mildly.

"Why did you call us here? Why taunt our fleet, when you
know what it would do?"

"My XO told you," Dryker shot back, meeting her gaze
evenly. "There is a greater threat, and that threat is located
here, in the Ghantan system. You'll see it as soon as you reach
our altitude. The Void Wraith are here, Fizgig, and they'll

exterminate all of us if we can't put our differences aside."

"Your recent actions make that impossible," Fizgig said, though her expression softened.

Dryker couldn't exactly ascribe human emotions to a Tigris, but almost he thought he saw regret there.

"Surrender," she continued, "and I will spare your crew. Your vessel must be destroyed, and your life is forfeit. But your crew will live."

"Captain, they're almost within grappling range," Emo called urgently. "Orders, sir? Should we retreat?"

"Negative," Dryker said, not breaking eye contact with Fizgig.

Long moments passed as the Tigris approached. Dryker knew it was impossible to run now--but then, he'd never intended to run.

"Very well," he said. "We surrender."

Whispers sounded between the bridge crew, but Dryker ignored them. This wasn't just the right thing to do, it was the only thing that might save them.

"Prepare to be boarded," Fizgig said, then terminated the connection.

Chapter 45- Stand Down

Hannan tensed, ready to run even though there was nowhere
to run. The Tigris vessel loomed larger on the view screen, then
began to fire. Harpoons shot from all four of its banks, each
slamming into a different part of the *Johnston*. The screech of
metal echoed around them as the huge tritanium barbs sank into
the hull.

There would definitely be no running now.

"Sir, are we sure about this?" Edwards asked, gesturing at
the packed shuttle bay. "At the very least, we should be armed.

All four squads of Marines had gathered here. If the Tigris
wanted to slaughter them, they'd meet almost no resistance.
Everyone capable of that resistance was gathered here, where
they could be easily controlled.

"I have no idea why Captain Dryker is showing his belly to
the Tigris, but I've served under him for four years," Hannan
said, pitching her voice loudly enough to carry through the
whole shuttle bay. "He says we wait here unarmed, so that's
exactly what we're going to do. I've never seen the captain make
a mistake, and he's one of the few survivors from the last
Tigris war. Trust him."

Some of the nervous chatter died away, but not all of it. The 14th fleet was a haven for malcontents, incompetents, and every brand of slacker the fleet had produced. Some of these people were good soldiers, but a lot of them were like the space debris that piled up around habited worlds: utterly worthless, and prone to ruin a perfectly fine re-entry.

"If you say so, sir," Edwards muttered. He sat heavily on a supply crate.

"This waiting is terrible, but it will be over soon enough," Hannan said, slapping Edwards on the back.

"Let's just hope 'over' doesn't mean 'permanently over,'" Mills said. He wasn't whispering but, as always, his voice was pitched low. As a sniper, everything he did was done quietly.

The *Johnston* shuddered violently, and Hannan looked up. "That's them docking."

"Crew of the *Johnston*." Captain Dryker's voice echoed over the ship wide comm. "Stand down and offer no resistance to the Tigris. Our surrender is unconditional."

That set up murmurs among the Marines. Hannan would have punched Dryker if the captain were within reach. She didn't know why he'd chosen to surrender, but that was the worst possible way he could have broached it to the crew. Several Marines were eyeing the weapons locker in the corner. Their posture had changed. They were ready to fight.

"Listen up," Hannan yelled. She leaped onto the storage
crate next to Edwards, making herself tall enough to draw every
eye in the room. "I know you're pissed off, because I'm pissed
off, too. We're Marines. We do the tough jobs no one else wants
to do. What's the toughest job? Turning the other cheek while we
let the cats take our ship. But you know what? That is exactly
what we're going to do. Stand down, people."

Then she hopped down, and turned away from her fellow
Marines. If she pressed the issue, they'd press back. But
embarrassing them into doing their duty would work, as long as
they were allowed to decide for themselves. The squads began
settling, and were approaching disciplined silence when the
Tigris finally arrived.

The first cat through the door was tall and lean, probably
six foot three. Her fur was mostly white, with little black
spots on her face. She looked a lot like a snow leopard that
Hannan had seen at a zoo back on earth. The cat eyed them
impassively, cradling a wicked-looking shotgun with a barbed
bayonet affixed to the end.

"Who is in charge here?" the cat asked, stepping into the
room. Several more cats prowled outside the door, but none
entered the shuttle bay. Most of those were Leonis, with the

dun-colored fur and large paws Hannan had come to fear.

"I guess that would be me," Hannan said, stepping forward. It wasn't technically true, as there were three other sergeants in the room. She had the most seniority, though--plus she could kick the other three squad leaders' asses. Hannan extended a hand to the cat. "I'm sergeant Hannan."

"I am Izzy Prideless," the cat said, accepting Hannan's hand. She had a firm grip, her furry paw more like a human hand than Hannan had expected. Izzy looked around the shuttle bay, releasing Hannan's hand. "This is all the soldiers your vessel possesses?"

"This is everyone," Hannan said, folding her arms. "Four squads is all we need to deal with...well, pretty much anything."

"Keep that in mind, cat," came a yell from the back of the room. Hannan thought she recognized Jinton's voice, but couldn't be sure.

Izzy merely smiled as her odd feline gaze roamed the room. She turned back to Hannan. "We will stay outside for now. As long as no one attempts to leave this shuttle bay, you will not be harmed."

Chapter 46- Boarded

Nolan's hand fell to his sidearm as the first Tigris ducked through the hatch into the CIC. He blinked in surprise when he realized he recognized this one. It was the golden-furred cat who'd filled the screen every time Dryker had verbally sparred with the Tigris. *Fizgig*, Dryker had called her. Nolan had expected guards first, and found it surprising that an enemy commander would risk herself this way.

Fizgig was a lot more intimidating up close. Her fur was short, and Nolan could see the corded muscle underneath. She wore a suit of simple black body armor that covered her torso and legs, but her arms and tail were free. Her golden fur lightened on her face, especially under the chin where it was as white as snow. It made Fizgig look ancient and venerable, a wise and canny general.

"Hello, Fizgig," Dryker said. He didn't rise from the captain's chair, instead greeting the Tigris with a nod.

"*Mighty* Fizgig," another Tigris corrected, this one larger than any of the others. He was at least six foot six and strongly resembled a male lion, complete with the thick mane. His arms were wide enough to crush Nolan's skull like a walnut.

"Hello, Dryker," Fizgig said, waving a paw in the male cat's direction. He subsided into silence, but glared sullenly around the room as if challenging someone to meet his gaze.

Nolan took up that challenge. He stared dead into the cat's face. This was his ship and, while he understood what Dryker was doing, he wasn't going to just lie down and take abuse from the cats. Even if the *Johnston* did need them.

"Tell me, Captain," Fizgig began, pulling Nolan's attention from the larger Tigris. "Why surrender? Why bait us, then run here? Is there really a threat so dire as you've claimed?"

"See for yourself," Dryker said, nodding at the view screen. "That's the enemy factory. You can see there are seven ships docked, ships unlike anything we've encountered before. I've seen one of those ships up close. It was a ship just like that that destroyed your science vessel. Not us."

"Are you trying to avoid your fate, Captain?" Fizgig asked. She walked slowly toward the captain, ignoring the rest of the bridge crew. "You know us better than that. Your fate is sealed. I have a duty, and I will do it."

"You have a greater duty--to your race, Fizgig," Dryker countered. He finally rose from his chair, standing almost nose-to-nose with the aging Tigris commander. "The Void Wraith have returned. They've planted agents in my government, and in yours.

They've even planted them among the Primo."

"Do you have evidence to back up that claim, Captain?"
Fizgig asked, her tail swishing slowly behind her. "I'm willing
to hear that evidence. It won't save you, but if you speak the
truth it could save your crew and prevent a war between our
peoples."

Nolan shifted from foot to foot, ready to fight if Dryker
called for it.

"The proof is in the patterns," Dryker countered. If he was
intimidated by the larger Tigris he didn't show it. "You're a
strategist, Fizgig. Look at the pieces being shuffled about the
board. How many colonies have you lost? What has your government
done about it? Doesn't it seem strange that they haven't
mobilized, strange that they sent a single vessel to hunt me
down?"

Fizgig was silent for a long moment. She studied Dryker
carefully, as if weighing him. When she finally spoke, her voice
was weary. "You're right. The prides are acting strangely, even
my own. We should have sent a fleet to deal with you, and we
should be more closely garrisoning our colonies. The
disappearance of one colony is a tragedy. We've lost four.
That's more damage than your entire race did in the war between
our peoples, yet the Tigris have done nothing. No reprisal, no

investigation."

"My government has reacted in the same way," Dryker said, shaking his head sadly. "We've lost six colonies, and there's been no reaction. As I understand it, the Primo have lost some as well. Entire worlds are disappearing, yet no one has done anything to stop it. Why? Why isn't anyone reacting?"

Fizgig didn't answer, but she did give a low growl. Her tail picked up the tempo, somehow conveying her agitation. "I do not know, and it troubles me deeply. If there really are spies, who do they work for? We are familiar with the legends of the Void Wraith. I cannot believe that we have been infiltrated by stories told to our kittens."

"What if I showed you proof? We recovered a Virtual Intelligence from some Primo ruins on Purito, one that predates recorded history," Dryker offered. He gestured behind him to the corner where Lena was standing. Until now she'd all but blended into the wall, and her eyes grew very large when the whole room focused in her direction. "Lena is one of your scientists, and she's been very helpful in learning more about the Void Wraith."

"Holy one?" Fizgig said. She growled low in her throat, her eyes narrowing. "Why are you still with the humans? Have they kept you prisoner?"

"No, mighty Fizgig," Lena said, bobbing her head. "I have

stayed of my own volition. These humans are the only ones trying to stop the Void Wraith, and if we cannot stop them then all of us are doomed. We're being harvested, our people *and* theirs."

"I see," Fizgig said. She studied Lena for several moments before shifting her attention back to Dryker. "You've presented a compelling argument. I am willing to release your crew. Your life is forfeit, and this vessel will be destroyed. Once that is complete we will travel back to Tigrana, and I will call a conclave of the prides."

Nolan considered drawing his sidearm, but knew it would be pointless. Their surrender had been total, and now they had to live with it. He watched Fizgig advanced toward Dryker, but his gaze was pulled to the view screen behind her.

At first he didn't realize what had drawn his attention. The massive factory was still there, and there was no visible movement from the enemy. So far as the Void Wraith knew, they were still safely hidden in the sun's corona, undetectable to all normal scans.

Then he realized what he'd noticed, almost subconsciously. "Juliard, set condition one. Battle Stations."

Dryker and Fizgig both whirled to face him. The Tigris raised their weapons, though fortunately they didn't fire.

"What the hell are you doing, Nolan?" Dryker demanded.

Nolan had never seen him look so angry.

"Look at the factory, sir," Nolan demanded, gesturing at the screen. "There were seven ships docked when we arrived. Now there are only six."

Chapter 47- Stealth Ship

"You heard Commander Nolan," Dryker bellowed at Juliard.
"Set condition one. Deploy turrets, and warm up the gauss
cannon."

"Captain," Fizgig said, a clear note of warning in her
tone. "If you arm this vessel, I will be forced to react with
extreme violence. Do not force my hand, not when you've worked
so hard to convince me of this threat."

"You don't understand," Nolan said, taking a step closer to
the Tigris commander. He stared defiantly up at her. "Those
vessels can cloak. They disappear entirely from both visual
detection, and scanners."

"He's right," Dryker broke in. He gave a heavy sigh.
"Listen, Fizgig...you've got us dead to rights. But if we don't
prepare for battle right now neither of us will be alive in ten
minutes. The Void Wraith use particle weapons. They're powerful,
nearly undetectable, and are almost certainly on their way now."

Fizgig's face tightened, and she watched Dryker
impassively. When she spoke, it was to the huge male. "Khar,
escort the captain to our vessel. If he resists, kill him.
Commander, what is your name?"

Nolan realized she meant him. "Nolan."

"Commander Nolan you will order your vessel to stand down, right now. If you do not I will be forced to order my troops to--" Fizgig trailed off, and her eyes widened.

Nolan spun around to see what she'd been distracted by. She was staring at the view screen, and it wasn't hard to figure out why. An enormous vessel was shimmering into existence, the same vessel that he'd seen departing Mar Kona. Its blue metallic surface glittered in the sun's brilliance as it swooped closer.

Then the twin wings began to glow with their own energy. A ball of crackling blue energy coalesced in the space where the two wings almost met, and it grew larger over the next few seconds. The Void Wraith vessel fired. Nolan winced, expecting the shot to hit the *Johnston*. Instead, it slammed into the Tigris vessel anchoring the *Johnston* into place. The CIC lurched wildly, and Nolan was knocked off his feet.

Chaos erupted as people staggered to their feet. Tigris aimed their weapons at humans, and humans drew their sidearms to defend themselves. Nolan ducked behind a console, and found himself standing next to Lena. She wore an agonized expression, as if not sure what side to join.

"Enough," Fizgig roared, so loudly that it hurt Nolan's ears. Everyone froze as her gaze swept the room.

The Void Wraith grew larger on the view screen, then the
Johnston shook from an impact similar to when the Tigris had
boarded.

"Sir," Juliard called, looking up from her station. "The
Void Wraith vessel has grappled us. It looks like we're about to
be boarded. Again."

"Mighty Fizgig," one of the cats called. "We must return to
the *Claw of Tigrana*."

"That may not be possible," Fizgig said, spearing that
soldier with her gaze. She turned to the large male. "Khar,
gather the warriors outside this doorway and await my orders."
Then she turned back to Dryker. "Why are these Void Wraith
boarding you when they could just as easily have blasted us to
atoms?"

"The data cube," Lena answered. Her tail drooped when
Fizgig focused on her, but Lena continued to speak. "We have a
VI from the first Primo empire. It contains all sorts of data
about the Void Wraith, and about the war that wiped out the
Primo."

"That still doesn't make sense," Nolan found himself
saying. "If they're concerned about the data, why not blast us
out of space? That deals with any potential leak."

"I think they want the cubes," Lena explained. "Every world

they've hit has had Primo ruins. I'm betting they're searching for these VIs. I don't know what they use them for, but for some reason the cubes are important."

"Assuming they're coming for the cube, they'll likely make their way here," Dryker said. He took two steps closer to Fizgig, staring up at her. "Are you willing to cede operational authority? I've dealt with these things, and we're going to be tripping over each other if we don't establish a chain of command."

"Done," Fizgig said, nodding. She raised her wrist and spoke into her comm. "Izzy, what's your situation?"

"We're guarding the human soldiers," a young female voice answered.

"Arm them, Izzy. Prepare for battle. We will be fighting alongside the humans," Fizgig explained, then turned to the captain. "Perhaps it would be wise to inform your crew of the situation?"

"Of course," Dryker said, running back to his chair. He glanced at Juliard. "Get me ship-wide. Now."

"Done, sir," Juliard said, a moment later.

"Men and women of the *Johnston*," Dryker began, "we're about to be boarded by the Void Wraith. The Tigris have agreed to fight alongside us, and you will treat them as allies for the

duration. Arm yourselves, and make best speed to the bridge.
We'll be setting up a final defense here."

"Aren't you worried that you might alert these Void Wraith
to your plans?" Fizgig asked. "They may have already begun
boarding."

"Quite the opposite. I'm counting on them fighting their
way here, especially if they believe we have the cube," Dryker
said, giving a sharp grin.

Chapter 48- Strange Bedfellows

"Izzy, right?" Hannan asked, nodding to the cat that seemed to be in charge.

"Yes," the cat said, her tail standing at attention behind her. She looked terrified.

"We're going to need to make a push for the bridge," Hannan said, slamming home the clip in her assault rifle. "We have four squads, each designed to operate independently. Because the corridors are narrow, it makes sense to split up. I'm thinking we divide your people into four groups, and send mixed units along different routes. Our people can show you the way to the bridge."

"All right," Izzy said, blinking. She turned back to the other cats, most of whom had entered the shuttle bay. They prowled around, each showing signs of stress. "You heard mighty Fizgig. We work with the humans against this common threat. Ragash, Tigren, and Vivica, you will each join one of the human squads. I will join Hannan's. Follow the humans' orders, and make your way to the bridge. For the Leonis!"

"For the Leonis!" echoed back a chorus of cats. They began filtering into the room, and the cats Izzy had named started pairing up with human squads.

"You sure about this, Hannan?" another sergeant called. She was the next most senior squad leader. "Might be better if we stick together and send the cats their own way."

"Mixed groups gives us the best shot of survival," Hannan countered. She stuffed four more clips into the pockets on her armor. "It may confuse the Void Wraith, and even if it doesn't the Tigris are going to need our help to get to the bridge."

"You've fought these Void Wraith before?" Izzy asked. She seemed calmer, but Hannan had a hard time taking her seriously. Her white fur and round face made her look like a teenager--if a cat could be a teenager, anyway.

"Yes," Hannan said. She climbed onto the supply crate again, hoping it was the last time. She needed to get her Marines up to speed. "Everyone listen up. You're going to be engaging Void Wraith shock troops--Command says they're called Judicators. They can cloak, but if you're careful you can still see them moving. They leave a motion blur. Head shots are best, as these things can keep fighting after losing a limb. And if you disable one, get around a corner or behind cover, because they detonate when they die."

"Oh, lovely," Becca called, rolling her eyes. "This just gets better and better. First we have to babysit cats, and now we fight exploding robots? I'm not getting paid enough for this shit."

"You're not getting paid at all if you're dead," Hannan shot back. She let her eyes roam the whole room. "This is it, people--the day we prove we're stronger than these bastards. Stick together, and watch each other's backs. Every person, and every Tigris, is needed. Put aside your bullshit. Let's move."

She hopped down from the crate and moved toward the door from the shuttle bay to the corridor. Mills and Edwards fell into step behind her, while Izzy walked right alongside.

"That was an impressive speech," Izzy whispered. "Your people respect you. Let us hope they will do as you ask, and work with my people."

"How about yours?" Hannan asked. "Are they willing to work with humans?"

"They'll do what they have to," Izzy said. They reached the hatch leading from the shuttle bay, and she paused to peer around the corner, then gestured at Hannan to proceed.

Hannan leapt into the corridor, scanning carefully for movement. There was was none, so she started advancing up the corridor, down B1. It wasn't the fastest way to the bridge, but she'd left those routes open for the less experienced squads. She was taking the long way.

Chapter 49- Machine Shop

Hannan waited patiently as Mills advanced ahead of her up the B1 corridor. Their path would bring them near the gauss cannon, but that was part of her plan. If she were the enemy commander, that would be one of her primary targets. She and her troops were heading for CIC, but there was no reason not to swing by and pop a few of these Void Wraith if they happened to be messing with the *Johnston*'s main gun.

"You sure about trusting the cats, sir?" Edwards asked. His voice was probably meant to be a whisper, but like the man himself it was larger than intended. He scrubbed at his beard, eyeing Izzy.

Izzy's ears twitched, but she didn't react. She was still crouched behind cover, just a few meters behind Mills.

"Get your head in the game, Marine," Hannan snapped. "We're in combat. We don't have time for bullshit questions."

Edwards nodded. He raised the barrel of his TM-601 and began advancing up the corridor. Hannan followed in the rear, darting frequent glances behind her. It was nerve-wracking, because they didn't know the enemy. Who knew what tactics the Void Wraith would use, or even what armament they'd brought?

There was no guarantee that the plasma weapons her crew had seen on Mar Kona were the full extent of what the Void Wraith could bring to bear.

"Contact," Mills yelled. Hanna's gaze snapped up to the sniper, who was at a T intersection ahead. That intersection led into the barrel of the gauss rifle, which they'd need to cross to get to C1, and then up to the CIC.

Bursts of blue energy shot into view, vaporizing sections of the bulkhead. Mills fell back in a full sprint, then dove into the hatch that led to the machine shop. That left Edwards and Izzy on point.

"Edwards, get ready to lay down suppressive fire," Hannan yelled. She dropped into a crouch, pressing her body against the right wall. There was no cover as such, so the best she could do was present a smaller profile.

"Should we fall back to a more secure location?" Izzy called over her shoulder. She'd raised the barrel of her bulky Tigris rifle. The bayonet at the end had begun to hum. "There's no cover here."

"They don't have cover either," Hannan yelled back. "Just gun down anything that comes around the--"

Something shimmered in the air near the corner, sort of a heat mirage. The same heat mirage she'd seen back in the jungle on Mar Kona.

"Light it up," Hannan bellowed. She depressed the trigger on her assault rifle, and sent a three-round burst at the section where she guessed the chest was. The cloaking field wavered where the rounds hit, temporarily exposing smooth blue armor.

Then Edwards's rifle drowned out all sound as he unloaded a stream of high velocity slugs. They caught the Judicator in the right knee, severing it in a spray of circuitry and bright orange fluid. Izzy completed the destruction, calmly sighting down her barrel and unleashing a single shot. Hannan wasn't sure what caliber the bullet was, but the Judicator's head exploded, spraying the wall with more orange fluid.

"Take cover," Hannan yelled, diving into the machine shop after Mills. Izzy came through a moment later.

Edwards had almost reached them when a sudden *whump* tore at Hannan's already damaged eardrums. A wash of flame and debris launched Edwards through the hatch, and he slammed into the wall with a sickening crunch.

Hannan rushed to his side, barking out orders as she inspected his body. "Mills, kill anything that approaches that doorway. Izzy, move a couple of those tables so we can use them as cover."

She didn't pause to see if they were listening, instead pressing two fingers against Edwards's neck. His eyes were closed, but his pulse was strong. There were no obvious broken bones, and no real damage to the armor.

"Come on, Edwards," she muttered, slapping him hard in the face. "Wake up, Marine. We need you."

"Sarge?" Edwards slurred, sitting up. His gaze was unfocused. "Why did you hit me?"

A rifle coughed behind her, and Hannan spun to assess the situation. Mills had fired, but there was no sign of whatever he'd been aiming at. The doorway was clear, though Mills had the stock of his rifle set against his shoulder and was clearly scanning for targets.

Something glided through the door, another of the near-invisible figures. It shimmered into view and extended a trio of crackling energy blades from its wrist, ramming them into the wall where Mills's face had been a split second before. Mills fell onto his back, attempting to raise his rifle in time to get a shot off.

Hannan knew he'd never make it, and she was too far away to stop the Judicator from ending her friend's life.

Then Izzy was there. The cat leapt into the air, her tail brushing the ceiling as she came down on the Judicator like a

whirlwind. She raked the claws of her right hand into the
Judicator's back, sending up a shower of sparks. Then she rammed
her rifle forward, burying the humming bayonet into the
Judicator's back.

The Judicator's cloaking field faded entirely, finally
revealing its appearance long enough for Hannan to get a good
look. The limbs were too thin to be human, and were obviously
made from some sort of composite alloy; it looked to be the same
alloy used on their ships. The thing had no mouth, just a pair
of glowing blue eyes. It looked robotic, though the orange fluid
leaking from its chest suggested it was organic.

It raised its rifle, aiming for Izzy. Before it could fire
Mills's rifle coughed, and the Judicator's chest caved in. It
stumbled backwards, and Izzy used the momentum. She swung her
rifle like a club, flinging the Judicator back into the hallway,
and dove to the right of the doorway just in time. Another wave
of flame and concussive force shot through the doorway as the
Judicator exploded.

"These things are a real pain in the ass," Edwards called,
pulling himself to his feet. He looked dazed, but otherwise
unharmed.

"Let's get moving, folks. We need to reach the CIC as
quickly as possible," Hannan ordered.

Chapter 50- Hold

Nolan had never seen Dryker's ready room so crowded.

Officers from both factions lined either side of the metal

table, and the chairs had been stacked in a corner to take up

less room. The table's surface displayed a map of the ship, with

red dots everywhere they'd had a report of a Void Wraith

encounter.

"They're definitely making a push for the bridge," Dryker

said, wiping sweat from his forehead. "We have teams on both B

and C decks that are making their way here, but I don't know if

they'll be here in time to push them back."

"The Void Wraith could have been here by now if they'd

wished," Fizgig observed, blinking down at the map. "I believe

they are being thorough, systematically wiping out all

resistance on their way here."

"She's right," Nolan agreed, tapping three different

locations on the map. "We've had fire teams go down here, here,

and here. They're clearing a path to us, and they're wiping out

everything they can between them and us. If they keep going at

that rate, they're going to hit us in the next few minutes. All

our Marines were in the shuttle bay, so we'll be virtually

undefended."

"Not undefended," the big male Tigris growled. "There are six Tigris here. We will hold this doorway until we receive reinforcements."

"Captain?" Nolan asked.

"Go with him, and take all able-bodied bridge crew with you," Dryker commanded. He gave Nolan a sober look. "Nothing gets through that door. Nothing."

"What about the cube?" Lena asked.

"That stays here with us," Dryker said. "And so do you."

"Acknowledged," Nolan said. "Juliard, Ezana, you're with me." He pushed past the Tigris until he reached the hatch leading back into the CIC.

"We're with you too, human," the male said. "I am called Khar. Remember my name. It will be the name that saves you."

Nolan ignored the cat, hurrying into CIC and giving the place a quick survey. The room wasn't designed as a fall back position. They could use monitors and computers as cover, but that seemed like a bad idea. If the computers were shot up, controlling the ship might not be possible. Of course if the crew were shot up, then there would be no one left to fly the ship anyway.

"Fan out," Nolan said. "Get whatever cover you can, and

make sure you've got overlapping fields of fire. We need to gun down anything that comes through that door." He moved for the Captain's chair, turning it around so the back faced the hatch leading into the corridor. It wasn't amazing cover, but he hoped the thick steel backing would ward off at least a shot or two.

"Commander," Juliard yelled, her voice tinged with panic. "The B deck hatch just opened. We don't have any fire teams in that area."

"Get ready for contact, people," Nolan bellowed. He gripped his pistol in both hands, ready to take a shot at whatever came through that doorway. "Khar, we've got nothing but small arms. You and your people are going to have to do the heavy lifting."

"Fear not, human." Khar gave a fanged grin. "My people will protect you."

Something shimmered in the doorway. Before anyone could react two bursts of blue energy shot into the room. The first took a cat in the face, and the Tigris dropped limply to the ground. She didn't rise. The second shot caught the monitor Juliard was hiding behind, sending up a shower of sparks and momentarily dimming the lights.

"Fire," Nolan roared, squeezing the trigger as fast as he could. The pistol bucked, sending a slug toward where he hoped the Judicator's head was. Its shimmering field dropped for a moment, exposing the emotionless metal face. Then other weapons fired--pistols from the humans, and the larger slug-throwing rifles the Tigris favored.

The Judicator staggered backwards, pushed through the doorway by the combined fury of both races. It staggered to the ground, crashing and not rising.

"Take cover," Nolan yelled. He ducked behind the captain's chair. A moment later a wash of heat and flame passed overhead. A mewling scream came from the near the doorway. Nolan glanced up. One of the cats hadn't gotten into cover in time.

Two more shimmering figures reached the doorway and began firing. Another cat went down, then another. Only Khar and two of his soldiers remained, all three behind cover. The Judicators were playing it smart, eliminating the largest threats first.

Nolan sighted down his barrel, then squeezed off two shots. He tagged one of the Judicators in the neck, sending up a spray of sparks. It ducked back into cover, leaving its companion alone in the doorway.

"For the Leonis!" Khar bellowed. He rose from cover, sprinting at the doorway. The Judicator fired, but the big golden cat was ready. He vaulted over the shot, twisting in the air, and came down with his bayonet extended. It sank into the Judicator's head, all the way to the hilt.

Khar pressed a button on his rifle, and the bayonet detached. Then he planted a foot against the Judicator's chest and kicked with all his might. The Judicator was flung back into the hallway, past its companion. Khar ducked back into CIC, taking shelter next to the doorway. A moment later another wall of flame shot through the doorway, this time not harming anyone.

"I told you, human," Khar said, laughing manically. "We will protect you."

"Movement," Juliard yelled. "I see at least four of them incoming."

"Damn it," Nolan muttered. This couldn't be their main force, but that might not matter. Most of the Judicators were still spread on the lower decks wiping out the crew, but even the handful they were facing seemed likely to overwhelm the bridge if they didn't get some help.

Chapter 51- CIC

"Let's move, people," Hannan said, grabbing Edwards by the forearm and hauling him to his feet. Izzy darted to the doorway, peering cautiously through the smoke. Her nose twitched, then her ears. Finally she turned back to Hannan, and gave her a nod.

Mills finished refilling his clip, slammed it into place, then joined them. He paused next to Izzy, meeting the cat's gaze. "You saved my ass back there. I won't forget it."

Hannan could only blink. Mills rarely strung that many words together, and she'd never heard him express gratitude before. And to a Tigris?

"We have a saying," Izzy said, clapping him on the shoulder. "The count is not done until the battle is done. You may return the favor, and if you do there is nothing to be thanked for. If not, thank me then."

Mills nodded, and Izzy leapt into the hallway. Hannan let Edwards and Mills follow, before finally bringing up the rear. Back when she'd been a private she'd loved taking point, but one of the first lessons her sergeant had drilled into her was the need for command to be in a position to assess. Those who led from the front usually died at the front, and when they went down their troops were either routed or wiped out. Smart

commanders knew that.

They moved up the corridor, turning down the T intersection

and finally entering the barrel of the gauss rifle--a smooth-

walled tube, twenty feet in diameter, that extended the length

of the ship. A quick glance in either direction showed no signs

of movement. Hannan had been worried that this might be a

potential target. The pair of massive magnetic generators at the

aft of the ship propelled a hunk of dense metal up the barrel.

If that happened with the barrel closed, the resulting kinetic

force would be transferred into the ship. It was as close to a

self-destruct as the *Johnston* had, and something she didn't want

to see exploited.

The doorway they'd entered from was set into a recessed

alcove, and there was a matching one on the other side of the

barrel. Since the place was empty, Hannan waved Izzy forward,

and the Tigris darted across the barrel to the other door.

Edwards moved next, then Mills, and finally Hannan. It all felt

a little easy, but she wasn't about to question her good

fortune.

As soon as Izzy opened the hatch, they heard the sounds of

gunfire. Bullets ricocheted off walls, and occasionally they

heard the telltale explosion of a Judicator detonating. The

screams became less and less frequent as they advanced up the C deck corridor. It was sobering, and they all knew what it meant. The Judicators were winning, and if something didn't change it would only be a matter of time before they took the ship.

"How much longer to your bridge?" Izzy asked. She'd paused next to an open hatchway that led to the aft causeway.

"Another hundred yards," Hannan called back. She paused next to Izzy, peering through the hatch and up the causeway. "Might take us four or five minutes."

"I don't hear any gunfire here," Mills said.

"Sounds like combat is mostly confined to A and B decks," Edwards replied. He leaned his M-601 against his knee, planting his butt against the wall. His chest was heaving from exertion, and Hannan could tell from his breathing that he was running on fumes.

"Less talk, more walk," she barked, jerking her head to indicate that Izzy should move through the hatch.

Izzy did so, and the others followed. Hannan brought up the rear. While she was just as exhausted as the others, she was very careful not to show it. Morale was the second thing her first sergeant had taught her about. It didn't matter how much you hurt. You never showed weakness in front of your men.

They crossed the causeway, which had short stairwells set

every twenty feet. They advanced over the engines, then began looping back into the main body of the ship. Eventually they reached a hatch leading to A deck. The hatch was closed.

Izzy knelt next to it, then turned to face them. "I can't hear anything on the other side."

"Open it," Hannan ordered. Mills slung his rifle over his shoulder, then bent to the hatch. He spun the wheel, pulling the door towards them.

Izzy was through the tube in a flash of white, quickly followed by Edwards. Hannan dropped to one knee, scanning the corridor beyond with the barrel of her rifle. She could hear faint screams in the distance, broken by sporadic gunfire. It was weaker here than it had been on C deck.

Once Mills was through, Hannan shot to her feet and trotted after him. Her squad leapfrogged their way across the starboard side of A deck. They circled wide, hugging the outer hull of the ship until they no longer had a choice. Then they shifted inward, making for the CIC set into the heavily armored core of the ship.

The gunfire grew louder as they approached the CIC, and a massive explosion echoed down the corridor. The gunfire paused, then resumed a moment later. It was mostly small arms fire, which Hannan found alarming. Fighting these things with pistols was a quick way to get killed. She was thankful that at least a few of the shots were the deep booms she'd come to associate with Tigris rifles.

"Izzy," Hannan called, softly. The cat's ear twitched, and she shot an inquisitive look Hannan's way. Hannan glided forward until she'd gathered all four squad members and they were crouched a few feet from the corner of a T intersection. "This is it. As soon as we round this corner, we'll have a view of the hatch leading to CIC."

"How do you want to do this?" Edwards asked.

"We wait until we hear another push. The Judicators engage the bridge crew," Hannan said. "Once they're engaged, we throw everything we have at them from behind. Down every target you can. If they pursue us, fall back around this corner."

"Simple, but effective. I like it," Izzy said, nodding. Her tail swished endlessly against the floor, which Hannan assumed was an indicator of stress. If so, Izzy hid it well.

"Get into position," Hannan ordered.

Chapter 52- Last Stand

Nolan glanced around at the remaining bridge crew. Emo,
Ezana, and Juliard had taken cover. A few techs were still up.
That was it. Khar was their last Tigris. They'd fought off three
assaults, but Nolan knew a fourth would be the last. There was
no way they could endure another assault.

"Prepare yourself human; they come again," Khar roared from
his place next to the hatch.

Nolan darted forward and scooped up one of the Tigris
rifles. It was heavier than he'd expected, and he struggled to
get the barrel aligned with the doorway. The foot-and-a-half
blade at the end threw off the balance, but fortunately it would
be hard to miss at this range.

A Judicator entered the doorway, its shimmering form
bending the light around it. Nolan squeezed the trigger, and the
rifle bucked. The stock slammed back into his shoulder, and he
grunted in pain. That was going to leave a bruise for days.

The Judicator staggered backwards, the shot temporarily
disrupting its cloaking field. It took a step back towards the
room, but Khar stepped into the hatch and ended the Judicator
with a head shot. Nolan clutched the rifle to his chest, and

dove behind a console. Heat washed over the top as yet another explosion detonated in the hall.

How much more punishment could that corridor take?

"Two more," Khar roared, though Nolan could barely hear him over the ringing in his ears.

He struggled to his knees, raising a hand to touch his right ear. A thin stream of something sticky flowed down his neck. He touched it with two fingers, then held them up before his eyes. Red. Blood. Nolan knew he wasn't thinking clearly, but everything felt so far away.

"Commander, we need you," Khar roared.

Nolan blinked, then shook his head. That caused massive pain, but the pain brought him back around. Another assault was beginning.

Two Judicators advanced on the doorway. The first was caught by small arms fire from the remaining bridge crew, each shot causing it to pause mid-step. The collective assault dropped the cloaking field, but the Judicator seemed otherwise unharmed. It raised its plasma rifle and fired off three quick shots. Two screams came from behind Nolan, but he didn't have time to see who'd gone down.

He raised the Tigris rifle, aligning the crosshairs with the now-visible Judicator's face. The rifle kicked again and he felt more than heard the shot. The butt drove into his shoulder a second time, renewing the pain there. But the shot was accurate. It took the Judicator in the face, and it crashed to the ground. Unfortunately, it crashed to the ground inside the CIC.

"Take cover," Nolan roared. He dropped back into a crouch, and covered his head with both arms.

Ezana leapt over Nolan, using his own body to covering the Judicator's. Nolan started to rise, desperately wanting to tell Ezana to get out of the way, but it was too late.

A wave of fire and shrapnel blossomed. Ezana's body muted the force of the explosion, but even with his body shielding the blast, shrapnel destroyed a number of key systems--including the view screen.

The stench of smoke, ozone, and gunpowder filled the area around Nolan, and he found himself coughing furiously. He tried to get to his feet, but it just wasn't going to be possible. He couldn't hear. Could barely see.

He'd landed on the floor next to the terminal he'd used for cover, and that terminal now had a gaping hole in the middle where one of the Judicator's limbs had punched through it. The hole showed four more Judicators advancing up the hall, their shimmering forms unmistakable amidst the smoke.

Then the first one slumped to the ground, becoming visible as it toppled. Its head had simply ceased to exist. The second and third Judicators pivoted to face the way they'd come, but it didn't save them. The first had both knees severed as the unmistakable roar of an M-601 pounded on Nolan's remaining eardrum. The third Judicator was launched backwards from multiple attacks. The fourth managed to get off several shots at its attackers, but the answering volley cut it down.

The resulting explosions, as all four Judicators went up at virtually in the same instant, shook the entire ship. When the shaking stopped Nolan, was unable to rise. Unable to think.

So he passed out.

Chapter 53- Desperate Plan

"Your plan is terrible," Fizgig said, looking down at the map Dryker had drawn. Dryker grimaced, but didn't respond--not immediately, anyway.

Finally, he sighed. "Do you have a better plan?" he asked. The sounds of gunfire were ever-present, even though they'd closed the hatch to the ready room.

"No," Fizgig said, sighing. "Which of us do you wish to have stay behind?"

"I'll do it," Dryker said, glancing at Lena as she entered the ready room from the opposite hatch. "She has to get to the Void Wraith vessel. Make sure that she does."

"Captain?" Lena asked, closing the hatch behind her.

"How many are there?" Dryker asked, withdrawing his sidearm and testing the action.

"Six," Lena said. "Each has a ninety-minute supply of oxygen."

"Perfect," Dryker said, starting for the hatch that led back into the CIC. It was hot to the touch. Not a good sign.

"Where are you going?" Fizgig asked, her tail thrashing in obvious annoyance.

"Back to CIC. They're losing out there; if they go down, the plan is for naught. We need to get the situation there under control, and get some armed personnel ready to escort Lena," Dryker explained. He spun the wheel on the hatch, pushing the door open a few inches.

The smoke was thick in the CIC, and the moans of the dying layered with the crackling of electrical fires. A quick glance around the room told the awful truth. There was no way the *Johnston* could fly. The nerve center that controlled her vital functions had been destroyed. That couldn't be helped. What *could* was the desperate plan he'd concocted. To pull that off, he was going to need something resembling a cohesive fighting force.

Dryker moved into the CIC, running in a low crouch until he found someone moving. He knelt next to a prone form. It was Nolan. "Commander, can you hear me?"

"Ow," Nolan said, his eyes fluttering open. They widened in alarm. "You have to get back into the ready room sir. We're about to lose the CIC."

"No, you're not," came a loud voice from the doorway.

Dryker looked up to see several figures striding through the doorway. Hannan was in the lead, flanked by Edwards and a white-furred Tigris. Mills crept in after them, then attempted

to close the hatch. It was so badly bent in its frame that the
best he could do was close it about sixty percent of the way.

"Hannan, sit rep," Dryker said. He seized Nolan's arm, and
hauled him to his feet. Dryker didn't know the extent of the
commander's injuries, but if the man could walk, Dryker needed
him on his feet.

"CIC is secure for now, sir," Hannan said, glancing back
through the hatch into the corridor. It was littered with bits
of metal and circuitry, and the walls were caked with soot from
repeated detonations. "I think we've stopped them for the time
being, but there are still teams all over the ship. They'll be
on us again in a few minutes."

"Everyone able to stand, get into the ready room, now,"
Dryker ordered.

He tried to help Nolan in that direction, but Nolan
shrugged off his hand. He picked up a Tigris rifle, then moved
to a male Tigris--Khar, Dryker remembered--who lay crumpled at
the base of a console. Nolan looked up at Hannan. "Get me a
medical kit, sergeant."

Hannan nodded wordlessly, pulling the red and white box
from the wall. She tossed it to Nolan, who caught it by the
handle. That was a good sign. Dryker had been worried that the
commander was too injured to keep fighting, which would have

made the next part of the plan tricky.

Nolan withdrew a syringe from the med pack, and slammed it into the cat's thigh. The Tigris yowled, his eyes shooting open. Nolan withdrew the syringe, and helped the cat to its feet. "Come on, Khar. You're not done protecting humans."

"The count is not done, Commander," Khar said, nodding respectfully to Nolan. He picked up his rifle, and limped after Nolan into the ready room.

Dryker made sure everyone else had cleared the bridge, then stepped into the ready room himself. He spun the wheel, and set the lock. The hatch wouldn't slow down the Judicators for long, but it would be long enough if his plan held.

"Eyes on me," Dryker yelled. A room full of exhausted Tigris and humans stared at him. Most sat, and those who didn't leaned against the wall. It was a pitiful crew, but it would have to do. "We're about to attempt something Fizgig considers suicidal."

"And foolish," Fizgig said, her tail swishing behind her.

"What do you have in mind, captain?" Nolan asked. He leaned against the wall, using the Tigris rifle like a cane to keep himself upright.

"The *Johnston* is lost," the captain began. "We can't fight off the Void Wraith. So we're going to take the fight to their ship."

"Come again?" Hannan said, looking up from the weapon she was servicing.

"How will we even reach their ship?" Nolan asked. "The Judicators aren't likely to let us by."

"You're taking a space walk. We have six EVA suits," Dryker replied. "Nolan, you'll lead a strike team over to the Void Wraith vessel. While you were fighting, Lena identified what appears to be a docking port near the rear of the ship. Since we're putting up heavy resistance, it's a safe bet that most of the fighting forces have left their vessel to subdue ours."

"Now I see why Fizgig thinks this plan is suicidal," Nolan said. He wiped soot from his cheek, but only succeeded in creating a larger smudge. "When do we leave?"

"Now," Dryker said.

"Wait a second," Mills said. The sniper pushed his bangs out of his face, meeting Dryker's gaze. "There are only six suits. What are the rest of us supposed to do?"

"Fight," Hannan said, glaring at Mills. "It doesn't matter if that means staying here or taking a space walk. We fight, regardless of where the captain assigns us."

"The following people will suit up," the captain said. "Lena, Nolan, Fizgig, Hannan, Edwards. Fizgig, we'll also send a second Tigris. You'll have to pick which one goes."

Fizgig looked at the two remaining Tigris. The first was the big, golden-furred brute Nolan had helped to his feet. The second was a lean, white-furred female who was sticking close to Hannan.

"Izzy, you will accompany us," Fizgig finally said. She turned to the large yellow. "Khar, your strength is needed here. You must stall the Void Wraith as long as possible. The longer they are here fighting, the more time we have to reach the bridge of the Void Wraith vessel.

"Captain, I can't believe you're doing this," Juliard said. She was cradling a broken arm, and her eyes were alight with fury. "How could you give two of those suits to the cats? We wouldn't be here if not for them. Those should go to loyal crew."

"None of us would be here without the Tigris," Nolan shot back, glaring at Juliard. "They saved our asses repeatedly on that bridge. You'd be dead right now if they hadn't helped us. Besides, this isn't a lottery for escape pods. The people putting on those suits need to invade the enemy vessel, fight their way to the bridge, and try to seize control of it. Most likely, we'll all die in the attempt. You're wounded. Could you even make the EVA?"

Juliard looked away from Nolan, slipping into sullen silence. A few of the other bridge crew looked just as angry, but none spoke.

"I know this is a tough pill to swallow." Dryker said. "No one wants to remain behind." He squared his shoulders. "But we're Fleet. We have a job to do. If that means we all die doing it, then so be it."

Chapter 54- EVA

"Listen up, people," Nolan said. Everyone swiveled to face him, including their new Tigris allies. They were in various stages of dress, each pulling on a suit of the bulky EVA armor from the *Johnston*'s armory. "Next to your suit, you will find a small grey pod, like the one Hannan has on her right wrist."

Hannan held up the pod, making sure they all saw it.

"Fix the handle to your suit's right glove before putting on your left," Nolan explained, attaching the pod to his own suit. "You'll notice two buttons, a red and a blue. The red button causes the pod to fire a thrust from the bottom, so make sure its angled away from you. The blue button will cause a smaller burst from the top, which will help slow your momentum if you are coming in too hot. We'll be using these to make the EVA."

The Marines all nodded, but the Tigris were a different matter. Lena, Fizgig, and Izzy all looked ready to throw up. Nolan couldn't blame them. The suits were human sized, and Tigris generally loathed tight, confined spaces.

"Here, let me," Hannan offered, stepping over to help Izzy fasten the pod to her suit.

Fizgig watched, then did the same to her own suit. Lena turned to Nolan with a helpless look. He gave her a smile, and helped fasten the pod to her suit. She smiled, fangs flashing, then held up a small black satchel. He showed her how to attach it to a pair of small rings low on the front of the suit, where it wouldn't get in her way. She nodded gratefully, then turned away to deal with her helmet and her other glove.

"Once you finish fastening your suit, a green light will come on in the base of the face plate. If this light turns red, it means the suit has been breached, and that you are losing oxygen," Nolan continued. He pulled on his own helmet, but kept the face plate open. "Each suit has a comm link, which you can access in the left glove with your pinky."

Then he closed the helmet and walked into the airlock. It was going to be crowded with six people, but they'd make it work. He stood by the control panel, waiting as each of the others finished donning their suits. About two minutes later, Fizgig stepped into the airlock. She was the last.

Nolan turned back to the panel, and keyed the lock button. The door leading into the *Johnston* sealed, and the scrubbers began sucking the air from the room. All six faces peered nervously at each other, though Nolan was careful to keep his neutral. What they were about to attempt was suicidal. It made

sense only because no better option existed. As his father would
have said, they were throwing the Hail Mary.

The light on the airlock panel shifted from red to yellow,
indicating that the atmosphere had been completely drained.
Nolan stabbed the *Open* button, and the outer doors rolled back.
They were looking at empty space, and it was terrifying. Not
because Nolan feared space; he'd done dozens of EVAs. No, it was
terrifying because below them lay the crackling inferno of a
star. He could *feel* it tugging at him, and knew that if he lost
his pod he'd be pulled relentlessly closer until he left the
Johnston's inductive field.

Nolan focused on his destination, the Void Wraith vessel.
It was perched over the *Johnston* like a preying mantis, its long
wings buried in the destroyer's hull. That meant that they only
needed to cross about a hundred and fifty feet of open space
before they'd reach the rear portion of the Void Wraith ship.
Once there, they could walk around to the airlock and force
their way in.

He turned back to the others and gave them a thumbs-up,
then kicked off the deck and into space. The star's gravity
immediately began to tug him, so he angled his pod and fired it
at full thrust. It righted his course, carrying him closer and
closer to the giant blue ship. Just before he reached it, Nolan

pressed the blue button three times, each two seconds apart. His velocity slowed, and he bent his knees. A small shock went through his legs as he hit the hull, then the magnetic clamps sealed and he was anchored.

Nolan turned back to the others and gave another thumbs-up. Edwards was the next into the gap, shooting towards him with unerring precision. Fizgig went next, then Lena. By that time, Edwards was landing.

"Edwards, you're coming in too hot," Nolan said over the comm. Edwards fired his pod, but it was too late.

He slammed into the hull, and began to bounce away. Nolan released his magnetic clamp and kicked off the deck. He grabbed Edwards's outstretched hand, which caused them both to spin. Nolan waited until the spin had carried him to the right angle, then fired his pod. The thrust pulled them back to the hull, and he whipped his feet down in time to lock against the hull. This time Edwards fared better, snapping onto the deck next to him.

"Thanks, Commander," Edwards said, his voice wavering. Nolan gave him a thumbs-up.

Fizgig landed gracefully a few feet away, the expression on her face full of pity when she looked at Edwards. She reached up as Lena approached, pulling the scientist down onto the deck next to her. Nolan was genuinely impressed, and gave her a respectful nod. After a moment she returned it.

Nolan looked back at the *Johnston*. Izzy was coming over next, with Hannan not far behind her. Izzy's thrusts were wild, and her quick shallow breaths grew more ragged over the comm.

"Relax, Izzy," Hannan's voice crackled over the comm. "I've got you."

Hannan glided up to Izzy, seizing the back of her suit. She fired her pod in short, controlled bursts, and the pair drifted to the deck not far from the rest of the team. Izzy's eyes were wild, but she seemed to be keeping it together.

"Let's move," Nolan said. He began slow, magnetic steps toward the airlock. Release, step, lock. Release, step, lock. It took long minutes to get to the airlock, and he tried not to focus on the *Johnston* during that time. The crew he'd just gotten to know was likely being slaughtered right now, and there wasn't a damned thing he could do about it.

Chapter 55- Gauss

Captain Dryker picked up the TM-601 and checked the action.
Edwards's weapon was scratched and dinged, the black paint
chipped in many locations. The internals, though, were extremely
well cared for. The weapon reminded Dryker of his time in the
infantry, a lifetime ago.

"How many rounds do you have left, Mills?" Dryker asked.

"Sixteen," Mills replied in that flat, emotionless voice.
Dryker had never been sure what to make of the dour sniper, but
at least he was calm. The others needed to see that right now.

"Khar, what about you?" Dryker asked.

"Eleven. After that I can use the bayonet," the burly
Tigris rumbled. He looked tired, and his fur was matted with
blood, but he was still on his feet.

"Juliard, you're left handed," Dryker pointed out, walking
over to his comm tech. Her left arm was in a sling, and she
clutched a pistol in her right. "Holster that thing. You're more
likely to shoot one of us than any of them."

"How am I supposed to defend myself?" Juliard asked. Her
eyes flashed a challenge, carrying the weight of anger and fear
she'd accumulated since they'd first encountered the Void

Wraith.

"You trust the Marines around you," Dryker countered, staring her down. Juliard broke eye contact. "I need you to do what you do best. Focus, lieutenant. Use your tablet. You're going to find us the safest route to the magnetic housing in the gauss cannon."

"Sir?" she asked, furrowing her brow. Then her eyes widened with understanding. "You're going to blow it up, aren't you?"

"That's right. For that to happen we need to move, and move quickly." Dryker didn't wait for the others to comment. He slung the TM-601's strap over his shoulder and moved to the hatch that led into the wreckage that used to be the CIC.

Dryker flipped the lock and spun the wheel, then kicked the hatch open. This was the critical moment. If the Void Wraith had already sent reinforcements they were done. He stepped boldly through the hatch, scanning the room with the barrel of his TM-601. Nothing visible moved. The place reeked of ozone, and streamers of smoke still rose from a few small electrical fires, making his eyes burn.

"Move, people," Dryker said, striding through the CIC. He stepped over Ezana's body without pausing, then moved into the corridor. Still no sign of resistance.

Dryker increased his pace, taking a right at the T

intersection. That took him towards the engines. It was out of the way, and he hoped that would mean fewer encounters with the enemy.

"Gunshots," Khar rumbled from behind him. "They're faint. Two decks down, maybe."

"Not good," Mills said, joining them. "More gunfire means more resistance. If it's fading, then so are we. They've moved into the cleanup portion of their attack. We need to keep moving."

"Take point, Corporal," Dryker ordered.

Mills trotted obediently ahead, and they moved down the corridor until they reached the first causeway. Mills paused at the door, holding up a clenched fist. A moment later he lowered it, and darted through the doorway. Dryker came next, with Khar and Juliard trailing after.

"Contact," Mills yelled from the far side of the causeway. He dropped to a knee, aiming his rifle at a target down the stairwell. The rifle kicked and a boom echoed through off the metal walls. Mills leapt to his feet, yelling even as he dove back onto the causeway. "Get down!"

A sharp explosion bloomed from the bottom of the stairwell. White and orange flame shot up the stairs, and the staircase distended as it heated. Dryker seized the railing with his free hand, and wrapped one leg around one of the metal bars anchoring it. Then the causeway snapped. The portion where Mills had landed dropped forty feet, and slammed into the floor.

Juliard wasn't able to anchor herself, and began sliding down the causeway. She picked up speed on the way down, struggling in vain to catch herself against the railing. Her training finally took over, and she extended both legs beneath her, knees bent. Juliard rolled with the landing, tumbling across the floor with a pained cry. She landed in a heap not far from where Mills had fallen. Juliard was still moving. Mills was not.

Dryker uncurled his leg, and used the railing to guide himself to the floor in a controlled fall. He landed easily, hefting his rifle as he stood back up. Khar landed next to him a moment later, still cradling his huge rifle.

"Where are we?" Khar asked, looking around him.

"Right where we need to be," Dryker replied, nodding towards the enormous magnetic generators a few dozen feet away. "That was a shortcut, though a costly one."

He moved to Mills, placing two fingers against the sniper's carotid artery. Nothing. The Marine stared sightlessly upward. Dryker sighed, then closed the Marine's eyes.

Chapter 56- Harvester

Nolan knelt next to the Void Wraith airlock, studying the
mechanism. It was unlike anything he'd encountered, just a
series of glowing crystals set into the metal. He thumbed his
comm, looking up at the others. "We might have to cut through,
unless anyone has an idea to get this thing open."

"I've got something we can try," Lena suggested. She
reached carefully down and opened the black satchel Nolan had
helped her affix to her suit, slowly withdrawing the data cube
they'd recovered from Purito. "The VI is similar to what we've
seen of Void Wraith tech. What if we wire it up to the lock?"

"If you think you can do that, give it a shot," Nolan said.
He stood back up, and took two magnetic steps away from the lock
to give Lena room. "Time is critical. I don't know how long
Captain Dryker can hold off the Void Wraith, and we need to get
inside and try to reach the bridge before their boarding parties
return."

Lena nodded, her golden fur floating around her in the suit
as she knelt next to the lock. She began attaching wires from
the cube to the door, her fingers moving more deftly than Nolan
would have expected given that she was wearing bulky EVA gloves.

Nolan glanced back at the *Johnston*, but there'd been no change. The destroyer was still grappled by the Void Wraith on one side, and the Tigris vessel on the other. The Tigris vessel had taken a lot of damage from the Void Wraith strafing attack, but still appeared functional. The *Johnston* was worse off, the cumulative damage from all the recent fighting painfully evident from this distance. Gaping holes dotted the hull, from the aft wing to the wreckage of the turrets on the starboard side. It was amazing she hadn't yet come apart.

"Fizgig, what are the odds that your crew would move over to the *Johnston* to help hold off the Void Wraith?" he asked, turning to face the grey-furred cat.

"They'd obey orders, but I'm not sure I should give them," Fizgig said over the comm. She blinked once, glancing at her ship, then back at Nolan. "If I broadcast a signal, it's possible the Void Wraith will pick it up. We shouldn't risk revealing our location."

"Point taken," Nolan said. He knew himself well enough to know that this was just his mind trying to find things he could control. He turned back to Lena. She'd wired up the cube, and was now feeding a wire into the comm unit mounted to the EVA's chest.

"I've got it," she called happily over the comm. "The VI is

linked to my suit via the comm panel, so we can issue orders.
I've told it to find a way to open the door."

A moment later, the crystals next to the door shifted from
red to white, and the door slid back into the hull. Inside was
an empty airlock, very similar to the one on any Fleet vessel.
Nolan jumped inside, the artificial gravity dropping him to the
deck as soon as he broke the plane to the airlock. He inspected
the inner airlock door; unfortunately, there was no window, and
thus no way to know what was on the other side.

"Everyone else inside. Edwards, you're last," Nolan ordered
over the comm.

One by one the rest of them dropped inside. Lena came
first, and she immediately started working on the inner door. It
took even less time, perhaps because she now knew how the VI
could interface with Void Wraith tech.

Edward dropped into the room, and a moment later the outer
door slid closed.

"It will begin pressurizing in a minute," Lena said. Sure
enough, they heard the telltale hiss of oxygen filling the room.

"That's interesting," Hannan said. "I wasn't sure these
things needed oxygen. The fact that they do is good. It's going
to be hard enough to fight our way to the bridge without wearing
these bulky suits."

"I can open the airlock door any time," Lena said, turning back to the group.

"Before you do, I have a question," Nolan said. He considered how best to ask it. "You said you've wired the VI to your comm system, right?"

"Yes, it's linked in. Any of us could talk to it, though right now it can't respond verbally," Lena explained. She cocked her head inside the EVA suit. "Why do you ask?"

"You said that the VI had a complete record of what it calls the final war," Nolan said. "That includes data about all the Void Wraith units they encountered, right?"

"It does," Lena said. She smiled. "I think I see where you're going with this."

"Excellent thinking, human," Fizgig said. Was she actually purring? "Lena, use this VI to share the tactical schematics over the comm. Commander, the visors inside the suits can be used independently, yes?"

"That's right," Nolan said, nodding. "If we keep the visors on after we remove the suits we'll be able to tell friend from foe, and our HUDs will show all the tactical data available in that VI."

"I'll take every advantage we can get," Hannan said. She reached up and popped the catch on her helmet, then tugged it off and dropped it on the floor. "Edwards, Izzy, let's get changed."

"Are we sure changing in the airlock is a good idea?" Izzy asked, making no move to remove her suit.

"Do as the human asks," Fizgig commanded. She removed her own helmet, and began working on the rest of the suit.

Nolan did the same, and less than two minutes later the floor of the airlock was littered with pieces of their EVA suits. He took a deep breath and turned to his makeshift squad. "Hannan and Izzy, you're first through the door. Fizgig and Edwards, you'll be bringing up the rear. I'll stay in the middle with Lena. Let's move."

Lena was now carrying the cube in one hand, and had a tablet in the other. She tapped the tablet, and the airlock door slid open.

Chapter 57- Captain

Dryker rose from the console, wiping the sweat from his eyes. It mixed with soot from the smoke, leaving an oily residue on his skin. "Okay, that will do it. In about six minutes the *Johnston* is going to tear itself apart from the inside."

"A noble sacrifice," Khar said, nodding. He'd set his rifle down and was now carrying Juliard. The comm tech had twisted her ankle during her landing, but was otherwise unharmed.

"Sacrifice?" Juliard asked, her voice rising half an octave. "Captain, are we going down with the ship?"

"Hell no," Dryker said, looking at Juliard like she was crazy. "I don't know about you, but I plan to live."

"How will we do that?" Khar asked, raising a bushy brown eyebrow.

"Your ship," Dryker said, starting up the barrel of the gauss rifle. "We can follow the barrel until we hit C junction, then take that to the tube where you boarded the *Johnston*."

Khar's eyes widened, then he began to laugh. It was the oddest sound Dryker had ever heard--part rumbling laugh, part purr. "Ah, you continue to surprise me, human. Lead on, and perhaps we'll survive the day."

Dryker took the lead, moving at a fast walk. Both hands were wrapped around his TM-601, and he was ready to gun down anything that appeared. The weapon was heavier than he'd remembered, and his back was already beginning to hurt. He was too old for this shit.

Several tense minutes passed before they reached the C junction. Surprisingly, the hatch was open. Dryker approached it cautiously, pausing to listen next to the hatch. Nothing. He turned to Khar. "Can you hear anything beyond?"

"No, all sounds of combat have stopped. Not a good sign. They'll be hunting for us," Khar replied, shaking his head. Juliard had buried her face against his armor. She'd begun weeping, probably from the pain. They needed to find a medkit.

Dryker stepped through the hatch, moving swiftly up the corridor. The walls were scorched, dented, and in some places ruptured by explosions or gunfire. It tore at him to see what a mess his vessel had become.

The *Johnston* wasn't a new ship. She wasn't a battleship. She was an aging destroyer. But she'd served proudly, and...damn it, she was *his* ship. Seeing her die, knowing he'd signed the death warrant, was one of the hardest things he'd ever had to face.

"Khar, how will your people react when we arrive?" Dryker

asked, pausing at another T intersection. He peered down both
sides, but saw no movement.

"They will allow us to board," Khar said. His breathing had
grown ragged, and his movement had slowed. "After that, I do not
know. They may imprison you. I am the second officer, and our
first officer will need to decide."

Dryker nodded, then started up the next corridor. They were
paralleling the outer hull of the ship, which was one of the
first areas the Judicators had cleared. Perhaps that was why
they hadn't met any resistance.

"How much further?" Khar asked, pausing to lean against the
corridor wall.

"Not much. About a hundred meters," Dryker said. "One more
push."

He started up the corridor, thankful that Khar moved to
follow him. He knew the Tigris was exhausted, but they didn't
have time to rest. Every moment they remained on the *Johnston*
was one moment closer to death. He checked the clock on his
comm. Two minutes until detonation.

Dryker redoubled his pace, moving at a near trot as he
crossed the last twenty meters. He stopped next to the airlock,
which was still coupled to the Tigris vessel. The outer airlock
door was open, so he stepped inside. The inner door was also

open, though the matching Tigris door that formed the seal was
still closed.

"Can you open this?" he asked, setting his M-601 against
the wall. It was doubtful the Tigris would let him keep it
anyway.

"I can," Khar said. Gently, he handed Juliard to Dryker,
then moved to the Tigris panel.

"How are you holding up, lieutenant?" Dryker asked, careful
not to jostle Juliard too much.

"My ankle is throbbing, but the arm is the worst," she
replied through gritted teeth. "Don't worry about me, though.
Just get us off this ship."

A sudden scream sounded in the distance, not more than a
hundred meters away. It was abruptly cut off.

"Hurry this up, Khar," Dryker said.

"I have it," the cat said, and a loud purr thrummed through
the airlock. The bronze Tigris door slid open, and they found
themselves staring at a half-dozen rifles leveled in their
direction. Khar stepped boldly forward, growling at the Tigris
soldiers. "Stand down. Once we are through close the door.
Metaza, I have need of you. You will take the wounded human to
our medical bay and sees that she receives treatment."

"Yes, mighty Khar," a tiger-striped cat said. It moved to

the captain, giving a slight bob of its head. "Allow me to
relieve you of this burden."

Dryker reluctantly handed Juliard over, meeting her gaze.
"It will be okay, lieutenant. You're going to get the treatment
you need."

"Come, Dryker," Khar said, starting up the wide, bronze
corridor. "I will take you to the bridge, where we can meet with
my superior."

Chapter 58- Alpha Judicator

Nolan sprinted low and fast down the Void Wraith corridor, struggling to keep up with Lena. Tigris were natural runners, and it had been a long time since Nolan went through PT. Hannan didn't seem to have any trouble keeping up with Izzy, and the pair were leapfrogging up the corridor ahead of them. Fizgig and Edwards brought up the rear, and each time Nolan glanced back he found Fizgig slowing to allow Edwards to keep up.

"Commander," Hannan called from up ahead. She'd stopped next to one of the wide, arched doorways that separated the Void Wraith corridors. They seemed vaguely Egyptian, though Nolan realized that was just his brain trying to find a comfortable comparison.

"What is it?" Nolan said, struggling to slow his breathing as he came to a stop next to the petite Marine. Izzy had taken shelter on the other side of the doorway, and was scanning the room within.

"Take a look," Hannan said, nodding at the doorway.

Nolan bent forward enough to see within the room. Wide stairs descended into a large chamber. The ceiling was at least thirty feet tall, and the walls were lined with giant pods. Each pod had a thick cable leading into the floor, and there was a small window on the front of each. He couldn't see inside the pod from here, and had no idea what they might be used for.

"Lena, what do you think?" he asked, quietly.

"No idea," she said, shrugging. "There's nothing in the VI's memory about this. They never made it inside a Void Wraith vessel, as the vessels self-destruct just like the Judicators."

"Well that would have been good to know before we decided to try to take one," Edwards said, rather sourly.

"Stow it," Hannan said. There was a hint of warning in her tone.

"Movement," Fizgig said, her voice just above a whisper.

A massive figure stepped into view below. It resembled the Judicators, but was taller and broader, and bristling with armaments. Nolan's HUD blinked, then began to display information. According to the data scrolling across his screen, this was an Alpha Judicator. It was apparently a cybernetic life form, and had the armaments and armor to take down heavy mechanized units.

"Fall back," he whispered. Everyone shuffled back a few steps, moving out of sight of the doorway. He turned to Lena. "Can you find us another way to the bridge?"

"I'm afraid not," she said, shaking her head. "I'm not even

sure this is the right way. We're going off guesswork based on the outside of the vessel. The Primos never made it to the bridge. We could try to make it around another way, but we'd be largely blind. I have no idea what we'd encounter."

"Okay, so we have to destroy this thing," Nolan said. He looked Hannan in the eye. "I need you to deliver me a dead Alpha Judicator."

"I'm not sure we have the ordinance for that, sir," Hannan said, going a little pale.

"Sarge is right, sir," Edwards said, holding up his assault rifle. "I had to leave the 601 behind. This pop gun isn't going to do shit to that monster."

"You're not going to be using your rifle," Nolan said. He glanced around the corner into the room below, then ducked back into the corridor. "Lena, those cables are conducting electricity, right?"

"Yes, I'm almost positive of it," Lena affirmed.

"Almost positive will have to do," Nolan said. He turned to Fizgig. "You, Izzy, Hannan and Edwards are going to distract that thing. We'll wait for it to walk back to the other side of the room, then flank it. Our crossfire probably won't do much to slow it down, but all we're trying to do is distract it."

"We can do that," Fizgig said, impassively. Her tail

swished behind her. "How do you plan to defeat this enemy?"

"I'll tear one of those cables out of the floor. When the Alpha passes my position, I'll dart out and plant the conduit against the Judicator," Nolan explained. He glanced at Hannan. "Can you keep this thing occupied until I get into position?"

"Can do, sir," Hannan asked, squaring her shoulders.

"Your plan could definitely work," Lena interjected. "We know that bullets disrupt the cloaking field. That field covers the entire outside of the unit, so I'm betting it's highly conductive. If it is, the conduit might overload the Alpha's systems."

"I do not believe we have any other choice," Fizgig said. She looked to Nolan. "The command is yours, of course."

"This is as good a plan as we're likely to get," Nolan replied grimly. "Okay, Hannan, this is your show. Give me a window to get to that cable."

Chapter 59- Larva

Kathryn awoke with a start and gazed wildly around the
room. She was not in her quarters; this room's flat metal walls
were completely unfamiliar. She began to thrash, but found
herself restrained. Thick metal bands pinned her head, forearms,
wrists, and ankles to the kind of chair that gave dentists a bad
name.

"Calm down," she said, forcing herself to take several
long, deep breaths. What was the last thing she remembered?
She'd gone to bed in her quarters, after seeding both the
Quantum Network and Quantum Lite with stories about Nolan and
the *Johnston*.

Someone must have broken into her quarters, drugged her,
and then brought her to a secure facility. It was textbook OFI,
designed to put an interrogation subject off balance. Placing
them in an unfamiliar situation outside of their control sapped
a subject's willpower, which made them easier to break.

The first method of fighting that was logic. She needed to
figure out where she was, who'd taken her, and what they wanted.
That meant gathering as much information as possible. She took
some time to look at the room she was in. A metal table sat next

to her, with an array of wicked-looking torture tools arrayed
prominently. A single high-illumination light shone on her from
above like a spotlight. That would partially blind her, allowing
her interrogators to stand in the shadows.

Kathryn closed her eyes and listened. In the distance she
heard voices. One of them was raised in anger, and she focused
on that one. She could make out faint words, one of which she
recognized immediately. Ghantan. That dropped so many pieces
into place. She'd already suspected that Admiral Mendez was
behind this, though she hadn't wanted to believe he was capable
of it. Did he think she knew something about the *Johnston* that
he could use?

"Dispatch the seventh. Make sure only loyal ships are
sent," Mendez's voice boomed. She knew her father well enough to
know that his tone meant he was close to panic. The admiral
always went on the offensive when angry. "They're to wipe out
the *Johnston*, and make sure there are no witnesses. No one
leaves that system alive, am I clear? If word gets out now, it
could ruin everything. It's too soon. We are not ready for war."

Footsteps sounded outside the room, stopping just on the
other side of what she guessed must be the door. A sharp hiss
confirmed her suspicions, and footsteps sounded inside the room.
There was only a single pair, and she knew exactly to whom they

belonged.

"Good morning, Admiral," Kathryn said cheerfully. "It sounds like things aren't going very well. Maybe because someone leaked information about your little coup all over the Quantum Network."

The footsteps approached until she could see a shadowed figure standing at the edge of the light. The admiral's bearded face was silhouetted by the light, giving him an even more sinister cast. She couldn't quite make out his eyes, but she could see the too-white teeth when he smiled.

"Ahh, Kathryn. I've suspected your true loyalties for some time, but that last little stunt was a bridge too far," the admiral pulled a metal stool next to her chair, then sat. He picked up a scalpel from the tray of tools. "Your flippant attitude is admirable. That's the product of OFI training, and I'd expect nothing less. I have no doubt it would take weeks to break you, if I used traditional techniques."

Kathryn considered quickly. This verbal sparring match would be short, and represented her only real chance to get information. After this the torture would begin in earnest, and she'd be in too much pain to learn anything of use.

"So why bother breaking me?" she said, turning her head as much as the restraints would allow. "You could have just

poisoned me in my sleep. A heart attack, like poor Admiral
Kelley."

"It's not sentimentality, I assure you. Our relationship
has nothing to do with you still breathing," Mendez said. He
leaned closer, until she could smell the tang of tobacco on his
breath. "You're alive because your incredible ingenuity has
allowed you to accomplish something no one else in the admiralty
has. To date, our little plot has gone completely undetected.
We've been operating for nearly a year without a whisper of our
activities reaching the wrong ears. Then you come along, tossing
wrenches into some of our best plans."

"I'd think that would be more reason to kill me," Kathryn
shot back.

"That would be a waste," Mendez said, eyeing her with an
unreadable mix of emotions. "I'd much rather convert you to our
cause, Lieutenant Commander."

Lieutenant Commander. Not Kate. Not daughter.

"And how is it you plan to do that?" Kathryn said, raising
an eyebrow. "I'll never work for you, not to subvert our
government. You have to know that."

"Of course you will," the admiral said, giving a booming
laugh.

Kathryn knew this stage of the interrogation was ending, so

she asked the most important question she could think of. "Why are you doing all this? You were a hero in the Tigris war. A patriot, through and through. What changed you so dramatically, and how did I miss it?"

"You'll understand our motives soon enough," the admiral said. He reached into the pockets of his uniform jacket, and withdrew two objects. The first Kathryn recognized. It was a hypo-stim, designed to inject any number of chemicals into a subject. The second was a small clear vial, but she couldn't make out the contents. "First, I need to ensure your loyalty. And I assure you, you *will* be loyal."

The admiral held up the clear vial, just a few inches from her face. Something green and slimy lay inside, a two-inch slug of a species she wasn't familiar with. It pressed against the glass, writhing as it attempted to get closer to her. "This is a Gorthian larva. It has several unique properties. The first is its ability to rewrite genetic material. It can modify both RNA and DNA, changing the host body to suit its needs. In the case of sentient species, that means rewriting your neurological pathways to fit desired patterns."

Kathryn could only stare in horror. If the admiral was on the level, this thing would quite literally brainwash her. That explained so much--why trusted members of every major race were serving the Void Wraith.

"Its next ability is the one I find most intriguing," the Admiral said, holding the vial up for his own inspection. "The larva acts as a quantum transmitter. It can both send and receive information, allowing the masters to orchestrate their grand design."

Mendez looked back at her, and gave a start. "You look terrified, Kate. Don't worry. I know that the bonding process is painful. I won't make you suffer through that."

He pressed the hypo against her thigh, and there was a sharp pain as the needle bit. Sudden warmth spread through her leg, and up into her chest. When the admiral spoke again his words were far away. "You'll sleep through the entire process, and when you've awoken you'll be one of us."

Chapter 60- Fried

Hannan took several deep breaths. She glanced around at her people. Everyone was ready. "Okay, let's do this. Fizgig, Izzy, into the hole."

The two Tigris darted down the stairwell, reaching the bottom in three superhuman bounds. The Alpha began to turn toward them, but they'd already reached the shelter of one of the pods.

"Nolan, let's go," she said. Hannan sprinted to the first landing, pausing to fire a three-round burst at the twelve-foot-tall Judicator. The rounds pinged off its face, but they got its attention. It turned in her direction, raising a massive rifle. That rifle took a moment to warm up, blue energy crackling around the barrel.

In that instant Hannan dove from the landing, rolling to safety behind a pod on the far side of the room from where Fizgig and Izzy had taken shelter. The Alpha's shot hit the stairs where she'd been standing, and the metal erupted into a spray of razored shrapnel that peppered the wall behind it. The pieces of shrapnel left a crater in their wake, both in the landing and in the wall where they'd hit. Jesus, that thing hit hard.

Nolan darted down the stairs behind her, popping off rounds
from his pistol as he did. The Alpha pivoted to face him, and
Hannan knew he was in serious trouble. Then Fizgig was moving.
She popped around her pod, firing a round from her Tigris war
rifle. The shot took the Alpha in the face, and actually knocked
the thing half a step back. It ruined the Alpha's aim, and the
shot that had been intended for Nolan wound up hitting the
ceiling instead.

Nolan dropped from the stairs, rolling to his feet near
Hannan. Their gazes met, but Nolan didn't slow. He ran low and
fast behind the pods, crouching near the one closest to the
Alpha.

Then Hannan's attention was back on their opponent. It was
stalking through the room, the barrels of its multiple weapons
scanning both sides as it sought targets. Edwards leapt into the
room, firing off single shots as he dropped into cover behind
the stairwell. The Judicator swiveled to face him, and began
advancing in Edwards's direction.

"For Fizgig," Izzy yelled, charging the Alpha from the
side. She made an impressive leap, grabbing the Alpha's shoulder
with one paw. She used the momentum to swing herself onto its
back, then buried her bayonet deep into the thing's neck. If the

wound caused any damage, the Alpha certainly didn't show it.

The Alpha paused, then reached back to remove Izzy. Hannan cursed under her breath, popping out of cover. She unloaded several more three-round bursts, each targeting the same knee. The first two bursts pinged off the tough metal, but one of the slugs from the third volley found something sensitive. The Alpha staggered, and the swipe it had aimed at Izzy missed by a good two feet.

Fizgig charged forward, burying her bayonet in the same knee. She squeezed the trigger of her rifle, and a loud boom echoed through the room. The scent of ozone intensified, but the Alpha seemed otherwise unarmed. It didn't go down. If anything, the wound had only annoyed it.

The Alpha swung its wounded leg forward, catching Fizgig in the chest. She was launched backwards, sailing toward the wall. Hannan winced, knowing Fizgig would have broken bones from the impact. Then Edwards darted from cover. He dove forward, catching Fizgig the instant before she slammed into the wall. The two went down in a tangle of limbs, but neither appeared to be harmed.

Edwards rolled to his feet, darting into cover near the Commander.

"Hurry it up, Nolan," Hannan ordered. Izzy was dancing away

from the Alpha's probing hand, but sooner or later the thing
would grab her.

"Got the cable free," Nolan yelled back. "You're going to
have to get it closer, though. This thing doesn't stretch very
far."

"Screw it," Hannan said. She ran toward the Alpha, popping
off single rounds from her assault rifle every third step. Each
shot tagged the thing in the face, and by the fourth shot its
beady blue eyes had focused directly on her. The Alpha took a
step closer, then another. Hannan skidded behind the pod next to
Nolan, panting as she glanced up at him. "I hope this works."

The Alpha stepped around the pod, leaning over it to aim
its rifle at her. It seemed to have forgotten Izzy, who was
holding onto her rifle with one hand while emptying her sidearm
into the back of its neck with the other. Hannan watched as the
Alpha's rifle got closer, until the barrel seemed to swallow her
entire vision. Energy began to crackle around that barrel, and
she knew she had only a few seconds to live.

Then the thing staggered backward. Hannan rolled away,
looking around the other side of the pod. Nolan stood right next
to the Alpha, and was holding the conduit against its wounded
knee. The Alpha's back arched, and electricity played up the
length of its body in tight, blue arcs. Those arcs caught Izzy,

who tumbled limply from the Alpha's back. Hannan dove, catching the Tigris just before she hit the deck.

"Commander, move," Edwards roared.

Hannan turned to see what was happening just in time to watch the Alpha topple limply towards Nolan. Edwards shoved Nolan out of the way, but was too slow to save himself. The judicator fell heavily atop the big Marine, crushing him under several tons of metal.

Chapter 61- Tigris Bridge

"You've brought a human traitor onto my bridge?" a black-furred cat roared at Khar. Dryker stood passively, knowing that anything he said would probably make the situation worse.

"Mighty Fizgig allied with this human," Khar spat back. The fur on the back of his neck stood up, and his tail swished angrily. "Dryker may be our only chance of survival. Let him speak, or I will challenge you right here, Skaan."

"Very well. Speak, human," Skaan said. His eyes narrowed distrustfully.

"In about twenty seconds an internal explosion is going to tear the *Johnston* apart," Dryker said.

Skaan's eyes widened, and he whirled to face his bridge crew. "Disengage the docking clamp. Now!"

"At once, mighty Skaan," answered a golden-furred female.

The ship rumbled, and Dryker could see a gap begin to form between the *Johnston* and the *Claw*. He winced inwardly as the *Johnston*'s hull began to buckle. Fire shot out of different points along the hull, while other sections collapsed inward. The whole vessel distended, then broke apart roughly midway down the hull. Seeing it break apart broke something inside of

Dryker. She was his ship, and she was dying.

Then the *Johnston* exploded. The brunt of that explosion was directed inward, but enough force remained to wash over both the Void Wraith vessel and the *Claw*. They were knocked back, and the screen went white for a moment.

When it cleared, the Void Wraith vessel was still there, seemingly unharmed.

"Mighty Skaan," the white-furred female called. "The other Void Wraith vessels are beginning to respond. They're moving away from the station, and heading in our direction. Two have already cloaked."

"Blast it," Skaan cursed, rounding on Dryker. "You've brought this on us, human. I'll see you dead."

Khar glided silently forward, seizing Skaan's head between both massive paws. The muscles in his arms tensed, and he gave a single twist. There was a sharp crack, then Skaan's lifeless body toppled to the deck.

Silence reigned across the bridge for several seconds, then the golden-furred comm officer called out. "Mighty Khar!"

The cry was taken up all over the bridge, until Khar raised his arms to silence it. He turned to Dryker. "Now, what?"

Chapter 62- Void Wraith Bridge

"Hang in there, Edwards," Nolan said, kneeling next to the burly Marine, who was still pinned underneath the Alpha.

"Sir, you have to get away. This thing could blow up now that we've killed it," Edwards said, in short pained gasps.

"I doubt that," Nolan said, looking at the Alpha. "The other Judicators detonated almost immediately. This one's been dead a good thirty seconds."

"Nolan is right," Lena said, approaching cautiously. "I suspect the Judicators have a different directive here. Why set them to detonate aboard your own ship? That could cause catastrophic damage."

"Excellent point," Fizgig growled. "That may serve us well. We should keep moving."

"What about Edwards?" Hannan said. Her face was set into the mask of determination Nolan was beginning to recognize. "We don't leave our own behind."

"There is no choice," Izzy said, placing a paw on Hannan's shoulder. "We lack the strength to move the Alpha."

"My legs are crushed, anyway," Edwards said, panting. The pain must be excruciating, if his armor couldn't suppress it.

"You need to leave me. Finish this, or everything we've done is for nothing."

"He's right," Nolan said, standing with a sigh. "Hannan, Izzy, take point."

"Sir," Hannan said, moving to stand in front of him. "We can spare two minutes to try to--"

"You have your orders, Marine," Nolan said. "I need you, Hannan. Get moving. Now."

"Yes, sir," Hannan said. She glanced at Edwards, and grew a shade paler. She kept moving, though. She and Izzy moved to the far side of the room, their weapons scanning the corridor that led in the direction they hoped the bridge was.

"Nolan, you might want to see this before we go," Lena called. She was standing in front of one of the pods.

Nolan approached cautiously, peering through the window. He could only stare. "My god, what are they doing?"

Inside was a human, or what was left of one. All that remained was a spine and a brain, and they floated in a viscous green liquid. The pod began to hum, and the bottom opened. Nolan peered down, watching as a shape rose into the liquid. A familiar metallic frame, with too-thin limbs.

"This is how they make Judicators," he said, horror turning his bowels to ice. "They're harvesting people to make more troops."

"This is barbaric," Fizgig hissed, peering into the pod.
She rounded on Nolan. "We must stop these things. At any cost."

Nolan gave a tight nod, then started trotting up the
corridor. Before, he'd been scared. He'd been tired. Now? He was
angry. These bastards were going to pay. He would find a way to
make them pay.

They ran up several flights of stairs, then through a maze
of corridors. Nolan let Lena guide them. She didn't have a true
map, but the info contained in the VI was the closest thing.
Minutes passed, and the anger continued to smolder. He could
read it on all their faces.

He expected to meet more resistance, but they saw no other
Judicators as they made their way closer and closer to the
bridge. Finally, they rounded a corner and found a room that
could be nothing else. A large black platform sat in the center
of the room. It looked almost identical to the one on Purito,
where they'd found the VI. The link between Primo technology and
the Void Wraith continued to trouble him.

"Okay, fan out and lock down the exits to this room," Nolan
commanded.

Hannan, Izzy, and Fizgig fanned out. There were two
doorways--the one they'd entered through and another at the far

side of the room. As with every room they'd passed through,
there were no doors, and thus no way to truly lock down the
room. If other Judicators were on the ship, they could assault
them at any time.

"Lena, what can you do to get us control of this ship?"
Nolan asked.

"Nothing," a metallic voice said. Nolan spun to see a
holographic figure appear over the black platform. It was Primo,
just like the VI they'd brought with them. "Your deaths are
assured, your efforts wasted."

"What the hell are you?" Nolan asked, instinctively aiming
his rifle at the hologram.

"I am Sentinel," it said, watching him impassively, "though
that information is useless to you. Wraith are already on their
way. Your existence will be terminated in four minutes and
thirteen seconds. Your genetic matter will be harvested, and
converted into more soldiers."

Nolan was silent for a moment. He glanced at Lena, but she
only shrugged. "Why are you attacking us?" Nolan asked. "What do
you get out of it?"

"I fulfill my purpose," Sentinel answered, metallically.
"Nothing you do here will matter. Your struggle is futile."

"You know," Nolan said, narrowing his eyes, "every time

I've heard anyone tell me something like that, it's because they fear me. If we're so powerless how did we reach your bridge? Lena, can you deactivate that thing?"

"It will take me a little time, but I think so," Lena said, moving to crouch next to the black platform.

"Your efforts will avail you not," Sentinel said, watching Lena.

"Maybe," Nolan said. "I believe otherwise. You fear us. You fear something we'd learn, otherwise why did you go to the effort of wiping out all those Primo ruins? You knew there was something that we could recover, something we could learn that would be a threat."

"Your arrogance is impressive," Sentinel said. It paused, studying Nolan. "I harvested the ruins to obtain more virtual intelligences. They are required to run vessels such as this. Their construction requires immense time and effort. Recovering them is a more expedient way of expanding my forces. This is why the worlds belonging to the race you know as the Primo Genitus were targeted first."

The wheels began to turn in Nolan's head, and a grin spread across his face. This thing had inadvertently revealed something vital.

"Your amusement will be short lived," Sentinel said, a hint

of emotion finally infusing its tone. "The other vessels I have created have nearly arrived. Even if they had not, over two dozen line units will soon be assaulting you."

Chapter 63- Allies

"Mighty Khar," one of the Tigris called. "Twelve vessels are emerging from the Helios Gate."

Dryker watched from his place in the corner, saying nothing as the view screen shifted to show a fleet emerging from the sun's corona. The vessels were tiny specs, too small to identify visually.

"Are they broadcasting an ident?" Khar rumbled. He hadn't risen since sitting in the captain's chair, which didn't surprise Dryker. Khar's fur was still matted with blood, and none of his injuries had been tended to. One of his eyes was swollen shut, and he bled freely from wounds on his chest.

"Yes, mighty Khar. It's the Fourth Claw of the Leonis pride," the comm officer said.

"Rejoice," Khar roared, giving a booming Tigris laugh. "Get me the lead vessel on screen."

A moment later, a black-furred Tigris face loomed on the screen. It stared hard at Khar before speaking. "Where is mighty Fizgig? We have come to aid her in battle."

"Mighty Fizgig is aboard the Void Wraith vessel near us," Khar said. He leaned forward in his chair. "She is attempting to seize control, with the aid of the humans."

"The humans?" the black-furred Tigris said, clearly

surprised. Then its gaze fell on Dryker. "I see you have one of

those humans aboard your ship, and not just any human either.

You've captured Dryker, the worm who destroyed one of our

science vessels. Why is he not restrained?"

"Because I'm not a prisoner," Dryker said. Letting Khar

speak for him would be a mistake, and he knew it. Tigris only

respected strength. "My ship is gutted, but with its destruction

Khar and I killed dozens of Void Wraith. Maybe hundreds. We gave

my first officer and mighty Fizgig time to invade their vessel."

"He speaks the truth, mighty Varr," Khar said, nodding

respectfully. "We do not have time to discuss this, though. Six

more Void Wraith vessels have left the station you've no doubt

seen on your sensors. They will engage us shortly."

"Interesting," Varr said, giving a feline smile. "We will

see what these fairy tales can do in real combat. My fleet is

moving to support you, mighty Khar. Fight with honor."

Then the view screen went dark. Dryker removed his tablet

from his pocket, reviewing the data he'd accumulated since

arriving in-system. The first massive structure was clearly a

factory, but what about the second--the one containing the vast

amount of that mysterious heavy element? It must be important to the Void Wraith, and he was afraid they'd soon find out why.

Chapter 64- VI Removal

"How's it going, Lena?" Nolan asked. He'd moved to stand just beside the doorway they'd entered through. He didn't see any sign of the enemy yet, but if Sentinel was telling the truth they'd be under assault by the ship's forces soon.

"I've exposed the panel, and I can see the data cube containing Sentinel," Lena called. She was bent over the black platform with an electro spanner in one hand.

The entire ship shook violently, and Nolan barely caught himself against the wall.

"What the hell was that?" Hannan called from the doorway she was guarding.

"That," Fizgig said, "was a massive explosion. Given the resulting kick, I'd guess we're no longer docked with the *Johnston*."

"Shit," Hannan said. She gave Nolan a sober look. "Do you think the old man blew up the gauss cannon?"

"It makes sense," Nolan replied. He glanced up the corridor. Still nothing. "If he detonated the gauss cannon, he'd take out all the Void Wraith forces--meaning they can't return to stop us here."

"A noble sacrifice," Fizgig said. Her tail drooped. "Dryker was the most feared human commander during our brief war with humanity. He will be sung about in our legends."

"Contact," Hannan yelled. She dropped to a knee, snapping her assault rifle to her shoulder. The sharp report of automatic weapons fire filled the bridge as she fired down her corridor.

Nolan considered running to join her, but resisted the urge. His job was to guard this doorway, and if he left it the Void Wraith could flank him from behind. He faced the doorway, his stomach dropping when he saw movement. Several shimmering forms were approaching. "We're about to have a lot more company. What's the status of deactivating that VI, Lena?"

"I need a minute," she yelled.

"We don't have a minute," Hannan called back. "Izzy, I need you over here."

The white-furred cat sprinted to join Hannan. The pair laid down continuous fire, and for the moment nothing was making it through their doorway. Nolan turned back to his. The shimmering forms were getting closer.

"I see at least three coming my way," he yelled, then carefully raised his assault rifle to his shoulder. He fired at the closest target, and the Judicator stumbled back three paces. Its cloaking field dropped, and Nolan used the opportunity to target the thing's head. He squeezed off a three-round burst, and the Judicator dropped to the deck.

The other two fired a steady stream of blue plasma, and Nolan had no choice but to duck behind cover. He waited two seconds, then ducked back into the doorway to fire another burst. Both Judicators fired the instant his head appeared, and it was only dumb luck that he got back into cover in time. The bursts of plasma shot into the room, one exploding a control panel in a shower of sparks.

"They've got me pinned over here," Nolan yelled. "Two bogies. They'll be into the room soon."

"I've almost got it," Lena yelled.

"Four targets inbound," Fizgig roared, firing down her corridor. "We are surrounded. I mean no disrespect, holy one, but if you cannot deactivate the VI we'll be dead in moments."

Nolan dropped prone, then extended his rifle along the floor. He fired blindly, then yanked the weapon back out of sight. A pair of plasma bursts cratered the floor where his weapon had been, sending up a spray of shrapnel that pinged off his armor. One of the fragments hit his visor, sending a spiderweb of cracks along the right rear portion. At least the HUD still worked.

"I've got it," Lena yelled triumphantly. Nolan risked a

glance. She was holding aloft a cube that looked nearly
identical to the Primo VI.

"They're still coming," Hannan yelled. "Whatever you did
didn't work."

Chapter 65- Engage

Dryker felt helpless, nothing more than a bystander in what could be the most important conflict in recorded history. He watched as the Tigris vessels fanned out, moving with the practiced precision that had given the Leonis pride such an advantage during their war with the humans.

The ships moved in unison, shifting formation to form a net around the *Claw of Tigrana* and the seemingly dormant Void Wraith vessel. Then it was a waiting game. They knew six Void Wraith vessels were out there, but their cloaking technology allowed them to choose the time and place they would engage. It was the type of advantage that a smart foe could use to devastating effect, and Dryker found himself holding his breath as he waited for the assault to begin.

It came sooner than he expected.

"Mighty Khar, three vessels have de-cloaked off our starboard port. They're moving to engage the fleet," the comm officer called.

The view screen shifted to show the three Void Wraith vessels. Each was charging their main weapon, the ball of blue plasma that did such catastrophic damage. All three fired at the

lead Tigris vessel. The first shot impacted against the shield,
which flickered, then dropped. The second and third shot both
hit the central line running down the Tigris vessel. The impacts
disintegrated huge chunks of the vessel, and it broke apart in a
fiery explosion. The remnants began drifting sunward, pulled by
the immense gravity.

All three Void Wraith vessels shifted to the next closest
target, unleashing a similar barrage. The second Tigris vessel
fared no better than the first, its remains joining the wreckage
floating toward the sun.

Four Tigris vessels moved to intercept, firing cable after
cable. They surrounded the first Void Wraith vessel, pulling it
into a web it could not escape. More Tigris vessels moved to
intercept, but the remaining two Void Wraith cloaked.

"Mighty Khar, we're under assault," the comm officer
yelled.

Proximity alarms went off, and the lighting on the bridge
changed from white to a soft red. Then the ship shook as
something impacted. A moment later, a second impact came, and
sparks showered from several terminals. The lights flickered,
then died.

"Damage report," Khar yelled.

"We've lost main power, Mighty Khar," a voice called in the

darkness. "Life support is operational, and we're working to restore secondary power."

"What hit us?" Khar roared.

"Two Void Wraith vessels de-cloaked off the aft side of the ship," the comm officer replied.

Dryker clenched a fist, wishing there was something he could do. The Void Wraith outclassed the Tigris. The Tigris might inflict casualties...but there was no way they could win this fight.

Chapter 66- VI Replacement

Nolan waited until the first Judicator stepped through the doorway, then jammed the barrel of his rifle into the place he suspected the face was. He fired a three-round burst, and was elated when the Judicator dropped to the deck with a clatter. He danced backwards, but then realized that they weren't exploding. If they had been, the fight would already have been over. Thank God for whatever directive made them less explosive aboard this ship.

"Lena, what have you got for us?" Nolan said, aiming his rifle at the doorway. The last Judicator hadn't stepped through.

"Uh, I'm going to connect the Primo VI to the ship," Lena yelled back. Her voice was nearly drowned out by the staccato of gunfire coming from Hannan, Izzy and Fizgig. "I have no idea what that will do, but it can't be any worse than where we're at right now."

"Do it," Nolan yelled.

The third Judicator stepped through the doorway. Nolan tried the same trick, but this Judicator was expecting it. It slashed down with a trio of blazing plasma blades, and the weapons sheared through the barrel of Nolan's rifle. He dropped the useless weapon, backpedaling as the thing advanced on him. He couldn't even see its face, since it was still cloaked. But he could see it raise the shimmering outline of a plasma rifle barrel.

Nolan drew his sidearm and began firing. The shots knocked the Judicator back, but he knew it wasn't going to be enough. He was dead.

The Judicator's head exploded, and it toppled onto Nolan. The weight of the body pinned him to the deck, and he struggled to kick the thing off him.

"You owe me, commander," Hannan yelled. "Now get back on your feet and secure the damned doorway. More of these things are coming. Izzy, go back him up."

The white cat bounded over, reaching down to tug the headless Judicator off Nolan. He could see her arms straining, and it reminded him of the much larger Judicator still pinning Edwards somewhere in the ship.

"Thanks," he said, accepting Izzy's paw as she helped him to his feet.

"I've got it," Lena called excitedly.

Nolan spun to the platform. The holographic display flickered to life, this time showing the same VI they'd met back on Purito. It looked down at Lena. "I have bonded with this vessel, and now control all vital systems. What are your

orders?"

"Turn off the Judicators," Lena yelled. "Make them stop

attacking."

"Acknowledged," the VI answered. It closes its virtual

eyes, and the Judicators advancing up the corridors shimmered

into view and then just...stopped. They froze mid-stride, some

with weapons still raised. "I've ordered all units to stand

down. They will take no further action until ordered to do so."

Chapter 67- More Allies

"Secondary power online," the golden-furred comm officer called. The lights flickered back on, though they were weaker than normal.

Dryker leaned against the railing that separated the rear deck from the main portion where the crew was performing vital bridge tasks. He longed to take action, but his role in this battle was over. He was an observer, and all he could was hope the Tigris found a way to prevail.

"Status report," Khar demanded.

"Five Tigris vessels have been destroyed, and one more is disabled," the comm officer said, his tone subdued. "At least two Void Wraith vessels have been destroyed, possibly three. The rest have retreated for now."

"They're falling back," Khar muttered. He spun his chair to face Dryker. "Why? Why would they do that, Captain?"

"They had the advantage," Dryker said, studying the view screen. "The only reason they'd fall back is if they expected reinforcements."

"Mighty Khar, the large structure near the factory has begun to move toward the sun," the comm officer said.

The view screen shifted to show the enormous vessel powering slowly toward the sun. It looked like a giant turnip, and if Dryker's data was correct it was easily the size of Earth's moon.

"Captain, do you have any theories about that thing?" Khar asked, turning to him.

"Not as of yet," Dryker admitted. "Our scans show that thing is teeming with some sort of theoretical element we've never encountered, but I have no idea what it is or what the Void Wraith intend to do with it. I guess that doesn't much matter, though. Whatever they want, we should oppose."

"We will destroy it," Khar said, clenching his fist and exposing his fangs.

"Mighty Khar, more ships are emerging from the Helios Gate," the comm officer's tone was shrill now. She sounded close to breaking.

"Ident?" Khar said, standing slowly from his chair. He was favoring his right leg.

"They're human vessels sir, OFI ident," the comm officer said. Khar moved to stand next to her, placing a comforting hand on her shoulder.

"It looks like four destroyers, and two capital ships," Dryker said, squinting at the screen. "I think that's the bulk of the seventh fleet."

"Then victory is once again within our grasp," Khar said, laughing. He turned to Dryker. "I will put you in contact with them so you can coordinate the battle. Comm, open a channel to the lead human vessel."

"They're ignoring our hails, mighty Khar. The human vessels are moving to interpose themselves between us and the large Void Wraith vessel," the comm officer said, her voice barely above a whisper.

"Treachery," Khar roared, slamming his fist into the view screen. A sharp crack spread from the impact point. Khar rounded on Dryker. "What is the meaning of this?"

"I can only guess," Dryker said, the exhaustion whispering a siren song: *Just lie down. Just give up.* "I suspect that the spies in my government have dispatched forces loyal to them. Forces that work indirectly for the Void Wraith. The same forces that tried to keep your fleet away from this system."

Chapter 68- Primo Online

"Lena, can you access communications?" Nolan asked. He limped over to the black platform, his breathing still ragged from the fight with the Judicators.

"Any of us can," Lena said, rising to her feet. "This VI will obey any of us."

"That is correct," the VI said. Its bulbous head turned to face Nolan. "I have complete control of Communications. What do you wish to know?"

"Monitor all communications in this system, and play them here on the bridge," Nolan ordered. "Can you give us a visual as well?"

"Of course," the VI said, as if insulted. A holographic display sprung up near the west wall, covering it from floor to ceiling. It showed a massive battle, which Nolan could barely get his brain around.

"What the hell?" he whispered.

"It looks like the Fourth Claw disobeyed the dictates of War Commander Mow," Fizgig said. Low, powerful purring came from her chest. "A large portion of our fleet has come to do battle on our behalf."

"Who are they fighting ,though?" Hannan said, resting the barrel of her assault rifle on her shoulder as she took a step closer to the holo display.

"That's the seventh," Nolan said. "Oh, God. The seventh is loyal to admiral Mendez. Kathryn warned me that he'd been compromised. Those ships work for the Void Wraith."

"Audio is now available," Primo interjected.

Static crackled across hidden speakers all over the bridge. That static resolved into a cacophony of voices.

"--main engines. Going critical," came a deep Tigris voice.

"--need to reach whatever that big ship is. It's making for the Helios Gate."

The overlapping voices were almost impossible to decipher, but Nolan could see from the disposition of the battle what was happening. The outnumbered and outgunned Tigris were trying to stop the giant ship from making it to the Helios Gate. They were failing.

"There are two potentially lethal situations you may wish to be aware of," the VI said pleasantly. "Would you like further details?"

"Yes," Nolan said, almost instantly.

"First, two Void Wraith vessels are attempting to dock," the VI said.

"Uh, Virtual Intelligence," Nolan said. "Can you engage this ship's cloaking device?

"Affirmative," the VI confirmed.

"Do that, then get us away from the two vessels attempting to dock," Nolan ordered.

A low whirring came from the bowels of the Void Wraith vessel. "Cloaking engaged. We are moving away from the two Void Wraith vessels, and they appear unaware of our current location."

"What is this second lethal situation?" Fizgig demanded, moving to stand next to Nolan.

"This vessel contains data regarding the massive structure moving for the Helios Gate. Using that data I have extrapolated the true purpose for the weapon," the VI said. The holographic display changed, now displaying an unfamiliar system. That system was dominated by a large G class star, and was taken from the perspective of a vessel orbiting the third planet. Countless other ships, vaguely Primo ships, were arrayed in a defensive perimeter. "This is a record of the first major battle in the final war, the battle that guaranteed the Primo could not win."

The color of the sun began to change. It went from yellow to a more pure white, then to blue. Then the star began to expand. At first that expansion was slow and measurable, but it

rapidly increased. The time index shifted forward, showing a
time lapse of the nova. It washed over the system, destroying
most of the ships docked there. The ship doing the recording
retreated ahead of the nova, presumably to carry the recording
they were viewing.

"What happened?" Izzy asked, raising a paw hesitantly
toward the hologram.

"The vessel you see moving towards the star is, in essence,
a bomb," the VI explained. "It contains a massive quantity of a
heavy element, more dense than anything found or manufactured in
our galaxy. This element is designed to cause an accelerated
reaction inside a star. Once that reaction reaches critical
mass, the star will go nova. The Void Wraith used just such a
bomb to wipe out our home world, and a large portion of our
fleet. It crippled us, ensuring that we couldn't mount an
effective defense. Then their fleets began to pour through,
attacking us everywhere at once. We were naked before the storm,
unable to defend ourselves."

"They're bringing it to Primo space," Fizgig said. She was
no longer purring. "If they detonate that in the Theras system,
it will wipe out the bulk of the Primo navy."

"Then we need to stop that ship," Nolan said.

Chapter 69- Down With The Ship

"Damage report," Khar croaked from his chair. He began
another fit of coughing.

Sparks flew from some terminals, while others had simply
gone dark. Dryker felt relatively safe in the corner of the
bridge--well, as safe as one could be on a critically-damaged
ship. He looked at the ops station, and realized the comm
officer was dead.

Dryker leapt over the railing, moving as swiftly as he
could to the Tigris panel. OFI officers had been required to
learn Tigris during the war, so he had no trouble deciphering
the data feed. It wasn't good.

"All three launch tubes have been destroyed," Dryker called
to Khar. "We've lost all decks C and below. Most of B deck is
depressurized. Armor on the stern is non-existent. If we take
another serious hit from anyone, we're going to come apart."

"That leaves only one course of action," Khar said,
coughing. He held a paw to his side, but was failing to staunch
the flow of blood. The few surviving bridge personnel looked
around at at each other. They all knew what Khar was going to
say. "Plot a course toward the largest human vessel. Accelerate

to maximum velocity."

Khar leaned back in his chair, closing his eyes. Dryker could see his chest rising in short, shallow breaths. The Tigris desperately needed a medic. Unfortunately, the ship's schematics showed that the bridge was cut off. There was a large depressurized section between them and the few surviving areas. The four of them were on their own.

"Course set, mighty Khar," called a white-furred Tigris, from the pilot's chair. She strongly resembled Izzy--a littermate, most likely.

The OFI carrier Adar loomed larger and larger on the view screen as they picked up speed. The carrier was currently engaged with another Tigris vessel, though it was clearly winning that exchange. That left it vulnerable, though. It was pinned in place by the first Tigris vessel's harpoons, which meant it wouldn't be able to dodge. If they could accelerate enough, they'd obliterate the carrier. With any luck, they'd leaving the human fleet leaderless.

"Void Wraith vessel de-cloaking off starboard," the white-furred Tigris yelled. "Orders, mighty Khar?"

Khar didn't respond. Nolan took a closer look, and realized that he could no longer see Khar's chest rising and following. Either he was dead, or he was close enough that it didn't matter. Dryker looked around the bridge. None of the three remaining Tigris seemed willing to take charge.

"Evasive maneuvers," Dryker barked, infusing his voice with as much authority as possible. "Try to get some distance from the Void Wraith, but keep us aimed at that carrier. If we're going down, we're taking them with us."

"Aye, mighty, uh, Dryker," the white-furred pilot said. "The Void Wraith vessel is hailing us."

Chapter 70- Promoted

"Primo, can you hail the *Claw of Tigrana*?" Nolan asked, studying the battle playing out on the holographic screen.

"I can, but to maximize efficiency I'd recommend appointing a captain," the VI said. "Otherwise, it is possible for conflicting orders to be received from multiple sources."

"Fizgig," Nolan said, turning to face the Tigris commander. "You've followed me this far. Will you keep following me if I assume command of this vessel?"

Hannan and Izzy tensed, both sensing the possible conflict for command. Nolan ignored them, staring hard at Fizgig. It was her opinion that mattered, after all. If she acquiesced he'd be in charge, if not...well things would get very interesting. There was a time just a few weeks back he'd have relinquished command to the venerable Tigris, but he was a different man now. He had a responsibility to see this through, and to keep his few remaining men alive.

"You've proven capable," Fizgig replied. She gave him an appraising look. "I will follow you into battle, as will Izzy."

"Lena?" Nolan asked, turning to face the scientist.

"I'd be dead if not for you. You have earned my trust,

Nolan," Lena said, giving him what was probably meant to be a warm smile. It was more than a little creepy, with so many sharp teeth.

"Hannan?" he asked, turning to face the petite Marine.

"I told you when we first met," Hannan said, shooting him a lopsided grin. "I'm tactics. You're strategy. Captain suits you, sir."

"Primo," Nolan said, facing the VI. "Register me as ship's captain."

"Done," Primo responded instantly. "What are your orders, sir?"

"Hail the *Claw*," Nolan commanded. He waited patiently for several seconds.

The holographic display shifted. Half still showed the battle, but the other half now showed the bridge of the *Claw*. It was a mess. A haze of smoke covered everything, and most of the crew was either dead or unconscious. Only the pilot's chair, and the ops station were occupied. The Tigris in the captain's chair wasn't moving. Nolan recognized him immediately. It was Khar.

"Nolan, is that you?" Dryker's voice called. He stepped away from the ops station, and into the center of the view.

"Yes, sir," Nolan said, grinning. He couldn't believe Dryker was alive. "Mission accomplished. We've seized control of the Void Wraith vessel."

"Sit rep?" Dryker asked. He looked pale and exhausted, but
his face was etched with grim determination.

"Dire," Fizgig called, stepping up to join Nolan. "I see
you've commandeered my ship."

"I'm sorry, Fizgig, but after Khar went down there was no
one else," Dryker said.

"It's understandable, especially with your own vessel
destroyed. The *Johnston* was a fine ship," Fizgig said, giving a
respectful nod.

"The very best," Dryker agreed. He gave a sad smile. "She
died well. We have a saying, one that dates back to the earliest
human navies. 'A ship is safe in harbor, but that's not what a
ship is made for.' *Johnston* was a destroyer, and she went down
swinging."

"Sir," Nolan interrupted. "We don't have a lot of time.
That big vessel powering for the sun? It's a bomb, and we
believe it's headed for Primo space."

"What do you plan to do about it?" Dryker asked. His bridge
shook again, and a wave of sparks erupted from a nearby
terminal.

"We're betting it's headed for Theras Prime," Nolan said.
He glanced at the battle map, then back to Dryker. "It looks

like you can circle wide, then make for the Helios Gate."

"You want me to retreat?" Dryker said. His expression turned sour. "I'm not even sure this ship can survive passage through a sun."

"We don't have any other choice," Nolan protested. "We need someone to warn the Primo, and you're the only vessel that can make it through the Helios Gate in time. The rest of the Tigris are engaged and being overwhelmed. This fight will be over in minutes."

"There is another vessel that can do it," Dryker shot back. "Yours."

"We've got a cloaking device, sir," Nolan said. He took a deep breath, realizing in that instant that he wasn't going to take orders, not from Dryker or anyone else. He knew what needed to be done. "I'm going to stop that bomb, or die trying. You're going to warn the Primo in case we fail."

Dryker's face was stony for a long moment, then he gave an affectionate smile. "You're becoming a hell of a leader, son. We'll do our best to reach the Helios Gate. Dryker out."

Chapter 71- Nolan

"Captain, there is an event occurring you may wish to be apprised of," the VI said, mildly.

Nolan closed his eyes for a moment, and took a deep breath. He wasn't sure how many more "events" he wanted to know about. "What is it, Primo?"

"Two Harvester-class vessels have de-cloaked and are moving to intercept us," Primo replied.

"Cloak us," Nolan shot back. "Now."

"They must have detected us when we de-cloaked to speak to Dryker," Fizgig observed. She folded her arms, studying the holographic battle map.

"Lena, we need a way to disable that bomb. What can you give me?" Nolan asked.

"I'm not sure," Lena said, her tail swishing. She looked at Primo. "Can you bring up a schematic?"

"This is the approximate makeup," Primo said, and a corner of the holographic wall showed a cutaway of the bomb. Data scrolled by next to it, a series of numbers and metrics that was gibberish to Nolan.

Lena moved closer to study the schematics, so Nolan turned

back to the battle. The Tigris were losing, badly. Only two of the human ships had been disabled, and three Void Wraith vessels were operational. At least the *Claw* had made it safely away. It had reached the safety of the sun's corona, and disappeared.

"I can't see a way to stop the bomb," Lena said, eyeing Nolan soberly. "This new element isn't explosive on its own. It's designed to work with a star's core, and is basically inert until that point."

"We could attempt to destroy the thrusters," Fizgig mused, studying the schematic with those unreadable eyes. "They'll likely destroy us in the attempt, unless we do it ourselves by ramming the bomb."

"I doubt that would work," Nolan said, sighing. "We might temporarily disable the engines, but the remaining vessels could tow the bomb into the sun. We need a more permanent way to stop it. Lena, what about the Helios Gate itself?"

"That might work," Lena said, blinking. "A Helios Gate can only sustain one wormhole at a time. If we open a connection to some other star, then the Void Wraith can't take the bomb to Primo space. They'd have to let it denote here, or in the star of our choosing."

"If we keep the connection open," Izzy said, hesitantly joining the conversation. "Wouldn't both stars go nova?"

"I hadn't considered that," Lena said, smiling at Izzy. "You could be a scientist, sister. If we open and sustain the connection, then the reaction would spread to both stars. This system *and* the destination would go nova."

"They'll try to stop us from keeping the connection open," Fizgig said. Her tail swayed back and forth. "I've never done battle in a Helios Gate. It will be tricky. If our shields drop, we'll be incinerated instantly."

"That will be true for the enemy as well," Hannan said. Nolan had almost forgotten she was in the room. "We could set the connection, go through, and then ambush anyone who comes through and attempts to sever the connection."

"That's workable," Nolan said, nodding. "Lena, how long will this reaction take?"

"I'm not sure." She turned to the VI. "Primo, when the bomb detonated in the final war, how long did it take?"

"Our measurements weren't precise, but given the data from that explosion and from this bomb I'd postulate that twenty minutes would be sufficient for the reaction to begin," the VI said. "Once the reaction begins, there is no way to stop it."

"So if we can keep the connection open for twenty minutes, then we win," Nolan said, smiling for the first time in what felt like days.

"There is a further consideration," Fizgig said. "What about us? Both systems will be destroyed."

"If we're fast, we might be able to outrun the nova," Nolan said.

"That still leaves us stranded," Izzy pointed out. "If the Helios Gate is destroyed, we'll have to use sub-light thrusters to reach another Gate. That could take years."

"Primo, locate two Helios Gates in close proximity. Ideally, within a light year of each other. Closer is better," Nolan ordered.

"Done," Primo said. "The Hexonis system is within a quarter light year of Nerat Prime. The two stars' proximity matches your criteria."

"Excellent. Set a course for the Helios Gate. When we get there we'll open a connection to Hexonis," Nolan said.

Chapter 72- Countdown

"We're entering the core, captain," Primo's pleasant voice said. "Total transition time, four minutes and fifty two seconds."

Nolan folded his arms, watching the holographic display. The Void Wraith vessel was far more efficient than the *Johnston*, and had made the trek through the star in approximately one third of the time a human vessel could manage.

"If it were me," Nolan mused aloud. "I'd move the bomb surrounded by the fleet, just in case. That would mean doing it slowly, at the speed of the human vessels. I'd estimate fifteen minutes if that's the case."

"I'd use the same strategy, were I in command of the enemy forces," Fizgig agreed. "That would mean that we'll need to hold the connection for five minutes after the enemy force reaches it."

"That also means that they'll probably use the human vessels as bait," Nolan said. The view screen showed a wall of super dense, super hot material. Then it faded to black as they entered the Helios Gate's protective bubble. The golden sphere sat in the very center of the star, surrounded by an empty space larger than the earth. "If it were me, I'd send them in first to engage. Once we de-cloak to attack them, I'd send in the Void Wraith vessels to overwhelm us."

"So how do you plan to deal with that?" Hannan asked.

"I'm not sure yet," Nolan said, thinking furiously. He'd been considered an excellent tactician back in fleet academy, but they'd never trained their personnel to deal with unwinnable scenarios like this.

"I have a suggestion," Lena said. She started purring. "All we need to do is power the connection, and cross through. Once we're on the far side we destroy the Helios Gate's limiter."

"Clever," Fizgig said, bowing to Lena. "You prove your intellectual superiority, holy one."

"Why is that clever?" Hannan asked, blinking at Nolan.

"The limiter is how the Helios Gate turns on and off," Nolan said, beginning to understand. "Without the limiter, they won't be able to turn off the Gate. They'd have to repair the connection."

"Exactly," Lena said, her tail rising slowly until it was over her head. It swished in a very satisfied way. "They could repair it, but if we're standing by we can attack anyone who makes the attempt. All we have to do is take pot shots at their repair crew. If we can keep them busy for five minutes, we win."

"Perfect," Nolan said. He was starting to think they might pull this off. "Primo, use the Helios Gate to establish a connection to Hexonis then move through."

The Helios Gate began to vibrate, and the harnessed singularity in the center flared white. On the other side they could see an identical Gate. Their vessel moved forward, entering the wormhole.

Chapter 73- The Core

"Primo, target the limiter," Nolan ordered. The view screen shifted to show a large sapphire triangle embedded in the Gate's golden surface. "We want enough power to disable that limiter, but not enough to further damage the Gate."

"Acknowledged," Primo said. The ship rumbled, then a ball of potent blue energy gathered between the wingtips. It was much less terrifying being in the ship firing one of those blue balls than it was being on the receiving end.

The ball shot forward, shattering the limiter in a shower of brilliant light. Nolan held his breath as he waited for the Gate to blow up. He'd never heard of someone intentionally damaging a Gate. Not only was it against every galactic law in every culture, but doing so was damn near suicidal.

"The connection is stable, and the limiter is offline," Primo said.

Cheers erupted around the bridge. Hannan and Izzy caught each other up in a heartfelt hug. Even Fizgig started purring softly. Nolan finally let out the breath he was holding.

"Focus, people," he said, ending the brief moment of jubilation. "Now we wait."

And wait they did. For several agonizing minutes they studied the connection.

"Two minutes until critical reaction is reached," Primo said, breaking the pregnant silence.

"Here they come," Hannan said, clutching her rifle to her chest.

Four human vessels emerged through the wormhole, each moving to flank the opening. Two showed signs of battle damage, though nothing critical. Then another ship emerged, this one an OFI carrier. It took up a position near the Helios Gate.

"Looks like they're figuring out what we've done," Nolan said. He considered what he knew of OFI protocol. "Primo, can you read the encryption protocol stored in my suit?"

"Affirmative," Primo confirmed. "How would you like me to employ it?"

"See if you can pick up chatter from those vessels," Nolan ordered.

A moment later panicked voices echoed across the deck. "-- looks like they've disabled the limiter. We're scanning it now, but there's no way we're going to be able to repair it in time."

"We don't have to repair it," came a strong female voice. "All vessels prepare to attack. If we destroy this Gate it will break the connection to the Ghantan star. They'll be able to open a new connection, and enact the masters' plans."

"Primo, move into position behind the carrier," Nolan ordered. Their perspective began to shift as the VI obeyed. "Once we're in position, I want you to unload everything we have on the carrier. Aim for the junction between the two engines."

"Why there?" Fizgig asked.

Nolan hesitated before answering. He knew a great deal about OFI vessels, but sharing that information with a rival race was risky. "I'm exploiting a design flaw, one I don't believe your people ever found. There's a conduit connecting the engines. That conduit runs back to the vessel's fusion core. If we can blow up the engines, it will probably force the core to go critical."

"Won't the resulting explosion take out the Gate?" Hannan asked.

"The Gates are far more durable than that," Lena supplied. "They're designed to withstand the stresses of being at the heart of a star. Only a concentrated assault on the outer ring will actually destroy one."

"We're in position, Captain. Shall I fire?" Primo asked.

"Do it," Nolan ordered.

They shimmered into view, the ball of blue energy already forming between their wing tips. Two seconds later, they fired.

The ball of crackling blue energy shot into the rear of the carrier. At first there was no reaction beyond both engines going dark. Then a pillar of flame shot out of the carrier's aft side. One pillar became two, then ten. The vessel detonated, and a wave of fire and debris washed over them.

The Harvester was knocked backwards, and Nolan toppled to the deck. "All power to the shield."

If the shield dropped, nothing would save them. Nolan shot back to his feet, glancing around at the walls. The fact that they were still alive meant that the shield had held. The same couldn't be said for the human vessels. The carrier's detonation had hit them with the same wave of force and debris, before any of them could prepare for the blast. Three of the four had lost their shields, instantly blossoming into balls of fire. That added to the explosion, which took out the fourth vessel.

A second wave of flame washed over the Harvester, but this one was weaker. They barely felt it.

"We did it," Hannan said, laughing.

"How long until the reaction is complete?" Nolan asked.

"Twelve seconds," Primo said.

"Get us the hell out of here," Nolan said, leaning against the wall. The adrenaline was already starting to fade. Damn, but he needed a nap.

"Acknowledged," Primo said. Their vessel began accelerating away from the Helios Gate, and into the star.

Chapter 74- Edwards

Hannan couldn't believe it. They'd done it. Not only lived, but found a way to stop the Void Wraith. The victory had been costly, but it was victory nonetheless.

"Captain, I have a piece of business you may wish to be aware of," the virtual intelligence said. It unnerved her, but she suppressed her distaste. The thing had saved their lives, after all.

"What is it?" Nolan said, looking up from where he sat slumped against the wall. He looked like death warmed over.

"The Judicators assigned to internal maintenance have located a surviving biological unit," Primo explained. "That unit is in critical condition, and scans indicate that its body cannot be saved."

"Edwards," Hannan said.

Nolan met her gaze, and she read the pain there. It mirrored her own.

"What shall I do with this biological entity?" Primo asked.

"What do you mean?" Nolan said. He rose from the floor, and approached the black platform.

"The entity can be recycled. We can remove his

consciousness, merging it with a cybernetic body.

"You're talking about turning Edwards into a Judicator," Nolan said. He looked back at Hannan. "What do you think?"

She wasn't sure how to answer. What would Edwards want? She didn't know. He'd want to live, but as a robot? That was a steep cost.

She looked at the VI. "What are the odds of survival if you don't make him into a Judicator?"

"Twelve percent," the VI replied immediately. "If he does survive, he will be completely paralyzed."

"Shit," Hannan said. She looked at Nolan, considering. "I'd say we do it. Edwards would want to keep fighting."

"All right," Nolan said, exhaling. Hannan could see the exhaustion, but the Commander's expression was resolved.

"VI, you can place his body into any Judicator?" Nolan asked.

"Affirmative, Captain," the VI confirmed.

Nolan smiled grimly. "Do it, then. Have him made into an Alpha Judicator, and when that's done have him report to us."

"Acknowledged," Primo said.

"How long until we reach the next Helios Gate?" Nolan asked.

"Eighty four days, using your calendar," the VI answered.

Hannan sighed. That was a long time to wait. Who knew what the Void Wraith would do in that time? They'd stopped them at Ghantan, but she had a terrifying certainty that this was only the beginning.

The real war was still to come.

Epilogue

Dryker came awake by degrees. There was a horrible klaxon in the distance, much higher pitched than the Johnston's. The Claw's bridge reeked of ozone, and the only illumination came from the occasional shower of sparks bursting from damaged terminals.

He tried to move, but his body was impossibly heavy, his head impossibly light. He was suffering from oxygen deprivation. The Claw's life support must have been damaged during the transit through Theras Prime's G class star.

Dryker gave a weak laugh that became a cough. He fished the Johnston's data core from his pocket, clutching it in his fist. They'd made it through the gate, and if Dryker succeeded then Theras was safe. That meant the Primos would find this vessel, and the data core clutched in his lifeless hand.

They were a curious, patient species. They'd dissect every byte of data, seeing everything he and his ship had seen in recent days. They'd know about the Void Wraith, assuming whoever found them didn't already work for the bastards.

His head swam as he forced himself into a sitting position. If he was going to die, it wasn't going to be face first on the

deck. He's die proud, sitting at attention since he couldn't
stand.

A bright light came on in the periphery of his vision. He
turned his head slowly, staring uncomprehendingly as the light
approached. A tall, thin figure ducked onto the bridge. It was a
blurry purple blob, and it was getting closer.

Dryker recoiled, but there was nowhere to go. He waited as
the blob approached, finally stopping next to him. It crouched,
and he tensed, expecting it to pounce. His breathing quickened,
but there just wasn't enough oxygen.

"Breathe," came an emotionless voice. Something settled
over his mouth, and he sucked in deep lungfuls of blessedly
clean air. His vision cleared a little, and he realized that the
figure next to him was a purple skinned Primo.

It studied him with those unreadable eyes, and long moments
passed before it finally spoke again. "You have suffered no
permanent damage. Can you understand me?"
"Kh-khar?" Dryker asked, moving the mask long enough to speak.

"I do not know that name. If you are concerned about the
Tigris there are several survivors on the bridge," the Primo
said, cocking its head as it continued to study him.

Dryker grabbed the railing behind him and pulled himself to
his feet. His balance was terrible, but the railing held him up.

He turned to face the captain's chair. Another Primo stood next

to it, a mask fixed to Khar's face. His chest rose and fell in

shallow breaths. Khar was alive.

"Why have you come to Theras? You trespass on Primo space,"

the Primo asked him, voice still emotionless.

"The Void Wraith are coming. We have to evacuate," Dryker

said. His throat burned, and he swallowed to relieve the pain.

He checked his chronometer. It had been hours since they'd come

through. "It should have already gone nova. Dryker must have

succeeded."

"You seem coherent," the Primo said, something like emotion

finally touching its voice. It seemed skeptical. "We will have

you and the survivors brought aboard the First Light. This

vessel can be towed back to Theras Prime. Rest now. We will

investigate this matter upon our arrival."

Dryker closed his eyes, but he didn't go to sleep. He had

to plan. They'd reached Primo space, and Dryker had apparently

succeeded. They'd stopped the Void Wraith fleet, and their bomb.

But the Void Wraith still had spies. Was this Primo working

for the void wraith? Or one of its companions? Dryker couldn't

be sure, and until he could it meant trusting no one. He slid

the data core back in his pocket, still clutching it when the

blackness overtook him.

Exiled

Thank you for reading Destroyer. It's my first Science Fiction novel, and I'm hoping you enjoyed it. If you did, please consider signing up to the mailing list. I'll send you a copy of Exiled, the Destroyer prequel. You'll find out how Nolan ended up on the Johnston, and a bit more about the Void Wraith and their motives.

Sign up for the mailing list

and read the Destroyer prequel for free.

You'll also be the first to know when book 2 is available:

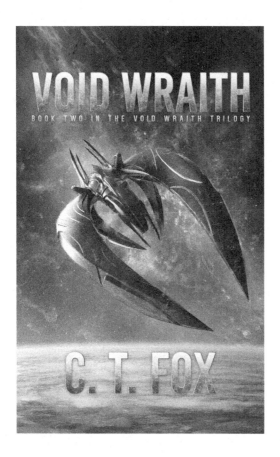

Want to connect?

Find me at chrisfoxwrites.com

<<<<>>>>

CPSIA information can be obtained
at www.ICGtesting.com
Printed in the USA
FSOW03n0650090516
20236FS

9 781530 628506